+OR

Max Sebastian is the bestselling author of *The Madeleine Trilogy*, *What's Mine is Yours* and *Marriage 2.0*.

He specializes in sizzling hot, romantic erotic stories that challenge the conventional boundaries of modern relationships, featuring naughty wives and insatiable girlfriends, along with the husbands or boyfriends who adore them.

Max lives in London with his wife and two children.

You can find Max online at MaxSebastian.net, and, you're always very welcome to contact Max by emailing Max@MaxSebastian.net.

facebook.com/writermax

twitter.com/maxsebastian

goodreads.com/maxsebastian

amazon.com/author/maxsebastian

ALSO BY MAX SEBASTIAN
WEB: MAXSEBASTIAN.NET

Anarchy of the Heart

The Madeleine Trilogy

What's Mine Is Yours

What's Yours Is Mine

The Game

Heidi, Corrupted

His Week With My Wife

Out of His League (with Kenny Wright)

Rock Her World

The One That I Married

Game Changer

Sharing My Sweetheart

Obsessive: Essence of an Affair

Obsessive 2: A Woman Shared

Obsessive 3: Claimed by Another

Marriage 2.0

The Truth About My BFF

A LOCKDOWN AFFAIR

MAX SEBASTIAN

maxSebastian.net

CONTENTS

PART I

CHAPTER ONE

THE KIDS WERE ALLOWED to stay up late on nights when Mommy was in London, so they could all FaceTime together. That was the way it had been even before COVID-19. But tonight was the first night Cam noticed something slightly amiss with the call.

'Daddy says you both did some good learning today.'

'Uh-huh. I did some English with Daddy and some history with Granny.'

'That's great! And you, too, Sarah?'

'I was drawing letters with Granny.'

A lot of the time, he didn't always pay too much attention to the FaceTime calls when the kids were chatting with their mother. He was always exhausted. Even with Marcie's mother, Flo, staying with them now, and helping out with the kids, he got to the end of a day and he was just shattered. It made him think that Francine, their au pair, must have done a superhuman job before she'd returned home to Rouen just before France went into full lockdown. But these days, cooped up at home, he was even exhausted at weekends, too, when Marcie and Flo were both able to take a share of the childcare.

Tonight, though, Flo was doing laundry, and Cam was sitting with Sarah on his lap and Henry by his side for the call with Marcie. And there was something slightly different about the picture he was seeing, but he couldn't quite put a finger on what it was.

'Did you guys go for a walk today?'

'Yeah, in the woods. Henry got stung by a nettie.'

'A net*tle*.'

'Oh no, Henry, were you okay?'

'It was pretty bad. But Daddy found a dock leaf and then it was okay.'

Here was Marcie, sitting at the table of their little flat in Bayswater, fairly close to Paddington Station so her commute was easy. The webcam from her laptop showed the kitchen area, the little smattering of clutter from her supper by the stove—the lonesome little box of mac 'n' cheese, the half-drunk bottle of red wine, cork still in the corkscrew lying beside it.

Marcie looked good, her shoulder-length blonde hair tied back smartly in a ponytail, her white work shirt still looking crisp and clean, the blue in her large, bewitching eyes opalescent, even in the relatively color-drained Face-Time image. But then Marcie always looked good on these FaceTime calls, it was like the opposite of everyone else. Cam thought it was possibly because she was usually still wearing makeup, which just seemed to sharpen up her features, and draw attention to her attractive face, whereas she rarely wore makeup when she was home. Maybe it was an absence making the heart grow fonder kind of thing— he did miss her during the three nights a week she was in London. Even though, at the same time, he quite liked having a few nights each week with the bed to himself, a little extra personal space.

'Okay, you guys need to go brush your teeth and get into bed.'

'Yes, Mommy.'

'Are you coming home tomorrow, Mommy?'

'No, Thursday, stupid. She always comes home on Thursdays.'

'Henry, don't call your sister 'stupid'.'

They were just about to say their goodbyes, and then end the call when Cam saw them. Over by the very edge of the screen, on the peninsula that divided the kitchen from the rest of the tiny one-bed apartment, right by the front door, was a set of keys. Ordinarily, it wouldn't have attracted any attention whatsoever—Marcie always dropped her keys on the counter right inside the front door as soon as she got into the apartment. He did, too, on the rare occasions he was in London, staying in the flat himself. Ordinarily, it really wouldn't be a big deal.

But tonight, there was a set of keys sitting there that were not Marcie's.

'Okay, sweethearts. Mommy will call you again tomorrow night, okay? Now you be good for Daddy and Granny. Promise me?'

'We promise.'

It was hardly even noticeable. Certainly, in the tiny window Marcie would have open on her laptop screen, showing how she looked to the other party, Marcie would not see it. But Cam did, and it made him feel an instant 'click' inside his head as the reason why he'd been feeling slightly odd about this call came into crystal clarity. Had his sub-conscious noticed it before his conscious mind had figured it out? That was weird. He tried not to react in an obvious way to what he was now seeing on screen, though he felt a strange heat shoot through his chest, an acid burn in his stomach.

The keys sitting by the front door included a car key with a visible VW logo on it.

'Okay. Good night!'

'Good night, Mommy!'

Cam leaned over the computer keyboard as the kids scampered away to find Granny to demand a story before bed. He smiled, doing his best to relax and look normal, despite the knots his stomach was being tied in inside.

'Everything good at work, honey?' He asked her.

'Oh, fine, fine, you know how it is,' she replied, flashing him a smile in return, though the energy she had in her face while the kids had been on the call had now faded.

Cam could never quite tell if she felt bad for leaving him with the kids while she continued going into London four days a week to work without having to worry about them—or if she slightly resented him for being able to stay home with the kids while she had to go to work. Whenever the subject came up—rarely, but occasionally she did seem to want to mention it—she always told him she felt guilty, because it always stressed her out to take care of the kids for more than a few hours at a time, and she really couldn't cope without her work. He always had to reassure her, even though it stressed him out a lot of the time, too. No, no, honey, it's fine. I like taking care of the children. And I can do an hour or two of work, here and there. Their arrangement was fine, except that occasionally he caught a slight coldness in her voice, or in her eyes, and suspected that perhaps the story wasn't as simple as she projected. Maybe she respected him less for being a stay-at-home dad.

'Have you been okay with the kids?'

'Yeah, it's fine. We're doing our best.'

There was once a time, long before the kids came along, when they'd call each other on FaceTime—or Skype, back then—whenever they had to be apart because of work, and they'd actually talk to each other all about their days, or whatever. These days, the FaceTime seemed mostly for the kids' benefit. And Cam found that he hardly ever said a word to his wife while she was away, beyond those calls with the kids.

But wasn't that just because they were so familiar with each other these days? They knew exactly how each other's day had probably gone, and so on. They didn't even really miss each other anymore, because they knew Marcie would be back from London every Thursday. It wasn't that they had any problems in their relationship, he told himself. It was just that they were so comfortable with each other these days. Some things didn't need to be said anymore.

'Well, good night, darling,' she said.

'Good night, honey.'

The moment before she ended the call, Cam pressed the shift and the command key down, along with the number '3', and took a screenshot of what he was seeing. Doing so meant there was a loud noise like an old camera shutter closing as the picture was taken, and for a moment he felt terrified she would figure out what he was doing. But the FaceTime image cut to black, the call ended, and Marcie didn't immediately call back to demand to know what he was up to.

He sat there for a moment, breathing slowly to calm himself down, listening to the sound of the kids running around upstairs while Granny attempted to corral them into bed.

Then he clicked on the image file that was now saved to the iMac desktop. He could zoom in, fill the whole screen with the image of those car keys. There was no doubting that was a car key for a Volkswagen. He wasn't mistaking the VW logo for something else. He told himself that there had to be an innocent explanation for it— perhaps Marcie's Toyota had broken down, though it had always been completely bombproof. Perhaps it was being serviced, and for some reason the dealership had given her a VW courtesy car so she could drive to the station to catch her train to London Monday morning. Wouldn't she mention it to him if her car needed to be serviced? She'd write it on the calendar hanging up on the kitchen wall, right?

He couldn't think of another reason that VW key would be there. This was the lockdown, friends were not allowed to visit Marcie. If a contractor needed to visit in order to carry out some kind of essential repair on something in the apartment, Cam would know about it.

Now he examined the car keys, he could recognize a metallic keyring as being in the shape of a Transformers robot face. This wasn't a key ring for a courtesy car—and it wasn't Marcie's own set of keys.

So who was staying at the apartment with her?

'They're asleep.'

Cam jolted out of his daze to find Granny had returned from upstairs. He was somewhat surprised to glance at the clock on the computer screen and find that half an hour had gone by since the FaceTime call. What?

'Thanks, Flo,' he smiled.

Granny—or Florence, among adults—made herself comfortable on the large sofa, ready to watch the new episode of *Better Call Saul*.

'Uh… I think I'm actually going to get an early night,' he said to her while the computer shut down.

'Good idea,' Granny grinned.

'You have everything you need?'

'Oh, yes, thanks, dear.'

He traipsed upstairs, feeling thankful to have a little space to himself, so he could process what he'd discovered during the FaceTime call. It seemed faintly ridiculous, the theory that was currently at the forefront of his mind. Could Marcie really be having an *affair*? But, what was it that Sherlock Holmes used to say? Something about the simplest explanation usually being the most likely one…

It was a shocking theory. But as he thought about it, it seemed that the shock was more about the fact that it just didn't seem like Marcie to *want* an affair, than anything else. She was so proper. She was so ambitious when it came to her work. She wasn't the type to let something like another man distract her from her goal to keep rising through the business world until she was a genuine titan. And ever since Sarah had come along, she'd hadn't really seemed all that interested in sex.

Or maybe it was just sex with her husband in which she no longer seemed interested?

His anger flared. It felt ugly, hot, powerful.

But he waited a few moments, and took a deep breath, and waited for the initial wave of emotion to calm a little so that he could really process what was going on. It was a little trick he'd learned over the years as a parent of small children—they could infuriate you at times, drive you absolutely crazy. But if he could just wait a minute or two, keep calm, and let reason take charge instead of emotion, then everyone was much the better for it.

Long, deep breaths.

If he was truthful, the main thing he felt right now was

stupid. Stupid that she'd pulled the wool over his eyes. Of course the opportunity was there for her to have an affair —she stayed in London, supposedly on her own, for three nights every week. Other than a regular—but usually quite brief—FaceTime call with the kids each night she was away, there was really no way for Cam to know how she filled the rest of her time she was staying at their London bolthole. He'd always assumed she just liked to watch TV, and maybe dial out for pizza, when she wasn't in the mood for mac 'n' cheese or scrambled eggs, or the rest of her fairly limited self-catering range.

He'd always assumed she worked so hard, that when evening arrived she just wanted to crash and sleep until it was time for another day in the office.

Upstairs, he took a shower, the hot water washing away the sweat and grime from a day of taking care of two young kids while the government banned them all from leaving the house, other than for essential shopping or one instance per day of exercise. Thinking, if there was another man staying with Marcie at the apartment in London, wouldn't that technically be breaching the Lock-down rules? You weren't supposed to visit friends during lockdown. You weren't even supposed to visit lovers. You were supposed to stay at home, with only the members of your own household, to help prevent the spread of the coronavirus, to help reduce the pressure on the National Health Service.

One of the government's top advisors on matters to do with the coronavirus had just resigned from his position because he'd been caught having a married woman over to his flat as part of a running affair.

Marcie still had to go into London to work, though she could work from home to a limited degree—and she did so on Fridays. She was one of the lucky ones at her company, part of the skeleton crew needed to keep the major national clothes retailer going, even though its stores were all closed. Part of the team of senior finance staff working to keep the business afloat while the lockdown devastated its income. Stressful work.

Cam dried off after his shower, and pulled on a clean pair of underwear and his sweatpants before climbing into bed. What was Marcie up to right now? Settling down on the sofa in front of the latest episode of *The Mandalorian* on Disney+—or scampering off to the bedroom with her lover?

He now felt somewhat naive to have made an assumption that she was simply by herself, watching TV until she felt tired enough to sleep.

Cam felt his stomach churning.

It felt more credible to believe that she was, perhaps, stripping off with her colleague, dragging him into the shower where she could press herself up against him as the hot water coursed down over their naked bodies. Kissing him while he rubbed soap into her bare breasts, her hands closing around his hard cock.

Strangely, lying there in bed imagining his wife being unfaithful at that very moment, Cam found himself getting aroused. Maybe it was because he was still in a state of shock. His cock stood up straight, while he lay there on his back, as tall and stiff as a fucking flag pole.

He hadn't been this aroused since… since… well, since before they'd been married. When they'd gone on a beach vacation to Tortola and Marcie had worn the kind of bikinis that would normally be the preserve of Playboy centerfolds.

Why did it make him feel so horny, to think of his wife being unfaithful?

He felt an odd queasy sensation in his stomach at the

same time, at the thought that Marcie had been lying to him, that she'd been seeing someone else behind his back. But he could not deny that he was turned on by the thought of her actually having sex with another man.

He thought of articles he'd read over the years, about people who had caught their spouses cheating. Tabloid pieces, usually—you couldn't escape them. Men whose wives had cheated, in particular, always seemed to say something like, *it wasn't the sex that was the worst thing, but the lying*. Now he could sort of understand that sentiment, in a way he never had before: the worst thing about the possibility that Marcie was cheating on him wasn't that she was having sex with someone else, but that she was breaking Cam's trust in her.

Actually, the sex part was kind of hot, if you disconnected it from the cheating part.

He started stroking his cock, tugging on it while closing his eyes, imagining some faceless man putting his hands all over Marcie's trim body, uttering sweet compliments to her about all the work she put in during her lunch breaks at the gym in her office building before it had closed, burying his face in her beautifully rounded breasts, pressing his cock up against her dripping-wet pussy.

What if you removed the cheating aspect, the lying aspect, from the whole adultery equation?

Marcie, sweetheart, I know you get lonely when you're staying in London, away from home. Maybe you should try and find a little company—you know, someone to have a little fun with, while you're in town. I wouldn't mind, so long as you didn't do anything behind my back.

It was such a powerful picture in his head. It made him feel like he hadn't had a proper sexual fantasy in years—he masturbated, sure. Didn't everyone? But for years, it had always been with pornography. Without it, he closed his eyes and it seemed so much more powerful. He could picture the excitement in his wife's eyes as she took in the sight of a muscled Lothario climbing on top of her. He could perceive the dark scent of her arousal as he pressed his big, hard cock up against her. He could imagine her erotic sigh as the man slipped his manhood inside her, inch by inch, slowly filling her completely.

And this man was making love to her with the expressed consent of her husband.

That was a weird thought, wasn't it? Husbands didn't let their wives cheat on them. Not normal husbands.

Cam lay on their marital bed and imagined another man pumping his big, fat cock into Marcie's eager pussy, again and again and again—both of them working up a sweat, their bodies glowing pink with the physical effort, sighs becoming moans, moans becoming cries, cries becoming yells before their orgasms approached, and the other man came inside Marcie's tight, wet pussy, filling her with his cream.

Oh. Em. Gee.

After that, he lay there in bed with his own come all over the place. But, strangely enough, he felt a little less angry that his wife had betrayed him, now that he had come. Maybe it was simply that he felt chilled out because he'd orgasmed. Maybe it was that he was still in a state of shock.

But the thought about allowing Marcie to see someone else, so long as nothing was done behind his back, no lying occurred, seemed like a powerful tonic to her actual cheating.

And, *Jesus*, for the first time in years—since they'd just started dating—he had actually made himself come by thinking of Marcie. For the first time in a long time, he thought about his wife with genuine, blood-pumping desire. Her adultery had, somehow, woken him up to the fact that he'd been taking her for granted for so long.

He was married to a beautiful woman.

He was married to a sexy woman.

He was married to a naughty girl.

CHAPTER TWO

HE WOKE up at five in the morning, and he wasn't feeling nearly as good as he had when he'd passed out the previous night.

He'd gotten out of the habit of waking that early—a couple of years back, the kids had woken he and Marcie quite often at such an hour, or even earlier. But Sarah was a little older now, so she usually made it through to 6.30, or even 7 if they were lucky. But this wasn't waking up because one of the kids was yelling for him or Marcie to go sit with them.

This was being woken up by fear.

By the cold light of the early morning, Cam wasn't feeling that strange eroticism from the thought of Marcie being naughty and sexy and oh-so horny—this was Cam suddenly desperately afraid that their sheltered, carefully constructed family life was about to be blown apart. The moment Cam awoke, he was breathing hard, almost panting, his pulse racing, his body wracked with chills and flushed with feverish heat all at the same time.

What if Marcie wanted to leave him?

He just had to calm down. He was going to have a panic attack if he wasn't careful, and that wasn't going to help anybody. For a few minutes, he tried to empty his mind, and just focus on breathing. Calm, slow, inhale followed by exhale, like there was some kind of yoga master in his head, telling him how to meditate. It helped a lot. But it didn't alleviate the fear.

He tried another approach. Perhaps, he pondered, he had jumped to conclusions about Marcie, unfairly. Perhaps her company had offered her the use of a VW rental car to ferry her around the city while the lockdown was in place, to get to urgent meetings to try to save the firm. That might explain the keys. After all, the Mayor had suspended the congestion charge and the Ultra-Low Emissions Zone while the lockdown was in place, to help as many essential workers as possible to travel without using public transport, where social distancing was more difficult.

But it just wasn't logical. She had her own car, the little Toyota. If her company had wanted her to drive around the city to get to meetings, she would have used that and just claimed back the mileage.

What if something had happened to the Toyota, and she'd been given a courtesy car while it was being fixed? She might have run into the back of someone, and been too embarrassed to tell him about it. That was highly possible, wasn't it? She could get someone to fix it before it was time to drive home to the Cotswolds, then her husband wouldn't need to know anything about her accidentally driving into the back of a truck when it braked suddenly.

He liked that theory. It gave him an ounce of comfort.

Marcie was proud, that was all. She didn't want him to think she could make a mistake. She didn't want to worry him about the state of her car.

Of course, that was it.

But thinking that—murmuring it over and over to himself, like some kind of mantra—didn't stop the doubts. And it didn't affect the feeling deep in his stomach. Before he'd been a stay-at-home dad and occasional features writer for various gardening magazines and websites, Cam had been a newspaper reporter, and he'd learned to pay heed to his gut. And his gut feeling right now was that that VW car key belonged to someone else. And if there was someone else hanging out with Marcie at the flat in London—during lockdown—and she wasn't telling him anything about it, then his gut said that it was a man, a lover, that she was keeping secret.

It was an ugly feeling, thinking that Marcie would start seeing somebody else while she was in London. And, yes, it wasn't the sex part that bothered him. The sex part was hot, even when he was feeling the fear. The part that bothered him most was the sense that she was excluding him from a fairly significant portion of her life.

Now, Cam didn't need Marcie to tell him about every little detail of her life when he wasn't around. He didn't need to know everything about her work, or even the people she worked with. But she would occasionally mention things about her job, or her colleagues, in passing, and it was enough for him to feel connected to her. Marcie had her own little circle of friends, too, and while she hadn't been able to see them during the many weeks of lockdown, when she did see them, Cam didn't have a problem with not being there with her. But at least he could ask about her friends, in passing, and she would give him the headlines on how they were, how life was for them—and he didn't feel excluded from that part of her life.

But if she had a lover, then that was a fairly significant

part of her life she was keeping from him. He didn't like that feeling.

And, knowing nothing about it, made him feel a lack of control over his own life, his own family. Because what if her lover was trying to persuade her to leave Cam, to leave her family, so she could marry him? And Cam wouldn't know anything about it until it was too late. He wouldn't be able to do anything to stop the implosion of their family.

God. He couldn't deny that it was arousing to think of her sleeping with a mystery man. Yet while their marital sex had not exactly been amazing in recent years—ever since Sarah had come along, actually—if Marcie had felt something serious was missing in her life, she could have told Cam about it.

They could have worked on it.

They could have tried counseling, or couples' therapy, or something like that.

Jesus. She could even have said to him, *I really want to sleep with this guy from work. He's just sex on legs, and I can't stop thinking about him.* And Cam could have said to her, *sure, go ahead, have fun. As long as it's just about the sex, and you still love me…*

Was that such a ridiculous thing? It made him smile. Maybe he was being a little fanciful, in retrospect. If she really had come to him and said something like that, would he have been so tolerant? Right now, his back was up against the wall. He was facing the end of his marriage, of course he felt he would have allowed her to just go off and have no-strings sex with some other guy, if she could guarantee it wouldn't damage their marriage.

He was out of bed, and quickly into, then out of, the shower. Then he was quietly searching through Marcie's drawers in the bedroom, looking for anything that might confirm, or rule out, an affair. Nothing unusual in the bedroom. He even checked the laundry basket, but the apartment in London had a little washing machine, so Marcie didn't need to bring anything home to wash.

He continued his search beyond the bedroom—in their little study, and then downstairs around the living room, the kitchen. He didn't really know what he was looking for, which probably didn't help. Got the sense that Marcie was quite compartmentalized in terms of what she kept in London, and what she kept at home.

He searched the family computer, to see if there was any way of tracking down communications between Marcie and some other man. But there was nothing he could find. She had her laptop with her, she took it wherever she went—if there *was* anything, it would be on there. Or on her phone, which, similarly, never left her person.

It was frustrating.

God, how it was frustrating.

As he searched fruitlessly, part of him was thinking that if she was being this careful about keeping her affair a secret, then it had to mean she wanted to protect their marriage. She was just having a little fun while she was in London—it was just sex. If she didn't care whether her husband discovered her affair, if she was so obsessed with her new lover that she was sloppy when it came to covering up their relationship, then that would mean bad things for her marriage. She was keeping everything secret because she didn't want to hurt him, because she still loved him, and saw her affair as just a fling while she had to cope with the loneliness of London nights.

But then again, she could have been keeping everything a secret because she was worried about losing custody of the kids. Could you even lose custody of your kids these days, just because you were the one being unfaithful?

He was a mass of confusion that morning. That whole day. Taking care of the kids after they got up, getting them their breakfast, getting them to brush their teeth and get dressed so they could do some home-schooling. Figuring out lunch. Finding something active for them to do in the afternoon. Sorting out supper. Through it all, he had the constant debate going on within his head as to whether Marcie wanted to stay in the marriage, or whether she was more likely to be heading for the exit.

And there was, during the entire time, a strange undercurrent of mild sexual arousal, as he considered the curious idea that if they ever had a big confrontation about Marcie's affair, one solution might be to tell her she could continue sleeping with her lover in London, so long as she still loved Cam, and so long as she continued to commit to their marriage.

No matter how queasy he felt about everything, or how much the fear got to him, he couldn't quite let go of the idea that the way to get beyond the broken trust of an affair was to accept that your spouse might occasionally get tempted by other people—and to just let her have a little outside fun when she needed it.

To let her cheat, with his consent. Then it wouldn't really be cheating, would it?

Then, after supper, it was time to call Marcie again.

He felt nervous, shepherding the kids in front of the computer so that they could FaceTime with Mommy. He hadn't felt this nervous in years. Did she still love him? Was she going to suddenly end their marriage, split their family into two households? He knew the uncertainty didn't help. Perhaps if she had fallen in love with another man, and was intending to steer toward a divorce court, it would just be better to know. So that he knew what he was dealing with, so that he could begin to prepare himself mentally.

But here she was, on screen, just like any normal evening when she was out of town.

'Hey, guys! How are you?'

Sounding perfectly cheerful, and happy, as normal.

'Hey Mom! We're good!'

'You didn't get too much sun today? It was a hot one.'

'No, Daddy made sure we put sun cream on. And he put the paddling pool in the shade.'

She glanced at him, and gave him a sweet little smile, and he couldn't help but return one back at her. Affectionate. She wouldn't smile at him like that if she was thinking about divorce, would she? She loved him. He felt the warmth from her, the sparkle in her big, blue eyes. You couldn't fake that.

'How's the home-schooling going?' She asked, and she was looking at him, pity in her eyes, that he was bearing the brunt of the stress of trying to educate kids who really did not want to be doing work while they were at home, surrounded by home comforts and distractions.

'Fine. They did a bit,' he said, and she gave him another one of those sweet smiles.

That made him feel so good inside. Massively reassuring.

'Well,' she said, 'Anything you can do with them is better than nothing. It's not easy.'

Then she was asking Flo how she was, and about whether her prescription medication had come in the mail, yet. Cam found himself searching the view of the apartment behind her to see if he could see even the tiniest clue that she was seeing someone else while she was in London. There wasn't anything he could see—certainly, those VW car keys were not in sight today.

It felt disappointing, it meant the uncertainty was still there. But the part of him that interpreted her care to keep her affair a secret as a positive thing—a sign that she wanted to keep their marriage going, that she believed her husband might never know about her little fling, and therefore would never be hurt by it—felt strangely hopeful that he wasn't noticing anything out of place.

Marcie looked good, didn't she? Did she always look this good on FaceTime?

But she wasn't wearing makeup, she was still wearing her work clothes, like she'd only just got home from the office—there wasn't anything about her that suggested she'd made an effort with her appearance just because she was going to be talking to her family on FaceTime.

She just looked *good*. He couldn't explain it. There was nothing he could identify about her that was particularly different—it was just that he noticed the attractiveness of her face, the high cheekbones, the big, soulful blue eyes, her kissable lips, along with the way her chest filled out that white shirt. Maybe thinking that some other guy was staying with her, sleeping with her, made Cam wake up to her beauty, shaking him from the fog of marital familiarity, so that he recognized he'd been taking her for granted for ages.

His desire for her had been re-awakened by the suspicion that she was having an affair, in a most unexpected way.

After the call was over, it was Flo's turn to help the kids get ready for bed, and Cam just ended up going up to the master bedroom to collapse on the bed. And there, the memory of seeing Marcie on FaceTime merged with the thought of what she would be doing now the call was over —the thought of her jumping into bed with another man. And he was back to pulling out his cock, stroking it to the thought of Marcie making out with another man, Marcie going down on another man, Marcie straddling another man.

Marcie crying out as another man made her come.

He was probably going stir crazy, cooped up in a house with the kids and his mother-in-law all the time. He was probably just craving something—anything—to break up the routine of all this house arrest, which was like an unending summer break, only they weren't actually allowed to go anywhere on vacation, and the kids couldn't even attend summer camps.

But a big part of him kind of *wanted* Marcie to be cheating on him.

CHAPTER THREE

THURSDAY. Marcie came home on a Thursday. This Thursday, he was nervous about her return. Again, it was more the uncertainty that made him feel queasy. The not knowing. He felt like he didn't want to be all affectionate with her, if she was secretly preparing herself to leave him, to tear his family apart. And yet, if he acted differently, then she'd know something was up—and he wasn't ready to confront her about her affair yet.

For one thing, he simply didn't have any real evidence. A cursory glance at a set of car keys in the background of a FaceTime call one evening. That was hardly cast iron. He didn't want to get into an argument if he didn't have much of a leg to stand on.

What if he was cold to her, and that made her harden her resolve to leave him? If she was in two minds, and he started acting as though he didn't love her anymore—it might push her away.

All day, he tried to keep calm. He tried to hold onto the positives.

Ever since he'd first suspected that she might be

sleeping with someone else, his desire for her had been building steadily. It didn't make sense, unless it was his subconscious trying to prepare him to win her back, making him desire her so much that when he needed to, he would be able to show her how much he loved her. He would be able to impress her in bed.

It made him realize he'd been neglecting that part of their marriage. It couldn't be just his fault, could it? But he hadn't been doing his part. He hadn't been putting effort into their sex lives, he had been sitting back and letting it happen, whenever it did, which wasn't so often these days.

Maybe this was all the chance he needed to make their marriage right again. To get back to where they needed to be.

He had to hang onto that desire he had for her.

But he had to be careful.

When they heard her car pull up in the gravel driveway, and the kids rushed out of the front door to see her, Cam held back. He had to do what he would normally do on a Thursday when she returned home from London. He had to do his utmost to act as normal—at least until he had something more concrete to go on, as to whether she was really having an affair.

Maybe he was being unfair to her. Jumping to a far-fetched conclusion based on nothing more than a set of car keys. How could he believe that of her, after they'd been together this long? Et cetera, et cetera. It was frustrating, not knowing, but at least he was now able to keep his eyes open for any signs, any clues, any tangible evidence.

He stayed in the kitchen, finishing up the cooking of supper, waiting until she came in to greet him—as per usual. Forcing himself to be calm, to keep his pulse from racing, to avoid seeming like he was as nervous as he was.

But then the door opened, and there she was, looking

spectacular in her white shirt and smart pencil skirt, her nylons and her makeup, her golden hair tied back in a ponytail.

'Hey,' she said, dropping her briefcase on the table by the fridge, walking over to him as he stood by the Aga, having removed a piping hot lasagna from the oven.

And as much as he tried to stay calm, to behave exactly as he would have done if he hadn't known anything different about her, it was too difficult. To his eyes, she was just *gorgeous*. It was ridiculous. If it was his subconscious trying to get him to work on re-heating their sex life, then it was being stupidly effective.

She walked over to him to greet him with the usual little kiss on the cheek—and he nearly swooned, for goodness' sake. This was his wife?

'How was your day?' she asked him, like normal, as her perfume filled his chest and made his soul sing.

'Oh, you know,' he said, trying to make his voice sound light, care-free.

She leaned in to kiss his cheek, and he found himself looking down her chest, a couple of buttons unfastened so that he could see her cleavage. Along with the scent of her sweet perfume, and the touch of her soft face against his cheek, it made him thicken up, it made him *want her*, desperately.

It made him realize that if this was a normal weekend, they might wait until Saturday night and then—only if the stars were properly aligned, and they'd had a good amount of wine, and dinner conversation had been interesting enough, and they weren't too tired, and no one had a headache, and only if one of them didn't have to get up early to get a little extra work done in the morning—they might have sex.

But he wanted her now. If he did something to break the routine, would she suspect that something was up?

'That smells amazing,' she said, peering over the food as it sat, resting, on the Aga's warming plate.

She was giving him another one of those sweet, affectionate smiles again. That wasn't normal, was it? He didn't remember it being a frequent thing, unless they'd shared a bottle or two of wine.

'Throw a bunch of cheese and meat together in a pan, you can't really go wrong,' he said.

Then, out of the blue, she kissed him again—this time, leaning in to connect her soft lips to his. It was brief, but it was warm and tender, sweet as candy. It shook him to the core.

'You're amazing, you know that?' she said, and he felt like blaming her for breaking with routine, though inside his heart was doing little pirouettes, and someone was in the process of letting off a bunch of wild fireworks inside his chest.

'You're pretty amazing yourself, you know that?' he said, and leaned in for another kiss—well, she started it.

She smirked, and was that a faint blush? *That* wasn't routine for a Thursday night. What was she thinking? Was she feeling guilty about her affair?

She stepped back, and for a moment, there was definitely some kind of chemistry between them, some kind of tension. What was that? He knew what it was on his side— he wanted her. Badly. But what was it on her side? As far as she could tell, nothing about him had changed, had it?

Then the kids came in, with Flo close behind them, and the moment was over. Cam was handing out dinner plates as everyone was sitting at the kitchen table, and Flo was starting to help Henry to some supper, Marcie was pouring Sarah a glass of water, and the family was settling into a nice dinner.

While trying to pretend everything was normal, over dinner Cam was left pondering that extra kiss from Marcie, along with her compliment. That kiss wasn't just a little peck on the lips, it wasn't even just a *hey, I love you* kind of a kiss. It had seemed like more than that. Had he been reading too much into it?

It wasn't easy, pretending to be normal. He constantly wanted to gaze at her, both to luxuriate in her beauty, now that he'd been re-awakened to it, and also to check her state of mind following that kiss. But in stopping himself from staring at her, was he being obvious in avoiding her? How much staring at her was normal for a dinner? He couldn't tell.

He would try to engage in any conversation that was going, because then he could glance at her freely, he believed. But was he too engaged with the conversation?

Occasionally, he caught a little look from Marcie, and he felt a jolt of terror shoot through his heart, like she'd discovered him looking at her a little too much. There were a couple of smirks, which almost seemed like she was signaling to him that she knew he was staring at her, that he wanted her. But maybe he was being paranoid.

And he knew he was being paranoid, but there wasn't much he could do about it. He told himself there was no way she would be able to tell he had suspicions about her.

The more he told himself that, the more he settled on the conclusion that the extra kiss she'd given him in the kitchen was about guilt. She felt guilty about cheating on him.

That was a good thing, wasn't it? It showed that she still loved him, she still wanted him.

As the family polished off the last of the lasagna, Cam wondered if he might be able to address a particular part of his central fear without even needing to prove, definitively, whether Marcie was cheating or not. Perhaps if he could take advantage of her guilt—and his own rekindled desire for her—he could work on reconnecting with her so that there could be no more doubt that she definitely wanted to stay in this marriage for the long-term.

Then, if she was feeling guilty about it, she could quietly bring a halt to her affair, and no one needed to even discuss it.

That would be the easiest thing, wouldn't it?

ONLY, after the kids were finally asleep, and Marcie came downstairs to sit with him and Flo, watching TV—and she actually snuggled up against him, Cam couldn't get it out of his head that she might have been sleeping with another man while she was in London.

For one thing, she didn't usually snuggle up with him on the sofa just to watch TV. That hadn't happened in a while, and it usually took wine to make it happen.

The second thing he noticed was that her perfume smelled slightly stronger than when she'd first returned home, when she'd given him that extra little kiss in the kitchen.

The third thing that made him feel she was breaking with their usual routine was that snuggled up to him, she put her hand on his thigh—and gently, oh-so-gently, she started stroking it while they all watched Netflix.

It made him fairly certain she wanted sex—and that was fine with him. His manhood started thickening up as her hand wandered closer and closer to the top of his thigh. He glanced down at her, to see if she'd glance back, perhaps giving him a little smile that said she was horny, and she hoped he was too. But she was looking studiously ahead, focused on the TV screen. Looking down, he was rewarded with a superb view down her white tank top. She was not wearing a bra. Just her white top, and a pair of gray yoga leggings. She looked so very fine. All those mouthwatering curves.

He was hard even before her fingers reached the bulge in his sweatpants.

And then her fingers did reach the bulge in his sweatpants, and started to stroke it. Still, she didn't move her head—she continued to focus on the TV, so that Flo would never know she wasn't simply watching it. But she did respond to his hardness. He could stare down her top and see her breathing deepen considerably. He could see her nipples stiff, pointing through her white tank top.

And there was the way she squeezed his cock through his sweatpants.

This was all great news regarding his strategy to strengthen their romantic bond without confronting her over his suspicions about her fidelity.

But while she was stroking his hard-on, and he was staring down her cleavage, and both of them were enjoying being just a little naughty while Flo was still in the room, Cam found that he couldn't let go of the thought that she was probably having an affair—and he really wanted to know about it.

He wanted her because he thought she was cheating. It wasn't *the* main reason, but it was *a* reason.

And when Flo excused herself, saying she needed to get to bed, and Marcie said they were going to bed, too, Cam found himself hoping that whatever happened, he might be able to stumble onto more evidence that she was, indeed, being unfaithful.

Why was that so exciting?

There was something wrong about it. Something forbidden.

CHAPTER FOUR

HE COULD HARDLY PRETEND things were normal now. But he could play the innocent.

'What's going on?' he said, deciding that if everything was normal on his part, and he suspected nothing about her time in the London flat recently, that he would have noticed her acting a little out of character this evening.

'Nothing,' she said, but she wasn't wearing her usual pajamas, emerging from the bathroom after brushing her teeth. That thin, white tank top and a pair of fairly plain, white panties. Plain, but somehow devastatingly sexy in that moment, because they drew his gaze to between her legs, and made him think about her guilt, her infidelity.

She walked slowly around the bed, knowing his eyes were following her. Knowing that he was taking in the sight of her wearing not much more than underwear, rather than nightwear.

Was she testing him? Seeing whether he was still attracted to her?

He quite plainly was, he didn't need to pretend when it came to that. But he was also nervous, very nervous. It felt curiously like the first time he'd ever had sex. He was nervous that he wouldn't be able to perform, and she'd take offense. That the pressure to please her, and to save their relationship, would bear down on his shoulders too much. He was also nervous that she would change her mind about him—that she would decide she loved someone else, not Cam, anymore.

'*Something*'s on your mind,' he insisted, his eyes returning to the book in his lap, trying not to seem as though he was horny as hell right now, trying to behave like normal.

'I'm just…' she was searching for something to explain herself, and he got the sense that she didn't want to lie to him, she just wasn't ready to tell him the truth. She put a knee onto the end of the bed, and he tried to keep calm and appear to be reading, though she looked so wincingly beautiful, clad in nothing but a thin layer of white cotton.

She asked him, 'Doesn't it frighten you, sometimes? All this virus stuff, I mean.'

A clever thing to say to him. Not wrong. Not a lie. But it might not have been the concern most at the forefront of her mind just now.

'Sure,' he said, looking up from his book, giving her a reassuring smile. 'But you can't dwell on it. It doesn't help anyone, getting scared.'

He allowed his eyes to linger on her, taking in the fine lines of her body, noticing the little buds upon her breasts, pushing against the thin cotton of her top. Hesitating as he looked upon her, at least long enough so that she knew he was looking and could take pleasure in his clear attraction to her. When his eyes traveled back up her chest, taking in the beauty of her face, meandering their way to connect with her own gaze, her expression broke into an affectionate smile.

'I don't know what I'd do without you,' she said, and it was reassuring to hear.

He felt his manhood stirring. What she said did, rather, confirm his suspicions that she was seeing someone else. Or had been, until very recently. Now, she was feeling guilt. She was quite clearly worried about losing him, though she could express such feelings through the disguise of concern about the virus, the pandemic.

'You don't have to worry,' he said. 'We're being careful, aren't we?'

'Yes, of course,' she nodded.

'We keep our distance from other people, and the risks are small.'

Was she keeping her distance from other people? He was getting more and more sure she hadn't been keeping her distance from one other person. And yet, if he was maintaining social distancing precautions, there couldn't be too much more risk, could there?

She smiled again, and now climbed onto the bed.

'I love you. You know that, don't you?' she said, crawling on hands and knees up toward him. Was this really the kind of thing she'd say if she was merely a little freaked out by the constant media coverage of the pandemic?

In his mind, it all confirmed his suspicions. And yet, it wasn't enough to act on. It wasn't enough for him to say, *I know you've been seeing someone else. I know, but it doesn't matter to me, so long as you keep loving me.* Because if it wasn't true, and he accused her wrongly, it could be devastating for them.

You could break trust in ways other than infidelity.

'I know,' he said, feeling like Han Solo.

Goodness, she was so sexy, slinking her way up the bed toward him.

'Sometimes I think I don't tell you enough,' she said,

swamping him with her perfume. Had she been re-applying it? She didn't do that normally, did she? Not even when it was a Saturday and they felt obligated to have sex.

He parted his legs, let her approach him, and kiss him. Her lips so warm, so tender, so sweet. A little tongue. Loving, but also needy.

Were these the lips of an adulterous wife?

Had she touched these lips to another man?

A shiver of pure lust flickered through him as he tasted her lips, her mouth. As he breathed her in. He was attracted to her, of course. But what got him so hard in that moment was the thought that she had been enjoying illicit attention in London. That she'd been naughty. That she was, somehow, unclean because of it—even if she smelled as fresh as a daisy, and she looked as perfect as the living day.

'It must be frightening, being in London during the lockdown,' he said, trying to reassure her, trying to understand her without referring to the thing that was really on his mind.

'It's just weird,' she said, and now she turned, so that she could sit between his legs, use him as her own personal armchair. 'The empty streets. I mean, there *are* people. Grocery shopping. Jogging. But it still looks so weird, in the middle of the day.'

'You feel safe at work?'

She leaned back, into him, and he put his arm around her. He could smell the freshness of her hair. She'd showered that morning, of course. After sex? Maybe. But she'd have showered anyway, affair or no affair. He stroked the smooth, soft skin of her upper chest. Gave her a little squeeze, kissed her cheek, albeit through a golden curtain of silky hair.

'Safe enough,' she said. 'We have meetings in the board

room, and there's so few of us we can keep our distance. Then, I have my own office, so. But, you know… I mean, we're all inside. The air circulates.'

'You could stop, if you were worried.'

'I guess.'

'Quit. Come home.' Was he telling her she could stop her affair?

She moaned quietly, enjoying their closeness. His hand drifted down to her breast, since that was naturally where it fell. But her little, quiet purring told him she liked him touching her there. Stroking her. Tracing circles around the little stiff bud pressing up through the thin cotton.

'I think I'll be okay,' she said, leaning back against him, her hand running down his thigh. Turning her head so she could kiss him, so her lips could find his.

Her kiss was so tender, so emotional. It conveyed her feelings toward him better than any professions of love, better even than a loving glance. The way a picture was worth a thousand words, a kiss could be worth ten thousand. A hundred thousand.

As he kissed her, he gently drew the hem of her top upward, exposing her bare breasts, her stiff nipples. Just stunning. And he could touch them.

Did she let another man touch them?

Her lover had to be in awe of her beauty. How could you not?

It made him feel proud. Stroking, squeezing her magnificent breasts. The other guy got to enjoy her, momentarily. But she was his. She had stood at the altar and committed herself to him. Until death do us part.

He was proud of her. Like he wanted to show her off. He wanted other men to see how incredible she was—and know that she was his.

Was it ego, on his part, that excited him about her potential infidelity?

Ego was such a driver in people, even people who believed they were comparatively unaffected.

She moaned as he touched her, and nuzzled into him. He swept one of his hands down her taut stomach. She had been doing well to keep in such good shape while people were no longer allowed to use gyms.

Had she kept in such good shape by fucking someone else?

'I love you,' he said, trying to give her a message, even if she thought he was saying it because she had expressed anxiety about the pandemic. 'I'll love you no matter what happens. We'll be okay. We can cope with anything.'

She smiled, kissed his mouth again, so sweetly. And his hand dipped down between her legs, feeling the thin cotton of her panties, the heat of her body there. The damp cotton over her sex. She was already wet for him. Or was she imagining her lover while her husband touched her?

Well, he couldn't profess to never thinking about someone else while he'd had sex with Marcie.

Now he slipped his hand down underneath the waistband of her panties, enjoying the smoothness, the softness of her skin, and the heat of her body, as he slowly drew it down between her legs, stretching the cotton of her underwear as it went.

And, to his surprise, the smoothness of her skin went on and on, over her mound and down until his middle finger dipped into the hot, wet vale of her sex. Where was her pubic hair? She'd always kept it fairly tidy, but right now there was no trace whatsoever. Her pussy was completely shaven.

Had she done that to please her lover? She had to have done. She'd never considered doing it before, in all the years they'd been together. When had she done it? Well, now Cam was trying to remember when had been the last time they'd had sex. Had it been so long ago? It had been a while, actually. He couldn't remember.

'You shaved...?' he said, quietly, because he felt that if this was a normal night, and he had no suspicions about her, he might notice that she'd gone and shaved her pussy.

She glanced up at his face, smiling, blushing, trying to determine whether he was in favor or not of what she'd done. 'I felt like a change,' she said quietly.

'Okay,' he said, running two fingers along her slippery folds, feeling her body writhe in response to stroking her there, hearing her soft sigh.

'You... like it?' she asked him.

'Sure,' he said, tracing his fingers over her mound, taking in the difference from what he'd known before. He'd never been with a woman who shaved her pussy completely. 'It's good to have a little change, sometimes.'

'Mmm...' she moaned, as his fingers slid back into her soaking pussy, and she just lay back against him, letting him move his finger inside her. Then her hand joined his, and she was pulling aside her panties to improve access, her hand on his, showing her what she wanted, guiding him to provide some attention to her clit.

She was so wet. He could smell her arousal, thick in the air. Was she always this wet when she made love?

But then usually when they made love, they didn't do this. They didn't spend time just touching each other like this. Long years of marriage had seen their lovemaking curtailed, shortened, made ultra efficient. It had turned sex into a brief snack, rather than a leisurely meal to be savored. Right now, she was showing him how she masturbated. It felt so intimate, he couldn't believe it. She was showing him, and he was trying it for himself, and then he was doing it for her—touching her, exactly as she liked.

He felt like an old dog being taught new tricks. But he was open to it. Never too late to learn how to please the woman you love.

'Mmm…' she said, after a while, like the cat who got the cream. Had she come? Her body had been constantly moving as he touched her, writhing, squirming. Her pussy so creamy as he worked it with his fingers. Perhaps she'd had something gentle, something that might lead to better.

But now she pulled herself up, turning so that she was kneeling between his legs, sliding her hands up his thighs as her gaze fell upon the bulge in his crotch. She swept her hands up his stomach, over his bare chest, then back down again, circling that beast between his thighs. She looked into his eyes, her pretty face full of brightness, just elated by how hard he was for her.

She hooked her fingers in the waistband of his sweat-pants, and he duly lifted his hips to help her slip it down, along with his underwear, freeing up his towering erection.

He smiled, amused at the surprise on her face, reassured by the delight in her eyes, joyous at the excitement in her broad smile.

She wasn't imagining her lover now. The way she was looking at his hard cock, the way she curled her fingers around it, touching it, exploring it. It was like she had to re-familiarize herself to it, she had to remind herself how it was in the old days, how much it could affect her.

Cam breathed out a long, slow breath as he felt her squeeze his hardness, and begin stroking it.

She flashed him a mischievous grin, as though reminding him how long it had been since they fooled around. Since they were young lovers, messing around on a lazy evening together, giving in to raucous desires. She looked playful like he hadn't seen in years—it made you so grown-up, didn't it, having kids? So awfully mature. But she was giggling, now, and pressing his thick cock against her cheek, before touching her lips to its tip, tasting it, taking it into her hot mouth.

'Oh God…' he moaned, thinking how he couldn't even remember the last time she'd done this with him.

The way she moved on his cock, the way she used her mouth on him—it didn't seem like she was rusty in any way. She made him feel she'd had recent practice at this.

'Oh my God…' she grinned at him, her mouth full of his cock, and then sank deeper on him, surprising him by how deep she could take him.

It had never been like this before, had it?

She licked his full length, from base to tip, watching how he groaned at the sensation. She swirled her tongue around him, she bobbed her head in a kind of twisting, spiral motion that just felt incredible. When had she learned to do that?

It all seemed like evidence pointing to her affair—and yet none of it was in any way definitive.

What if she'd simply been watching a lot of porn while she'd been on her own during those London nights? What if she'd been reading self-help books on how to improve your blow-job technique?

She seemed to enjoy going down on him like she hadn't before. Perhaps she was merely performing, to make him feel that she was really into this, because of her guilt. Because of her fears that their marriage could collapse. But she didn't seem like she was acting. She seemed relaxed, and genuinely happy. Closing her eyes as she sucked on him, like it was turning her on as much as him.

He watched her pretty face as she took his hard cock in

her elegant mouth, and he wondered what he was up against.

Did her lover have a big dick?

It shouldn't matter. He wasn't worried that the guy had such a monumental cock that it would make Marcie want to leave him. There were other reasons—like love—that made him nervous she'd want to leave him, but not that. He was just curious about that. And actually, when he thought about it, he rather preferred the idea that she would take a lover who had a big dick, than one who wasn't so gifted in the trouser department. If she was going to have an affair, then she might as well have a searing hot affair.

He actually liked the idea of his wife having an adventure with a guy who was hung like a horse.

Maybe, another positive, would be that it would be comparatively easier for her to go down on her husband. It could be a more pleasurable experience for her.

Jesus, did she look like this with her lips wrapped around her lover's cock? So beautiful, her golden hair now trailing down over his hip. He stroked it out of her face, and she looked up at him, smiling albeit with her mouth full.

He urged her up from his lap with a gentle hand supporting her jaw, and sat up himself, kissing her lips, feeling the affection, the love in her kiss, seeing the bliss in her eyes as he kissed her. Continuing to tangle with her lips, he pulled her onto him, making her giggle again, but then he was hauling her over, making her squeak with surprise as he turned her onto her back, so that he lay over her, sucking on lips he believed had been used on another man.

She was just magnificent, a goddess. How could he have ever taken her for granted? How could he ever have become overfamiliar with her, to the point that sex had been inconsequential?

But his eyes were open now. It might have taken her adultery to do it, but they were open now. He gazed at her, ran his hands down her bare chest, reveled in seeing her nipples so stiff on her glorious breasts. He knelt up between her smooth thighs and tugged on her panties, feeling a little buzz, a little throb between his legs as she lifted her hips and allowed him to peel down her underwear, then part her knees to reveal the breathtaking sight of her bare pussy.

Had she taken another man in here?

When had she last fucked him? Last night? This morning?

He swept his hands over her stomach, and up to her breasts, and she smiled broadly. He could see in her bright expression she thought him about to slide inside her, to finish this. But while normally he would, no doubt, tonight he felt differently. He was more certain, now, that she was sleeping with another man than when they'd started making love. The little things had all added up to confirmation, in his mind, though there was no way they added up to enough to confront her about anything. They were enough, though, to make him see her differently. To make him want her differently than normal.

He refrained from lying over her, from sliding his hard cock inside her to get on with it. He slid down, his head descending between her raised knees, his hands holding her by the waist. He had to get a closer look at her shaved pussy.

Her cheating pussy.

The scent of her arousal was almost overwhelming, this close up. Her pussy seemed so pristine, so tidy. So pink.

Glistening in the light from the bedside table lamps. Did her lover insist she keep it this way?

He leaned forward, kissed her beside her navel, once, twice, feeling the softness of her skin, the wonderful warmth. The little tremble in her frame. Was she nervous? Or just horny?

She stroked his head, the back of his neck, affectionate, but somehow uncertain. She wasn't sure what he was up to. He was breaking from his normal routine, just as she had been breaking with hers. But she knew why she was being unpredictable tonight, she didn't know why he was.

'I've never seen you like this before,' he said, overtly gazing at her hairless quim, staring at it like a bear of very little brain might stare at a honeypot, making her feel that his departure from normal behavior might be the result of hers before him—in particular, her new look down below.

'You like it?' she smiled.

'I liked it before, too.'

She laughed at that. 'Diplomatic,' she said.

He dropped down, taking a long, slow, deep breath to savor that exhilarating scent, his mind reeling as the word *adultery* spun round and round inside it. Gently, he kissed her just beside her pussy lips, taking in the strange softness, where he might ordinarily expect a dusting of golden fur.

'What are you doing?' she asked him, quietly, her voice sounding strangely far-off, dazed.

'Enjoying myself,' he said, and now drew the tip of his tongue slowly through her pussy lips, all the way up to her clit, tasting her, as though for the first time.

'Mmmm…' she moaned, as he pressed his hot mouth against her sex, sucking on her folds. 'That's nice…'

It had been a long time since he'd gone down on her. It seemed much easier with her fur gone. He put his hands on her upper thighs and French-kissed her there, and from the very beginning she was responding to his every touch with free abandon. He didn't exactly consider his technique—he just gave in to his lust, lapping at her copious juices, loving how she moved under him, and if she responded particularly well to something he did, he kept on doing it until she was squirming and whimpering under him.

She stroked his head as he tongued her. She closed her eyes, tilted her head back, and moaned so loudly he thought he might have to warn her that their kids were asleep elsewhere in the house. But she did manage to control herself, limiting her vocal expression to a desperate panting as he sucked forcefully on her pussy lips, and nudged his nose into her clit.

Soon enough, she was thrashing around underneath him, and it seemed that his entire face was sticky with her emissions. As her orgasm struck, she had both hands pressing his head to her body, and she was jerking her hips, practically fucking his face, though he was the one on top.

It was intense, but so sexy.

He wondered whether it had been this good before. He wondered if it was the fact that she'd shaved her pussy that made it so good this time, or because he kept thinking of her giving this sweet pussy to another man. He was leaning toward the latter.

When her orgasm hit her, she was laughing, and he wasn't entirely sure why, but it seemed like she hadn't been expecting to come this way—she hadn't expected her husband to suddenly want to go down on her, she hadn't expected him to be as effective as this.

After she had had time to recover her breath, he knelt up between her legs, and she parted them as wide as she could, encouraging him in. She had a wonderfully satisfied smile on her face, and they weren't even finished.

'I should have shaved my pussy a long time ago,' she said with a naughty grin.

'Maybe,' he chuckled.

And inside, he was thinking, maybe you should have had an affair a long time ago.

Maybe she had, and he'd never had a clue.

He tapped the end of his cock against her open flower, then touched the tip to her entrance, coating it in her wetness.

Thinking, what did it matter if she had had an affair? If she was still as into him as this, that was the main thing. That she still loved him, that she still wanted him.

But this wasn't just about forgiving her for past indiscretions. This wasn't just about tolerating her infidelity. Cam stroked his cock against the dewy petals of her flower, and he wanted her to have enjoyed this kind of attention from another man. He liked to think of her having such an illicit adventure.

'Please,' she said softly as he teased her with his manhood without, yet, dipping inside her, and it seemed almost as though she was pleading for his forgiveness.

But then she said, 'Please... fuck me. I need you to fuck me...'

And he grinned, and then sank his cock deep inside her.

———

LATER, he played those moments over and over in his mind as she lay there beside him soundly asleep. He remembered how it had been, thrusting into her, the movement of his cock so easy because she was so wet.

Thinking, had she ever been that wet with him before?

Thinking, she was soaking wet because she had two

men fucking her these days, one in the city, and one in the country.

He lay awake in bed and remembered how Marcie had not finished with her surprises for him when he had started fucking her. She had another little change to their routine for him, urging him up so she could turn onto all fours, present herself to him like an animal in heat, an animal ready to mate. He had knelt there behind her, grasping her stunning rear with both hands, taking in the delicious sight of her from the rear, gently stroking her pussy with a hand before lining up to drive his hard cock back inside her.

They really had paired their marital sex down to almost nothing. Almost always missionary. When had he last taken her from behind?

She had quickly pulled off her tank top, and then he was working it, thrusting into her over and over again like it was a workout routine. Both of them getting sweaty, Marcie rocking back and forth under him, so that she was almost doing more of the pounding than he was.

Then she was on top of him, riding him like a stallion, just magnificent as she rocked back and forth, her gorgeous breasts bouncing, her hips working, her face contorting as another orgasm swept through her.

But then at the last moment, she was off him again, dropping down to lie between his legs, to take his shaft in one hand, just before it started bucking and jerking and letting go. She slipped the end of his cock between her lips, and he was coming inside her mouth, and she was swallowing every last drop, as though she needed it to sustain her.

CHAPTER FIVE

AFTER THAT, he felt better. There was less of the anxiety, less of the butterflies. The whole of that weekend, he felt like he was walking on clouds. Every time Marcie looked at him, she smiled sweetly, *lovingly*. That wasn't fake. She, too, seemed to be lighter of step, and more cheery of heart than normal. It was noticeable, though both of them seemed to be trying to act normal around Flo and the kids.

It felt almost as though they were newlyweds again. Honeymooners. Permanently tipsy on their rekindled passion, drunk on their professed love.

It made Cam feel more settled than he had been even before noticing that set of VW car keys in the background of the FaceTime call to Marcie in London. He felt practically bombproof, in fact. And it wasn't just Cam who seemed to feel different—stronger, bolder. Marcie had this wonderful confidence about her, this constant cheer, a kind of energy that Cam, as a newspaperman from the turn of the millennium, might have suspected was cocaine-related, though he knew full well it wasn't class-A drugs that perked her up like this.

As he had got over his fear—fear of losing her—through their rekindled desire, Marcie seemed to have pushed past her guilt. And it made it that much clearer to Cam how guilty she must have felt beforehand. How she had been afraid, too—of losing him. But through that weekend, through their lovemaking, he had been murmuring expressions of love to her that he had directed toward her guilt, that subconsciously might have felt like he was forgiving her for her past transgressions.

I'll always love you, you know that? No matter what.

He saw his words impact on her. He didn't just see the rosy smiles from a woman to whom he'd been pledging his heart. There was an easing of the tension on her face, a dilution of the concern in her eyes, as he made it clear that whatever life threw at them, whatever circumstances changed for them both, personally, Cam was hers, and hers completely, without question or condition.

Every night, that weekend, after the kids were asleep, Marcie snuggled up to him on the sofa as they watched TV.

They hadn't been coupley like that beforehand, not for years.

Flo didn't seem to notice, or else, if she did then she didn't comment on it.

Marcie gave him little secret touches as she cuddled up with him, stroking him where she could without Flo seeing. It felt furtive, exciting, as though they were in the presence of parents but were not yet married.

And then when Flo went to bed, each night they would wait five or ten minutes, and then Marcie would give him a naughty look, seductive. They'd scamper upstairs as quietly as they could, seal themselves off in the master bedroom, then tear off each other's clothes.

And when they had torn off each other's clothes, things

were still different than they'd been before. Marcie's self-confidence seemed to boil over into her lovemaking—she seemed to like to take more charge than ever before, telling him exactly what she wanted, how she wanted it, and never simply lying there and taking it. Was this the influence of a new lover?

Whether or not she had learned lessons from a new man, he found her new confidence thrilling—and knowing exactly what she wanted as he made love to her was a blast. It took the guesswork out of pleasing her, took the pressure off his attempts to read her signals. It also seemed to mean guaranteed orgasms for her.

But then it came to Sunday night, and the fear returned.

She was going back to London the next morning. It was all very well feeling this renewed sense of connection with Marcie, and he had certainly embraced the erotic thrill of believing she had been sleeping with another man on the side—but the simple fact was that she was still keeping the truth from him. As many times as she had told him she loved him that weekend, and it had been many times, she was still hiding a big secret from him.

And as the time neared when she would be leaving home once again to commute into London, where she would be joining her lover—Cam came to the realization that his thrill about her having sex with other people was somewhat reliant on him knowing that she was, on him consenting to it, on him being involved, at least in sharing in the details of her adventures.

When he thought about her infidelity, it turned him on only to the point where he was reminded of the ugliness of her deception. If only that part of her infidelity could simply disappear! She could come clean with him, tell him she was seeing another man during her nights in London

—and he could tell her it was okay, she could sleep with whoever she pleased, so long as she didn't keep her husband in the dark about it.

He was turned on by merely suspecting she was being promiscuous. Imagine if he knew for certain she was. Imagine if she told him about her liaisons. Imagine if he could ever see glimpses of her with another man, either pictures or in person.

He could imagine that another man might not want his lover's husband hanging around while he was with her, let alone watching when they had sex. But the main point, as he thought about it during that Sunday, was that he wanted her to be open with him about everything that happened.

And that started with an admission.

He just didn't want to have to force an admission out of her. And even more scary was the possibility that he could accuse her of infidelity and that she would deny it— and then what would be worse for him—that she was lying, or that she was telling the truth and he'd have falsely accused her?

But how to get through that truth barrier?

That final night, he even tried to make light of it, to see if he could get her to open up, to help them both through that truth barrier.

'God, I'm going to miss this until Thursday,' she said, standing by the end of their bed as he knelt on the carpet, head tilted upward between her thighs so he could worship her perfectly hairless pussy.

'I could sneak down to London late at night,' he joked. 'Make you come and then sneak back before anyone knew I was gone.'

'Mmm…' she moaned, stroking his hair as he worked the tip of his tongue around the apex of her pussy, and sucked gently on her clit. 'What if the police stopped you, and asked you why you were breaching lockdown?'

'I'd say I was an essential service,' he said, his hands clutching her gorgeous rear as he lapped at her sex.

She laughed at that. 'I'm not sure they'd agree with your definition of… *ohh*… essential…'

'I could show them a picture of you. They'd probably agree it was essential to make you happy.'

A giggle. She had both hands on his head now, stroking him as he sucked on her pussy. Perhaps gently pulling him to her, to encourage him.

'I'm serious, though,' he said in between mouthfuls. 'I could come down one night. If you're finding it difficult being alone.'

'No,' she said quickly, perhaps a little more quickly than she'd meant to—a touch more startled than she'd meant to appear. As though she was worried he genuinely would come down to London in the middle of the night, only to find that she was not alone. Then, perhaps realizing she'd been a little abrupt in her reply, she softened it by adding, 'It's not so difficult. Really.'

'The chances of being stopped by the police have to be pretty slim,' he said.

She held his head a little more firmly in her hands, and now she was moving her hips a little, too, guiding his mouth against her sex. Maybe even controlling. Maybe even trying to stifle his talk, to distract him from the thought about coming down to London to see her at night.

'Oh yes… just like that…' she moaned, and he sucked on her tangy goodness as she gently rubbed her sex against his face.

Gazing up her body from this angle was just breathtaking. How could he not want to show off this incredible woman to other men? To prove what he had. The nerd in school who had grown up to marry a cheerleader.

He said, 'It'd probably do the car a world of good, to have a little run down to London and back.'

But she stopped him, gazed down at him, said, 'It's not worth it. You know they can fine you nearly £2,000 for breaking lockdown?'

He nodded, but wondered whether she considered that she was breaking lockdown, potentially, by seeing another man when she was in London.

He laid a soft little kiss on her clit, and gazed up at her. 'I worry about you being on your own at night.'

'I'll be okay. It's only three nights a week.'

He lapped at her a little more, enjoying her wetness, savoring her flavor.

Then he looked up at her and said, 'Maybe we could find you a companion. You know. To stay over.'

She stopped him when he said that, peered down at him quizzically. 'What are you talking about?'

He grinned, as though he was quite obviously making a joke. 'All of those colleagues of yours who've been furloughed—maybe one of them could do with a roof over their head until the economy gets going again?'

'Maybe a nice young stud?' he laughed.

She knelt down, ran her fingers through his hair, her hands sliding down to cradle his jaw just as she leaned in to kiss his mouth. 'You're a funny guy, you know that?' She said, kissing him forcefully, and he wondered whether the gentle flush in her cheeks was from him getting perilously close to the truth about another man staying with her in London—or simply because he'd just been sucking on her pussy.

'It wouldn't need to be a big deal,' he said, as she stood up again, presenting him with another glimpse of heaven.

'You know, what happens in lockdown stays in lockdown...'

He leaned in to kiss her pussy again, and she gave him a smirk that told him he was saying crazy things, then she turned around, and he ended up kissing her pussy, briefly, from the rear. She giggled at that, and then climbed onto the bed, pausing on all fours to wait for him to join her.

He sighed, realizing that a touch of humor was no way to get into the serious topic of her actual infidelity.

But now wasn't the time to figure out what he should do next. Now was time to climb onto the bed behind her, and slide his hard cock inside her, taking care of that most pressing need.

CHAPTER SIX

AND THEN SHE WAS GONE, again. Back to London.

Cam stood at the bedroom window and watched her drive away, and he just felt empty. Totally empty.

She hadn't said a thing about her affair.

He knew she'd been feeling guilty, all weekend. He could tell. The guilt had driven her need to get close to him, to be close to him from Thursday to Sunday. To recommit to him, to reignite the sex between them. The guilt had been eating at her, all the time, under the surface—even while she'd embraced Cam's renewed desire for her, his clear attraction, his newfound love of foreplay, his devotion to her newly-shaven sex.

Perhaps she assumed his rekindled passion for her might be related to her own push to initiate sex between them, her own change in attitude towards sex? The fact that she was more willing to take charge, to tell him or show him exactly what she wanted, rather than leaving it to him and his male ego to control things. Or else, maybe, he was just particularly taken with her now perfectly hairless pussy. Or a combination of both.

She could know nothing of his excitement concerning her infidelity. He could hardly understand it himself, though through the weekend he lost any shred of capability for denying it in his own mind.

And yet, though he now accepted that he was aroused by her adultery, it still hurt that she left that Monday morning, on her usual early-morning commute to the city, and she hadn't come clean about the real driver for change within her. It hurt that though they had spent so much effort connecting, and professing their love for each other, that she could return to London without giving up the secret that was dominating her life.

He was surprised just how much it hurt.

———

'EVERYTHING OKAY, DEAR?' Flo asked him, and he realized he'd been sitting there at the breakfast table, not eating his cereal for God knew how long. Distracted. Dazed.

He nodded, and smiled, vaguely. An idea had formed in his head, but words were now coming out of his mouth before he could even really process the idea fully.

'I have to go out today,' he said. 'For work.'

'For *work*, dear?'

Work. Flo gave him an odd look. His kids looked at him like he was being funny, too. They didn't really think that he ever *worked*. It was Mommy who worked. But while these days Cam didn't get to be the newspaper man he had been when he'd first met their mother, he did continue to spend a few hours a week, where he could snatch them, writing. Though these days, his topic was gardening, rather than retail business, since the garden was so much easier to access when he was a stay-at-home dad.

'I'm visiting a gardening center,' he said, lying out of his ass, but saying the first thing he could come up with to explain his need to go out for the day for work.

'A gardening center?'

'They're giving me a tour so I can see how the lockdown is affecting their business—all the plants they can't sell since they're not allowed to open to customers.'

'Oh, of course,' Flo said, 'they're going to have to throw out a lot of plants, aren't they? This time of year.'

Cam nodded sagely, feeling the lie really warming up now, locking into a firm state of credibility. 'Even if they try to sell things online, they can't get enough staff to do all the packing and shipping—and they still have to meet all these social distancing requirements.'

Thank goodness for his mother-in-law, huh. Flo was completely fine about taking care of the kids. She had more parenting experience than either he or Marcie, even if she was a little rusty here and there, with a predilection for giving the children too much candy or snacks.

And then Cam was safely in his car, driving off toward London.

Jesus.

Was he really doing this? What was he going to say to Marcie if she found out?

Well, he figured he'd stick to his cover story about the garden center. She didn't delve too much into his work— she'd never been much interested in the garden, or his rebirth as a horticultural writer. She just left him to it.

He drove along the A40 to Oxford, but as he was doing so, he thought about all the reports about people being stopped by the police and fined for breaking lockdown rules—for traveling without a 'reasonable' excuse. What would he say if he was stopped by the police? That he was working? He didn't have any evidence that he was on his way to a work assignment, of course he didn't. As of that morning, the police had issued 3,493 fines for alleged breaches of coronavirus lockdown laws—ranging from people sitting on park benches and not 'exercising' to families driving hundreds of miles for vacations.

After Oxford, he avoided the motorway and used back roads to get to London. It took more than twice as long, but better to be safe than sorry. And there was a lot less traffic than normal, of course. That helped.

And here he was, creeping into Bayswater, praying that there wasn't some coincidental reason that Marcie might have decided to stay in the apartment today, or that she might have some need to pop back to the apartment to get something while he was there. He parked two blocks away, in a shady little corner, so that there would be less risk that Marcie might walk along and recognize his car. At least lockdown meant that finding a parking space was pretty straightforward. Then, he walked to the flat, constantly glancing around to check for danger.

He was actually surprised to see quite a number of people around—the streets weren't completely deserted, as he had assumed they would be. Sure, there was very little by way of traffic. But there were people out carrying shopping bags, and people apparently going for their daily allocation of 'exercise'. Plenty of runners, certainly. But there was nobody out who would recognize him.

Quietly, he slipped into the apartment building, and then headed upstairs like a cat burglar, hoping he didn't run into any neighbors.

His heart was pounding like a military drum as he slid his key into the front door lock, and turned. For a moment, there was a little resistance to his efforts to turn the key in the lock, and he had a panicky thought that she might have changed the locks. But why would she do that, if at any time the lockdown could be lifted by the government, and maybe one day he would officially need to go to London for a meeting, and need the apartment himself?

A little extra wiggle, and the front door unlocked with a satisfying click.

He was in.

Inside, the place was clean, tidy, just as expected. Marcie was a tidy person. Cam breathed deeply, recovering from the climb up the stairs to the apartment, but also trying to keep calm. The air smelled faintly of Marcie's perfume, and he could pick up an underlying scent of cleaning products. Of course, there was no sign of those unidentified car keys lying around. A little food in the fridge—a few takeaway boxes half-filled with leftovers, a bottle of white wine. Nothing amiss there.

Had Marcie been ultra-careful in cleaning up this place? Had she taken pains to hide any sign that anyone else had been here, in case her husband suddenly visited? Why would she be so suspicious?

No, Marcie was just this clean, this tidy. She didn't like living in a mess. Cam nosed around the living room, and found no evidence of anyone other than his wife being there. He started to feel an unforeseen sense of disappointment, that Marcie *hadn't* been sleeping with someone else, that there really had been a valid reason for her to have those Volkswagen keys, that he had been mistaken and she was still the same old highly-efficient, highly predictable, highly ambitious businesswoman she had always been, and she didn't have a secret dark side, a sexy alter ego as an adulterous seductress.

He laughed at himself. God, what an idiot. And he'd come all this way, too, for nothing.

Then he walked into the bedroom, opened one of the drawers in the chest over by the wardrobe, and found it full of men's underwear and socks. And he almost had a seizure.

CHAPTER SEVEN

AT FIRST, he was stunned. Shocked. He couldn't breathe. He felt like somebody had kicked him hard in the chest.

Then he felt stupid. He even blushed, fiercely, though there was nobody there to see. He'd been building himself to find exactly this, and yet now that he was here, seeing it, he wasn't reacting at all the way he expected. Sure, there was that vague arousal underpinning everything—he was even getting hard. But somehow, seeing all these clothes— these male clothes packed neatly away in the chest of drawers—simply emphasized the hurt he felt because Marcie had been keeping the truth from him.

Even if the thought of her having sex with another man was strangely erotic to him, he couldn't quite get over the fact that she was betraying him.

Part of it was the sense that his gut feeling about her, that she couldn't possibly do something like this to him, had been wrong. Part of it was the sense that he had missed out on a significant event in her life, he simply wasn't a part of it.

Even though, if they'd talked about it out in the open,

about her genuine need for companionship, or even a desire to have sex with someone she'd met, Cam might well have been open to her going through with it, she had never given him the choice. She had never given him the chance to consent to it.

He stood there, frozen for a good minute or two. Then he breathed, and tried to keep calm.

His rational mind even tried to find an explanation for what he was seeing. Like, maybe Marcie had packed a load of male clothing into the drawers of this chest so that Cam could simply drop by the apartment any time, and not need to bring a huge suitcase with him.

The next drawer down was full of female underwear— but it struck him almost immediately as different from looking in Marcie's underwear drawer at home. It was all lacy, or satin, even some velvety items. Black, white, bright scarlet, crimson, purple. He took some things out, and found that along with bras and panties, here were stockings, and garter belts, and babydolls, and bodysuits.

Cam plucked out a pair of white satin panties, only to find he was holding a g-string. Here was another one. And a thong—when had Marcie started wearing thongs?

It was like someone had crammed a branch of Victoria's Secret into a drawer. Where was all the sensible underwear? The big panties, the plain bras, the standard cotton or polyester?

His heart was hammering against his chest wall, trying to get out. His rational mind was reeling, searching for some kind of explanation. Marcie just liked wearing expensive lingerie when she was working. It made her feel sexy, powerful, special. She just did it to make herself feel good while she worked. But if she felt like that, why didn't she have any of this stuff at home? Why did she never come home wearing sexy underwear, or dress in lingerie on a Monday morning before commuting into the city?

Why did she never wear anything sexy, like this, when she was in a mood to have sex with her husband?

True, sex for them wasn't as common as it had once been, but most times nowadays, on a Thursday night she'd come back from the city with an inclination to drag him to bed and jump his bones—but when she stripped, she was always wearing something very ordinary-looking in terms of underwear.

Here was a drawer full of men's clothing—polo shirts, jeans, t-shirts. Sure, Marcie could wear men's clothing if she wanted to, but she didn't at home. Maybe these were emergency clothes in case Cam was in town—but why so many outfits? Surely he'd only need one drawer with a couple of pairs of underpants, a t-shirt or two, a pair of jeans.

It wasn't even, really, the kind of clothing Cam would wear, in London or otherwise.

The closet had male clothing within it, too. Not a huge amount—but a couple of suits, a jacket or two, a few smart shirts. Again, just too many items for it to be an in-case-Cam's-in-town deal.

Were these the clothes of a man she was having sex with while staying here in London?

He felt a little nauseous, thinking about Marcie going behind his back like this.

But he did also feel some remorse, a quiet shame that in their marriage, despite the pressures of having two young kids, he had somehow failed Marcie. He had taken her for granted. He had looked at her with over-familiar eyes, and had not paid her enough attention, sexually.

In recent months, in recent years, sex had even seemed like a bit of a chore. Something necessary for Marcie—and maybe for himself, sure—but no longer something particularly special. It was so familiar. She was so familiar. He'd assumed and accepted that it was just what happened when you were in a relationship long-term, when you were married for seven years and more.

Her adultery had opened his eyes to her beauty, it had suddenly given her an intense *value* that he had been overlooking for years. Something to do with knowing that other men wanted her, other men could have her if she let them, other men could show her the kind of devotion her husband ought to be.

The shock seemed less distressing as he quietly poked around the bedroom, and the en suite bathroom, where there were men's toiletries that proved someone was living here; men's clothing in the laundry basket, which showed that the clean clothes in the chest of drawers were not for Cam to make use of while in town.

He was calming down. The full hard-on he was sporting was beginning to influence his feelings.

He heard a bang from behind him, and nearly jumped out of his skin.

Now, he was looking around for a place to hide, his heart beat on rapid-fire, cold sweat breaking out on his forehead. Could he fit in the closet? What would Marcie be doing coming back to the flat now, in the middle of the day? He couldn't think where to hide, where he might be safe. He froze, like the proverbial deer in headlamps.

But after a moment, there was only silence.

He started to relax again.

Had it been a car back-firing, outside?

He calmed down, even managed to laugh at himself for being so jumpy. Somehow, the sudden jolt had eased the pain he'd been feeling inside—or, at least, distracted him from it.

Then he sat down on the bed, on his wife's side, and he opened the little drawer in her bedside table and the first thing he laid eyes on was a box of condoms.

Now his heart was beating hard again, and his erection was at full strength. He and Marcie hadn't used condoms since they'd started dating. Since she'd gone on birth control pills so they didn't have to use them. Still, he found his rational mind looking for an innocent explanation—had she got them in case her birth control pills ran out, and it took longer for her to get a repeat prescription because of all the delays in the delivery system during lockdown?

In which case, why did she have the condoms in her bedside table, here in London? If they were for use with her husband, why weren't they stashed in the medical cabinet in their en suite bathroom at home in the Cotswolds?

Jesus. Here at the back of her drawer was a pair of silver handcuffs. And what were these things? Restraints? And something he'd assumed to be an eye mask, something to help Marcie sleep—although, admittedly, she never used such things at home—now made him think it was more likely to be a blindfold.

Marcie was into bondage?

These could only be sex objects. The innocent, naive angel on his shoulder could only sit there and shrug as the devil sitting on his other shoulder laughed smugly. The evidence had reached incontrovertible levels.

Cam had to sit on the bed and just breathe for a minute or two. His feelings were so confused. Excitement, fear. Pain, desire. All mixed up.

His wife of so many years wasn't quite the woman he'd always taken her to be. He couldn't hide from that. Why had she never opened up to him about any of this stuff?

Maybe she assumed he'd be hurt by finding out about her affair—and she'd be right, although it wasn't as simple as that. But if she was into handcuffs and blindfolds—and crazy-sexy underwear—why had she never mentioned anything to him?

Trying to imagine things from her ee, he figured she'd been switched on to all this by her new lover.

Well. Imagining things from her perspective made him less upset about it all. Less angry. It helped free his mind to enjoy the thrill of discovering his wife's sexy secrets. Why would he be so excited at the thought of Marcie having sex with another man? He couldn't exactly say. Maybe porn had primed him to find promiscuous women sexy, since the assumption was that all the porn stars you watched online had plenty of sex with plenty of men, and now you were turned on watching them. Maybe he just liked the idea that Marcie had a secret sex life, it made her more interesting.

Maybe he just liked the thought that she was having a little secret fun while she was here in the city, and not being all lonely and sad away from home.

Who knew why? But here he was, sitting on the bed with a pair of handcuffs in his hands, and a boner the size of the Empire State Building within his pants. He couldn't deny that he was turned on. And he liked feeling turned on.

He left the bedside drawer as he'd found it.

He explored the rest of the apartment, now with a new attitude toward it. A man was living here—maybe not every day of the week, but certainly a regular few nights each week. Here were two toothbrushes in the bathroom, shampoo that wasn't Marcie's, and wasn't his own. Cologne in the cabinet, for goodness sake—Cam hadn't used cologne in a long while. Maybe he needed to start using it again. The guy's things weren't hidden away because Marcie was worried that they'd be discovered—they were hidden away because she was just the same clean and tidy person she'd always been.

Back in the kitchen, there were food items that Marcie would never buy—balsamic vinegar, brown sauce, mayonnaise. There were two plates and two glasses—with two sets of silverware—in the little half-size dishwasher.

In the living room, he searched through the little magazine rack, and in amongst the issues of *Vogue* and *Tatler* and *Cosmo* was a *Top Gear* magazine, a copy of *Four-Four-Two*. Marcie didn't care tuppence about cars, and couldn't even tell you the difference between football and rugby.

In fact, Cam was a little blown away by how confident Marcie seemed to be about having another man staying here at the apartment. She really was making a big assumption that her husband would never need to suddenly come to London and stay in the apartment any time soon.

Lockdown had made her over-confident.

And the weirdest thing was, Cam felt jubilant, ecstatic, that he had discovered all this. It was like finding out he'd gotten into Oxford. It was like waking up on Christmas morning as a kid to unwrap a huge box to find that his parent had given him Optimus fucking Prime.

But he glanced at his watch, now, and it was already past one o'clock. He couldn't stick around. He would have to get going very soon. It wasn't so much that he was worried that Marcie would come back to the apartment—it was that he needed to get home to the Cotswolds in time for the nightly FaceTime call with the kids and their mother.

He went back into the bedroom, wanting another good look at everything, at all the evidence. Marcie really was a very tidy person, there was nothing out of place, no clothes on the floor, even when she had another night here before heading back to the Cotswolds. At home, Cam left everything lying around, right up until Thursday afternoon when there was a mad dash to get everything tidy before Marcie got home. Here, everything was in its proper place. The clothes were all either folded up in drawers, hanging in the closet, or dropped in the little laundry basket in the bathroom.

His heart skipped a beat as he laid eyes on the laundry basket again.

He stepped into the bathroom, wondering if he was taking this too far. Intruding into his wife's privacy. But here was some of the most telling evidence of all. Cam peered into the little laundry basket and found a jumble of worn men's clothing along with some of Marcie's work shirts—and various items of her underwear, which were all chic and sexy like the ones in the chest of drawers out in the bedroom.

Jesus.

He plucked out a little black lacy thong from near the top of the pile, his thoughts racing as he pictured another man peeling these off her—or perhaps even leaving them on while he made love to her.

He touched them briefly to his nose, and recoiled a little, the scent of female arousal was still so strong on the material.

Wow.

This wasn't a pair of fancy panties Marcie just wore to work so she'd feel special in a male-dominated field. This wasn't even simply an overly tiny pair of underwear worn inadvisably for a workout, or for a run around nearby Kensington Gardens. This was a scrap of lace that had been soaked in Marcie's come, drenched by sex with another man, pressed up against her adulterous pussy while she rode her suitor's big dick.

Cam drew in another breath, a full chestful of air through the luxurious black lace, not recoiling this time, but reveling in the wicked scent, feeling the adrenaline coursing through his veins as he savored the unflinching evidence of Marcie's infidelity.

It suddenly felt so wrong, being there. It was his apartment, too, and he had his own keys to get inside, but it felt dangerous to be there. This was Marcie's domain now. This was where she stayed with another man. This was where she cheated on her husband. The darkness he felt only seemed to fuel his lust, his arousal even more.

He couldn't help himself.

He flicked open the fly of his jeans, dragged them down, releasing the monster inside.

He lay on the huge bed—king-size bed, it took up most of the floorspace of the little bedroom—the bed in which Marcie violated her marriage vows with someone else.

He grasped his rock-hard shaft in one hand while he jammed Marcie's worn panties against his face, inhaling a deep chestful of that wicked, sinful scent. Then he was stroking it, squeezing it, slowly pumping it as he savored every detail of that dark, spicy aroma, like a connoisseur assessing the bouquet of a complex, rich and highly valuable red wine.

It felt so good, tending to the tension he had been feeling, responding to the vicious excitement he felt now that he knew Marcie was a red-hot, sexy-as-hell adulteress. Yet he didn't completely lose his mind over that little scrap of extravagant black lace in his hands. He was still in a place that did not feel safe. He couldn't completely relax. He got very close to a powerful climax, but then he considered how problematic it would be if he started spraying come everywhere.

He pulled himself up off the bed. Thinking, maybe he needed to just finish with a handful of toilet paper, and be done.

But then he glanced at his watch again, and he was aware that he didn't have much time to linger. He had to go. He knew how it was with masturbation—you gave in to the temptation, you indulged when you believed it would just be a quick release of the sexual tension that had built up inside you, and then when you were done, you'd lost much more time than you expected. He'd be late.

He pulled up his pants, straightened himself out, despite the massive bulge that made it difficult to zip up his fly once he was squeezed into his jeans again. Now, time for a quick scout around to make sure he'd left everything as he found it: straighten the pillows a little, shake out the duvet to remove the imprint from where he'd lain. In the bathroom, he made sure to replace the laundry basket in its proper position, and leave the clothes therein in a similar fashion to the state he'd found them in.

But he gave in to a base impulse, and did not put Marcie's sex-stained panties back into the basket. Instead, he tucked them into a pocket, before carefully leaving the apartment.

CHAPTER EIGHT

HE DROVE HOME ON MOTORWAYS, feeling less worried about police stopping him to find out whether he had a valid reason for driving long-distance. M4, M25, M40 to Oxford. He figured that if he was stopped, he'd say he'd been working in London and was now headed home to the Cotswolds. They wouldn't ask him for proof he lived there.

Actually, there was a surprising amount of traffic around—were this many people really defying the lockdown? But then again, the government guidelines about the lockdown had never been completely clear—and people were told that if you needed to go in to work because your job could not be done working from home, then you should go into work.

So he figured he was unlikely to be stopped by the police tonight. Chances were as likely as getting into a car accident..

The bottom line was, even if he was fined for breaching lockdown rules, and Marcie found out that he'd made a secret trip to London, he didn't have to feel guilty about popping into the apartment to check up on her. Sure, it was a little intrusive, and it was behind her back.

But Marcie was cheating on him.

That trumped everything.

God, he felt awful. He was driving down the motorway bitterly regretting what he'd done. Jesus. How embarrassing. What if they knew what he'd done in that apartment? What if there was some trace of evidence he had missed when he'd cleaned up, a telltale sign that would give the whole game away? What if they found out he'd laid on that bed and beat off, jacking his cock like an idiot as he sniffed the used panties of his adulterous wife.

The deep, sweat-inducing shame sapped all his sexual energy. It meant that on the long drive home, he had none of the erotic distraction that had, so far, underpinned his consideration of her infidelity—and that meant there was nothing much there to keep the fear and the hurt and the heart-wrenching sense of betrayal in check.

He felt like he was driving back to the Cotswolds with a big hole in his chest. Marcie had betrayed him. She had gone behind his back to enjoy another man. And she'd done it despite the possible risk to her family. He could just about understand that she may have carried on the affair in secret because she didn't want to hurt Cam—and she obviously believed quite firmly that she could keep it a secret from him.

But she had to have known the risks involved.

What if he'd been the kind of jealous, angry husband who would take the news of her having an affair and immediately demand a divorce, breaking their family apart? What if he'd been the type of husband who would feel such sorrow, he'd never be able to lay eyes on her again without his wounds re-opening, constantly reminding him of her betrayal? She had to have known that there would be a risk of discovery—there always was with adultery, wasn't there? She had to have known there was a risk that it would mean the end of their family as it currently was. Why would she take such a risk?

That made him angry.

He wasn't angry about her having sex with another man. It was just sex. He wasn't even angry that she'd done it all behind his back—he assumed she wanted to avoid hurting him. But he was angry that she'd go and do something stupid that risked the end of their *family*.

The whole way on the M25, he was angry. But he dealt with it. He knew anger wasn't going to be helpful in this matter. He knew how ugly the anger was, how terrible it made him feel. Thankfully, by the time he reached the M40, and the traffic volume reduced, and the speeds went back up to the national limit, he had managed to calm down. The reduction in traffic probably helped. But also, he made himself try to see it from her perspective. It couldn't be easy, commuting such a long distance, staying half the week away from the kids. Working so hard to give them a comfortable lifestyle. And her job had turned into a nightmare as her company struggled to stave off bankruptcy.

This affair had been how she was coping with it.

And it *was* only sex, right?

And putting himself in her shoes, he figured that Marcie had probably considered what kind of person her husband was, and had decided that he wasn't the kind of person who would want to end their family just because he discovered she'd been having a little fling with somebody from the office. She knew him well, right? Better than anybody, probably. So she trusted that he wouldn't turn into a raging monster on learning of her infidelity, she trusted he wouldn't turn into a suicidal or manic depressive person, capable of doing dangerous things that would threaten the family.

She couldn't have known that he'd be sexually aroused by the discovery of her adultery—but she did trust him enough, and she did believe him to be rational enough that she could mitigate the risks of her affair.

And sex hadn't been great with Cam for a while. Before the previous weekend's renaissance, at least. It had been pretty awful for years. Whenever it had happened, it had usually been like they were going through the motions, and it only ever happened because they had assumed the other person needed it occasionally. It hadn't been for the fun, or because they got so horny spending time with each other.

He'd been an idiot. She'd gotten bored of sex with him. And now, when she was feeling alone, probably depressed, and vulnerable, she had sought out a little secret sex with somebody else to keep herself sane.

No, he couldn't be entirely angry with her.

By the time he turned off the M40 outside Oxford, to continue on the A40 toward the Cotswolds, the sexual desire was returning. He was starting to think more of Marcie's beauty, and the erotic aspects of her adultery, rather than the family responsibility aspects. He thought about what he'd seen when he'd searched the apartment, and dwelled less on the shock of finding another man's personal belongings all over the place, and more about how he'd discovered Marcie's secret sexy underwear, the condoms, the handcuffs, the blindfold.

He remembered finding those panties, pressing them to his face, breathing in the incontrovertible evidence of his wife's adulterous sex with another man.

By the time he turned into the driveway of their little cottage in the Cotswolds, the sun was beginning to disappear over the horizon, and Cam was sitting in the driver's seat with an erection making his jeans feel rather tight and uncomfortable.

He even found himself wondering if everyone, all round, might end up being better off if he allowed Marcie to go on believing that he knew nothing about her affair. To let her go on conducting it in secret, trusting that she would end that particular relationship when necessary, and meanwhile he would work his socks off to make sure their newfound sexual connection did not ever wither again.

But then he pulled up outside the cottage, and when the front door opened, there was Flo, but there, also, was Marcie. Standing beside her mother. And quite clearly, Marcie had been crying her eyes out.

CHAPTER NINE

IT WAS A SHOCK, seeing her home on a Monday evening. Seeing her mascara smudged, her eyes red from crying. As he switched off the ignition and glanced up, he saw her step forward tentatively, and even saw a glistening of moisture on her cheeks.

Despite everything, his first instinct was that Marcie's company had finally gone bust. That she'd lost her job. That they, as a family, were now in financial trouble, they'd have to move out of the house, get somewhere cheaper, without the garden that had become a lifeline in this lockdown.

And yet they knew the company was going to file for bankruptcy, that if lockdown continued, it would never survive—and they'd prepared for it. They had the savings needed to keep their mortgage paid for up to two years if everything went wrong. She wouldn't be upset if the company went down—that was the general expectation.

What if something had happened at work, and she'd been fired? She might be upset at being fired, she might be fearful about her prospects of getting another job after being fired.

But she looked distraught, frightened. As he opened the car door to climb out, he looked up and saw her face was so pale, and her breathing was labored—panicky, you might even say.

He glanced at Flo, who looked grim, but her emotions were guarded, concealed. Flo didn't give him a little reassuring smile, as he might have expected if something bad had happened at Marcie's work. The kind of smile that said, *don't worry, we'll all get through this.* There was nothing on her face at all, she was impassive. It made Cam more fearful than even Marcie's distraught appearance. Flo made him feel like *he* had done something wrong.

Had Flo figured out what his trip to London was really about? Had she told Marcie that he'd lied about going to a garden center for an article, that he'd probably gone to the London apartment because he suspected Marcie of cheating?

How could Flo have possibly known any of that?

Had Marcie figured it out on her own? And now she was going to tell him their marriage was over, because he had invaded her privacy like that?

Or maybe, quite by coincidence, Marcie had made the decision to leave him, to move in permanently with her lover in London—and Flo looked grim because she knew it was all over.

In those brief moments, as he got out of the car, a world of awful possibility whirled around his head, and Cam regretted ever going to London to find definitive proof of Marcie's affair. But for now, he felt the need to act the innocent again, to conceal his true knowledge and his true feelings.

'Hey, honey, what are you doing here?' he asked her as he got out of the car. 'Did something happen at work?'

She didn't rush up to greet him with a big hug or a kiss, as he might have expected after what had happened between them at the weekend. She kept back. She was hugging herself—her arms tight around her chest—in a very defensive position.

'I… I came home,' she said, her voice shaky, fragile.

He quietly took a deep breath. Was she angry at him? She didn't seem angry at him. Not really knowing what to say, he said, 'Oh…'

She wasn't wearing her work clothes—she was dressed in a hoodie and jeans, very dressed down. It made him feel she'd been home for a while. She'd probably helped put the kids to bed, and then she'd been talking with Flo about heavy issues.

God.

Was their marriage really over? Like this?

She said, 'I… I need to talk to you.'

He nodded. 'Okay.'

'There's something… I need to tell you.'

Here it came. He could feel a strange clamor in his ears, dread and fear and panic and anguish all convening in his head. She was going to leave him. He felt his stomach churn, his heart slow to limping speed.

'What is it?'

He glanced at Flo, and thought at first that Marcie had her mother here in case he got angry, in case he got abusive. But she knew he wasn't like that. Yet as he glanced at Flo, his mother-in-law did give him a mild little smile— pity, empathy, and, yes, perhaps a hint of warmth, like she was telling him he didn't really deserve this. Then to his surprise, Flo stepped back, leaving them to it.

He looked back at Marcie, and saw that she was

waiting until her mother had gone, slipping quietly back into the house, before continuing.

Was she going to do it here?

Was she going to tell him to leave? Maybe his bags were even packed already. Did he not get to say goodbye to the kids?

It felt like the time he'd lost his job as editor of one of the fortnightly political rags, because it had been bought by a new owner who didn't share his politics. He'd been called in to a short meeting informing him that his services were no longer required, and then he'd been escorted out of the building by security—he hadn't even been allowed to clean out his desk. The new owners were worried he'd somehow steal sensitive company information if he was allowed back to his desk to prepare himself for leaving the job.

'What's going on?' he asked.

Marcie glanced over her shoulder, making sure Flo was gone. She even looked up at the windows on the second floor of the cottage, to check the kids weren't somehow awake and eavesdropping. Then she turned back to him, and he saw the moisture in her eyes bubble over, a tear tumbling down her cheek.

'I... I don't know how to say this...' she said, and it didn't seem very much like her, to be like this. Marcie was a strong, independent woman. She didn't get overwhelmed by her emotions. She paused a moment, and seemed to recognize it herself, that this wasn't like her.

She sniffed, and looked at him with a more firm gaze.

For a moment, he caught his breath, waiting for her to order him out of their house, out of their lives.

Then she said, 'I'm just going to say it. I... I've been having an affair.'

He waited a moment, for what she was going to say next.

But nothing else came.

He said, quietly, 'Oh.'

She looked up at him, her watery eyes seeking out his, searching for clues in his face as to what he was thinking, how he was reacting to her bombshell news.

He waited for her to declare that she knew all about his trip to London, that she was disgusted by how he'd violated her privacy, that if he'd suspected she'd been having an affair he could have just come forward and asked her about it, rather than sneaking away to London to ransack her belongings.

She said none of that. She was looking to him to respond now, she'd given him her news.

But his mind was blank. He didn't quite know what to think, what to say. When it started sinking in, what she'd said, the first real emotion he felt was relief, strangely. She didn't seem angry at him, at all. And then beyond that, she'd said she'd been *having an affair*, not that she'd fallen in love with another man. That, and the clear regret imprinted in her expression—along with severe anxiety, distress and pity for him—made him suppose that she did still love him, she still did want to be with him.

He said, 'I don't understand…'

And, perhaps, he was even *happy* that she'd admitted to her affair, because that had been the worst thing about it, hadn't it? The deception, the secrecy.

She gave a little nod, accepting that this must be an enormous blow to him, that it had come from nowhere—particularly since they'd reconnected so strongly at the weekend.

'I've been feeling so awful recently,' she said, glancing down at her hands, which were clutched firmly together. Then she looked up, as though realizing it was hardly time for her to try to garner sympathy from him. She said, 'I know, it should never have happened, but—'

He said, 'When did it start?' Trying to keep his voice soft, anything but angry.

Now that it was out there, he didn't want to be angry about her deception. The important thing was that she should want to be with him, that she should want to commit to her marriage, not be scared away.

She said, 'A few weeks ago. No more.'

'You've been breaking lockdown rules?' Cam said, leaning back against the car. In his mind he was making a gentle joke about Marcie breaking the rules, when she was the last person you'd expect to break the rules. It was partly why having an affair was so surprising for her.

But in her mind, he was concerned that she was bringing risk into their family, seeing someone from outside their household socially. Sexually.

'He lost his job, so he doesn't really come into contact with anyone else,' she said. 'He's been, you know, looking for a new job, but the applications, the interviews… it's all done online.'

Cam nodded.

So he was staying in their apartment, huh? He really was living there. A live-in lover for her during lockdown.

Cam's manhood thickened. He wasn't angry with her, as he might have expected. He'd moved way past that. There was no point in anger. Fear, though—there was still plenty of fear. Fear, along with that strange tickle of excitement that he didn't really understand.

He wanted to forgive her, to tell her it was all right. To admit that he had mixed feelings about her affair, that he had suspected it, that it made him feel oddly aroused to think it might be true. Secrets were bad, weren't they? The secrets were the things that threatened him and Marcie.

But now didn't seem like the time to confess to his own weaknesses.

'Why are you telling me this now?' He asked her. 'You know, after what happened at the weekend…?'

She nodded, and attempted a weak little smile, remembering how hot they had been together at the weekend.

'I've been talking to my mother a lot,' she said, and Cam felt a little twinge of horror and disappointment at finding out Flo had known about the affair before he did. 'She knows me so well, she could tell something was up,' she explained. 'She guessed what had happened. But by then I was feeling so guilty about it all, I had to talk to someone. I had to talk to her.'

'And what did she say?' He asked her, nervous, afraid that Flo had told Marcie to leave her husband.

Well, Marcie hadn't actually clarified that point yet.

'She told me to end it. To stop seeing Michael—'

Michael. So that was his name.

'—and stop being an idiot.'

'But you didn't want to end it?'

She sobbed, and now Cam was worried that she did, after all, have feelings for Michael.

He asked her straight out, 'Do you love him?'

She shook her head immediately. It was immensely reassuring. 'It's just… he makes me feel good. When I'm in London. It makes such a difference. I mean… I've been lonely for a while, and I always tried to deal with it by just working as late as I could while I was in town. But—'

'It must have been quite frightening being in London on your own with the pandemic going on,' Cam said, gently.

She smiled, surprised and touched at his empathy.

He quietly suggested they go inside, and she seemed grateful for the opportunity to go into the warm. It was getting a little chilly, despite the searing-hot May they were having.

Inside, there was no sign of Flo. She'd gone to bed, it seemed; left them to it.

In the living room, Marcie sat in the armchair, leaving the sofa for Cam.

'So what happened when you talked to Flo?' He asked her.

She smiled, but not with any joy. 'When I hesitated about ending things with Michael, she gave me this big talk about how you have to work at marriage, and if there's something lacking in the bedroom, you have to work at that, too.'

'So this weekend,' Cam asked her. 'That was you working at it?'

She smiled, 'I guess. I wasn't expecting it to go quite as well as that…' He enjoyed the little look she gave him then —a look that said she was thinking about their lovemaking that past weekend, and that it had somewhat knocked her socks off.

'So you decided to come clean. But you couldn't wait until Thursday to have this talk with me?'

She laughed, but again, with no humor. 'My mother called me this morning. Phoned me while I was at the office, since I didn't really get to talk to her about all this at the weekend. She said I needed to tell you the truth and end things with Michael. She said she thought you might suspect the truth.'

'She's very perceptive.'

'She says she recognized some of the looks you were giving me from the way it was with my dad, when he discovered her affair.'

'Wow,' he said, not knowing that Marcie's father had once been in a similar position to him.

'So you did know about it?' Marcie was surprised.

'Vague suspicions.'

'What made you suspect?'

He sighed. Rubbed his chin. 'One of our FaceTime calls last week,' he said. 'There was a set of car keys on the kitchen counter, behind you.'

'Car keys?'

'VW car keys. I knew they weren't yours.'

She nodded. 'Michael's.' Then, 'Why didn't you say anything about it?'

He shrugged again. 'I didn't want to accuse you of something without having any real evidence.'

'Why would I have a set of VW car keys on the kitchen counter?'

Well, wasn't that what he'd thought at the time?

'You seem very calm,' she said then. Confused about it, nervous about it. Imagining it meant he was going to leave her, that he'd already decided, and this final definitive proof, her confession, was all he needed to make that choice.

'Well... I mean... it's all a bit much to take in,' he said, and she nodded, meekly, making sure he knew she was taking in what he was saying, and opening herself up to whatever emotions he wanted to throw at her. She seemed prepared for his anger, his shock, his disgust, his sorrow, his hatred—but he gave her only quiet calm.

'It's a shock,' she agreed. 'I mean... you've worked so hard to keep this family together... and you didn't deserve any of this. I'm so sorry. I've been so stupid... so selfish...'

The tears were coming again. She really looked wretched—and it was difficult for someone as attractive as her to look so truly wretched.

He didn't know what to say to her.

He could have said, don't worry, it's okay, never mind,

all is forgiven. He could have told her he understood the reasons why she'd started her affair, and he didn't have a problem with it. But he still felt hurt, he still felt sore that she had done it behind his back. The pain was there, the loss of trust, the fear that she had done something that had imperiled their family unit—what if she decided to do something like that again?

He was confused, that was the problem. If he thought about the two of them having sex, he was aroused. But he was still shocked by all this, and he was still hurt by the loss of trust.

So for a while, he just sat there, breathing, trying not to break down himself, while she quietly sobbed.

Then she said, quietly, 'Do you want me to leave?'

And when he said, 'No, of course not,' she actually looked relieved, very relieved. That was reassuring.

The thing was, it just didn't seem like the right time to be wholly forgiving. To let her off with a mild warning. He didn't want her to get the wrong message—that it was okay what she did, that if she felt like going behind his back again someday, it would be fine.

He liked the idea of her sleeping with someone else. What he didn't like was the idea that she would do it in secret. That seemed like the most dangerous situation.

She pulled herself off the chair, and went down in front of him, kneeling. He was afraid she'd start begging for his forgiveness, but she didn't. She gazed up at him and said, 'I never meant to hurt you. It was just… it was stupid. I was on my own, I was tired, I was afraid…'

He nodded, trying to seem understanding.

'Do you love him?' He asked her.

'No, of course. I love you.'

'You can love two people,' he pointed out.

'It's just sex,' she said, and then corrected herself: '*was* just sex. It was just… a distraction.'

He nodded again. 'And you still want me?' He asked her. 'I mean… you know… more than just for my child-care capabilities?'

He smiled, trying to lighten the tension between them. She smiled, too, and said, 'Couldn't you tell I want you more than just because you're the world's best father, since we spent most of the past weekend fucking?'

'Well, that's what it seemed like.'

Her bottom lip quivered. He'd never seen that before. It really hit him how damn *scared* she was. He'd never seen her like this before. She whispered, '*I'm so sorry*.' And she just about managed to get it out, she was shaking so much.

'Hey,' he said, pulling her up for a warm hug, his heart going out to her. She might have broken their trust, but that didn't mean he wanted to see her like this.

She knelt up between his legs, and they embraced. He breathed her in, and felt the first little warm fizzing feeling of healing inside.

'Come on,' he said, at last. 'I think we both need to get some sleep.'

CHAPTER TEN

THEY WENT TO BED, but they didn't make love. It didn't feel right, yet. They held each other, but they didn't touch each other. They kissed, occasionally, but it was conciliatory, not passionate.

They lay there together, but there wasn't a lot of sleeping that night. There was a lot of crying, a lot of talking, a lot of apologizing. But there was also a lot of reassuring, and Cam felt a lot of healing, too, after a while.

Holding each other close, she helped him get over the shock of discovering that she'd been cheating on him by explaining, in detail, how it had all happened. Taking him step by step, from the moment one of her close friends at work had found himself out of a job because of the first round of redundancies at the company, to her offer of a couch where he could stay, rent-free, until he found something else. She'd explained how lonely it got in that apartment, all on her own, in the middle of a thriving city that now found itself torpedoed by the global pandemic. How the presence of her friend, Michael, on the couch, had been a powerful comfort as she had had to cope with everything.

How the lack of real satisfaction in her marriage had led to temptation when she occasionally glimpsed Michael around the apartment in various states of undress.

It helped Cam see that her completely shocking behavior could be explained, and that if he'd known what was going on as it had happened, he could see that it had even been predictable. That took the edge off his feelings of shock at what had happened.

And as Cam understood how it had happened, and encouraged her to talk it out to the point where everything she had done had seemed almost inevitable, that helped Marcie cope with her guilt.

He even agreed that their marital sex had been lacking, up until the weekend gone by, when it had suddenly exploded into life again.

But the most important thing, as they lay there together, talking but not fucking, was that they both felt strongly that they were still together, and that neither was leaving each other, or the family. Michael was just all about the sex. She wasn't in love with him.

Cam even got to say the standard line about it 'not being about the sex', that it was more about the deception.

He did ask about the sex, though. About how good it was. And though she was a little evasive at first, mainly because she feared the full details would be painful for him, eventually she gave in and admitted Michael was good in bed. Very good in bed.

'But you know, I don't need him. I showed that with you this past weekend,' she said.

He liked hearing that. But at the same time, he liked hearing that she'd had incredible sex with Michael. That part forced him to hide an erection from her—he didn't

want her to feel that from him, not for now. It didn't feel
like the appropriate time for sex.

They eventually fell asleep.

———

IN THE MORNING, when he woke, it almost felt as
though it had all been a weird dream brought on by the
stress and anxiety of lockdown. But there she was, lying
next to him in a baggy t-shirt and sweatpants, on a
Tuesday morning.

At least it didn't feel so painful, the next morning. He
didn't have such awful anxiety, things didn't feel quite as
uncertain.

'Hey,' he said when he saw that she was waking
up, too.

'Hey.'

'You going into work?'

She wrinkled up her nose. 'I can stay home,' she said,
peering at the alarm clock. 'I can stay with you.'

'They'll let you have days off right now?' he asked,
surprised, since it was a critical time for her company, and
she was a critical part of the finance team needed to keep
it going.

She shrugged. 'If I tell them I'm sick. I have a fever…'

'They'll make you self-isolate for two weeks,' he
pointed out. 'And if you stay away two weeks, they'll probably figure they can afford to get rid of you.'

She sighed. It was still early—6am. Even if she took an
hour to get herself ready, she still had time to get to the
office, off Oxford Street, for a 9am start. She said, 'I can
commute this week. Drive home every night, sleep here in
this bed.'

Cam shook his head. 'Four hours of driving each day?

Probably five hours, actually, let's face it. That's pretty heavy.'

'I'll tell Michael to stay in a hotel.'

'Hotels aren't open during lockdown,' Cam pointed out.

She groaned.

'It'll be okay,' he said.

'I can sleep on the couch,' she said.

He smiled. 'You don't think you'd be able to sleep in the same bed as him for a couple of nights, without having sex?'

She gave him a wry look. 'I think the issue is whether you'd worry about us having sex if we were sleeping in the same bed.'

Cam stroked her, tracing the delightful curve of her lower back under her t-shirt. 'I wouldn't worry about it,' he said.

She laughed. 'You're insane. You'd worry. I just told you I've been having an affair, and you think you'd be okay about me sleeping with him a few more nights?'

'I told you, didn't I? It's not the sex I worry about.'

She paused a moment, and he realized that what he'd said might be a little more revealing than he'd meant. Or at least, he'd kind of meant it as more jokey than it was.

Then she said, 'I don't understand. It's *not* the sex you worry about?'

Her question made him doubt he'd been very clear in how he'd explained himself the previous night. But while he'd been telling her about his concerns about her not telling him the truth, or hiding significant things from him, he had generally avoided the whole issue of her having sex with another man. He hadn't commented outright about what he thought about that.

He took a deep breath.

'I worry about you keeping things from me,' he said. She didn't jump in with any assurances or promises to change, and he realized she was giving him space, letting him speak, and allowing what he said to fully sink in.

He said, 'I worry about you forming a close relationship with someone I know nothing about.'

She turned a little more, so she could look at him, so he could see her paying full attention to him.

'I worry about you getting bored of me because your lover is better,' he went on. 'I worry about you falling in love with someone else. I worry about you deciding that life would be better if you left me, whether or not you decided to take the kids with you.'

She was silent a moment, thinking about everything he had said.

Then she said, 'I promise I won't keep things from you ever again.'

He kissed the base of her neck, just where her bare skin was exposed, and just listened to her soft, soothing voice.

She said, 'I promise I won't ever form a close relationship with someone you know nothing about.'

He traced a hand down between her shoulder blades, down to her lower back, where her t-shirt didn't quite cover, and he could touch bare skin.

'I promise never to get bored of you,' she said.

'You can't possibly promise that,' he smiled.

'Okay… how about… if I ever got bored, if I ever got close to being bored with you, we'd talk about it, and try something else so that I wouldn't be bored. So that neither of us would be bored.'

'Sounds acceptable,' he said, his hand sliding slowly down over her behind, taking real pleasure in the roundness of her bottom, to seek out the warmth between her legs.

'What are you doing?' she murmured quietly.

'Nothing,' he said, gently stroking her sex through the fairly thick material of her sweatpants. 'Listening to you.'

She breathed, experiencing his touch, appreciating it as though she was about to embark on a long period of chastity.

Then she said, taking her time so that she really emphasized how much she meant every word, she said, 'I promise I'll never fall in love with someone else. I promise, I *could* never decide life would be better if I left you, even if the kids came with me.'

He grazed a fingernail along the groove in her sweatpants made by her sex, and she gave a little shudder, a little groan.

Then she turned slightly more, so that she was lying properly on her back, so that she could gaze down at him, look him in the eye. She said, 'I'd never want to stop being with you, being with our family, just like this.'

He nodded. 'Good,' he said. 'Then in that case, I'm not worried about the sex.'

He kissed her just below the navel, luxuriating in the softness of her skin against his lips, the warmth of her body, her sweet personal smell and the faint remnants of her perfume.

'You're not worried about me going back to London, and seeing Michael?' she asked him, clearly not understanding him fully.

'Not particularly,' he said, sliding a hand under the waistband of her sweatpants, finding the thin elasticated waistband of her panties.

'I had an affair,' she said. 'I hid it from you. I *cheated* on you. But you think I should go back to London and stay overnight with him?'

He slipped a finger down further into her panties,

feeling only soft, warm, smooth skin where there ought to have been a soft tangle of pubic hair—the change in his wife, in that respect, giving him a little thrill.

He said, 'You don't love him, do you? You said that last night.'

'No, I definitely don't love him.'

'So, as long as you don't hide anything from me anymore, we don't have a problem.'

He liked this. He liked being open with her like this. It felt so cathartic he almost felt slightly drunk. His finger ventured lower in her panties, feeling the temperature rising. The way she responded, by parting her legs a little more to give him easier access, thrilled him.

'We don't have a problem,' she said, mulling over the words. 'You wouldn't be back here, while I'm in London, paranoid about whether Michael was really sleeping on our couch, or whether he was in bed with me?'

He slipped his finger further down, the tip finding her sex, already open for him, already wet. She drew in a deep breath as he touched her there.

'I don't think I'd worry if you were in bed with him,' he said. 'That couch isn't exactly very comfortable for sleeping on.'

She moaned as he dipped his finger a little deeper into her pussy, feeling the heat, and her oily wetness. 'You shouldn't joke about that,' she said, and quietly gasped as he slid his full finger inside her. 'It would be like me telling you if you had to, I'd be okay with you sleeping in the same bed as Natalie Portman.'

'Hmm… Natalie Portman, huh?' he laughed, and withdrew his finger from her sex, to spread her wetness over her pussy lips. 'Are you telling me Michael looks like Natalie Portman?'

She giggled. 'No…' she said, propping herself up on

her elbows to watch what he was doing. 'But if you imagine the reaction you'd have to having Natalie Portman in your bed… in her underwear… and that's how I would feel with Michael in mine.'

He chuckled.

'You know I prefer blondes,' he said, cupping her pussy in his hand, detecting the growing need in her, in the way her body pushed back against his hand as he pressed it against her sex.

'I'll bet Natalie Portman could do blonde.'

'Can I assume you have a thing about Natalie Portman?' he asked, amused, and kissed her below the navel.

'No, I just assumed you do.'

'Me?'

'You liked that movie *Closer*. I assumed she was the reason.'

'It's a *good movie*,' he laughed.

'So you don't think she's attractive?'

He slid his hand out from her panties, and shivered a little as he detected the scent of her arousal in the air. He gazed up at her, and slipped his finger in his mouth, tasting her wetness.

He said, 'If you don't keep any secrets from me, if you tell me everything. Why should I have a problem if you sleep with him?'

His heart was hammering inside his chest.

The truth was, he wasn't telling her that the thought of her having sex with another man turned him on. He was telling her that the thought of her having sex with another man didn't bother him. There was a world of difference in those two. One was a pervert, and one was merely a highly tolerant husband. And while terrified him to be venturing this far in telling her it was okay to continue seeing Michael, it wasn't as degrading as admitting to her that he found the idea arousing.

'Most husbands would,' she said.

'I'm not most husbands,' he said, kissing her just above her hip.

'You're telling me to sleep with him. With Michael?'

'I'm not telling you to sleep with him. I just don't think you should be throwing the poor guy out on the street during a pandemic.'

'So you're trusting me to sleep in the same bed with him while I stay in London, but not to *sleep* with him.'

It was funny how people used that phrase, 'sleeping' with somebody, to mean sex. All part of society's strange awkwardness with sex as a whole.

'I'm saying it's your choice,' he said. He kissed his way up her stomach, pushing up her t-shirt as he went. 'If we trust each other, it doesn't matter what you decide.'

'Is this a test?' She said. 'You're saying it's my choice…'

'Not a test,' he shook his head, and pushed her t-shirt up to expose her gorgeous breasts. 'I'm saying if we trust each other… and I know that you love me, not him, it doesn't matter if you want him when you get back to London.'

'It doesn't matter if I *want* him, or it doesn't matter if I *have* him?'

She moaned as he took one of her stiff nipples into his hot mouth. She seemed to be lying there, as though letting him do whatever he wanted to her without question. Leaving it all to him, though she was enjoying his attention. As though, after what she'd done to him, she had no right to be in control just now, even if she'd shown how sexy it was when she was in control the past weekend.

He said, 'As long as we don't have secrets anymore, as long as you're not in love with him, I'm okay with it.'

'You're… okay with it?'

He said, sitting up, 'I don't have a problem with the sex. Not if we trust each other.'

She looked down at him, confused, as he knelt between her legs. It was a difficult concept to grasp. Made more difficult because he couldn't quite bring himself to admit that he wanted her to have sex with Michael because the thought of it turned him on.

Was he being stupid? Was he being an idiot?

She said, 'Plenty of husbands would say we couldn't have trust… if there was sex.'

He looked at her straight. 'I'm saying that the important thing is that you love me, not him, and that you don't keep *anything* a secret any more. Nothing else matters.'

'Nothing else?'

'Nothing else.'

He reached forward, grasped her sweatpants at the hips, and hauled them down, along with her panties. She seemed to be in a state of stunned surprise. Well, he had probably thrown her a curveball by saying she could continue to sleep with Michael. To *sleep with* Michael.

'What?' he smiled up at her, as he removed her clothing from the waist down, which she didn't entirely seem to notice.

'Uh… I *think* my husband just told me I can still sleep with the man I was cheating on him with,' she said.

He laughed, 'I told you, I was never upset about the *sex*.'

'Yeah, but people say that when they've been cheated on, they don't *mean* it.'

He dropped down between her thighs, her bare, shaven sex filling his vision. Breathing her in, inhaling that spicy scent from her growing excitement, he gazed up at her. 'Maybe some of them do mean it.'

He kissed her soft skin close to her pussy, but not on it.

'You get lonely when you're in London,' he said, and kissed her again, around the edges of her sex.

'I do,' she moaned quietly.

'You get depressed, you get frightened.'

'Sometimes I do,' she said, sighing as he continued to circumvent her pussy with little kisses, breathing on her, but not yet touching her sensitive folds.

'So you need someone to keep you company,' he said, surprised at how bold he was being in telling her this.

'I do,' she said, and she did seem to mean it. As many times as she'd tried to explain herself and her affair during the night, she'd never actually said anything about still needing companionship when she was in London. But he got the feeling she would. She might go forward with intentions of maintaining a chaste existence in London, because now they had trust again, and she didn't ever want to break it again—but that didn't mean she'd stop being lonely and depressed when she had to stay in London away from her family day after day.

She sighed as he breathed hot air over her pussy.

He said, 'So then, we're all straightened out, aren't we?'

He touched his tongue to her pussy lips, and she moaned. She said, 'Michael's... going to keep me company... and if he demands sex?'

Cam licked her pussy, slowly, from the bottom to the top, his tongue flat, feeling how wet she was already getting. She groaned, breathily.

'I've told you. If it's just sex, we don't have a problem.'

'Just sex?'

'Just sex, not love.'

He licked her some more, enjoying her flavor. Enjoying

the silky sounds of her breathing as she responded to his attention.

'I don't love him,' she said, earnestly, as he continued lapping at her. 'I mean it.'

'So then, it would be just sex.'

He touched the very tip of his tongue gently to her clit, and flicked it lightly, like he was using a feather. She gasped.

'You're crazy, you know that?' She said, somewhat breathless, panting by now. Then she was whispering, 'Oh yes… oh *please…*'

He paused, for a moment just looking at her pussy, taking in her beauty, letting it sink in that he was letting her have sex with another man. Letting her use this gorgeous pussy on another man.

But it felt much better, didn't it? Letting her, rather than having her do it behind his back.

He took her clit in his mouth, and gently sucked on it, and for a moment she just moaned and breathed, deep and slow, still watching him going down on her with a kind of stunned expression on her attractive face.

'I just want you to be happy,' he said, withdrawing from her far enough so he could gently touch a finger to her clit, then stroke down to her pussy and back up again.

'Oh *God…*'

Then he licked her while he was stroking her like that, and she quietly gasped again.

'You know… you're not going to make me want to go into London… if you do this to me,' she said.

'You've got plenty of time,' he said. 'It's early.'

He sucked on her clit, slid his finger deep inside her searing-hot pussy, stroking her, thrusting into her, working up a rhythm that seemed synchronized to her breathing. He flicked the tip of his tongue against her clit, and now added another finger inside her pussy, feeling it tightening on his fingers.

'God that feels *amazing*…'

Flicking his tongue, left-right, right-left, over her clit, then sucking it, drawing out her moans, her body beginning to move under him, writhing, her breathing deepening, into deep panting. He stroked his fingers inside her, playing her like a musical instrument, loving how she was responding to him.

She was moving her whole body under him, now, jerking her hips back and forth, thrusting as he moved his fingers inside her, as he sucked on her clit.

'Fuck…'

Lifting herself, now, pressing herself against his face.

'Oh it feels so good…'

Moaning, gasping for breath. 'Oh fuck… *oh*…'

But now he picked himself up, knelt between her legs, placed his hard cock down against her moistened groove. She looked up at him with fresh flames in her eyes, and her hand slipped in between her legs, her fingers curling around his shaft, pulling it against her burning sex.

He started rocking, back and forth, stroking his full length against her sensitive folds without, yet, entering her. Spreading her wetness over his shaft as he caressed her with his rock-hard manhood.

Then he plunged deep into her, and it seemed to him that the pure relief of knowing he still loved her, he still wanted her, and he still wanted their marriage to be real and physical somehow set her off like he'd never seen her before.

When she came, she came hard, and it made him wonder if there had been times—plenty of times, perhaps —in their marriage that she had faked it for him. But this was no fake. As she came, he felt her pussy clamp tighter around his manhood, pulsing with the jolts of the climax she experienced, her pussy getting so much wetter he wondered if she was actually squirting.

Then he was coming, too, profusely, pulling his cock out of her as he did so, to finish off firing his thick, white cream all over her pussy, her stomach, her breasts.

Marking her as his territory.

PART II

CHAPTER ELEVEN

SHE HAD breakfast with the kids, and they were a little confused at first, but they said Mommy hadn't been feeling good the previous day, so she'd come home so she could get better again, and now she was feeling much better—and that was the only explanation Henry and Sarah needed.

'Are you sure you're better?' Henry asked her.

Marcie looked at Cam, and he gave her a warm, loving smile, and she smiled back, telling Henry, 'Yes, much better, thank you.'

'We usually stay home a few days when we're sick,' Sarah pointed out.

'Mommy wasn't feeling sick,' Marcie explained to them. 'Just a little… sad. She just had to come home for a little bit. To see Daddy.'

Henry looked at her, and then at Cam, and then back at Marcie as though he was watching a tennis match between them. 'Did Daddy make you feel happy again?' he asked.

'Yes,' she said, beaming at her husband. 'Daddy made Mommy very happy.'

After breakfast, Marcie cleared up the kitchen with Flo, and Cam left them to talk amongst themselves, knowing that Marcie was going to update her mother on the whole situation between them, though he wasn't quite sure how much she was going to share about what they'd agreed.

Then she was headed back out the door, having said goodbye to the kids, who were disappointed that her flying visit wasn't going to last longer, but understanding that she had to go to work—since Sarah and Henry had their own work to be getting on with, in the form of home learning.

As Cam walked Marcie to her car, she revealed, 'I told my Mom the affair's over.'

'Okay,' he said. 'Did you tell her you'll still be seeing Michael?'

She put a hand on her car roof, and turned to look him in the face—and he saw that she was determining if he was really, honestly, serious about her continuing to sleep with Michael. He maintained a serious expression, his eyes connected to hers, assuring her this was no joke—and this was no test.

'I... don't think she'd fully understand,' Marcie said, but in many ways it seemed that Marcie was the one who didn't fully understand.

Cam nodded. Well, it probably wasn't easy to understand. He didn't fully understand himself why he was turned on by the thought of Marcie sleeping with someone else—he suspected pornography might have some part to play in why he would want to watch her having sex with someone else, and yet his turn-on wasn't just about watching her. He was turned on just thinking that she might sleep with Michael, even if he didn't get to see it happen.

Marcie turned to him, put her hands delicately on his shoulders, and gazed earnestly into his eyes. 'You *are* serious about this?' she said. 'I *can* tell him to leave. Or sleep on the couch at the very least.'

He smiled. 'I don't want you to be lonely.'

'So call me,' she said. 'Text me. All the time.'

He chuckled. 'I should do that anyway. It wouldn't stop you being on your own…'

She paused, letting it sink in, giving him a last few moments to change his mind.

Then she gave a little nod, and leaned into him, tilted her head and kissed him softly on the lips, sharing such warm affection it made him tingle all over. He kissed her back, and made her smile while she continued to kiss him, her hands gently circling his head as she sucked on his lips a little more forcefully, and slipped her tongue deftly into his mouth, somewhat surprising him considering the fact that this was so public, right in the middle of the driveway.

Sometimes, a kiss could be more erotic than an entire night of good sex—when it was tender, passionate, and full of meaning. Just then, the way Marcie kissed him seemed to make the ground shake under him. It made the hairs stand up on the back of his neck, butterflies flutter in his stomach, and his blood pump twice as quickly around his body.

Afterward, she pulled back, leaving him breathless, and perhaps a little stunned. She was just exquisite, and her kiss had him so turned on he felt like his insides were on fire.

Was he really letting her drive away to another man?

Yes, he was.

But this was no longer a secret love affair she was conducting. It was just companionship. Just a little human contact to fend off the loneliness.

It was just sex.

Would she ever understand, if he ever managed to admit to his own dark secret? Would she be horrified, would she treat him with contempt?

Now she was the one with the clean conscience, and he was the one feeling guilt.

She looked him in the eye and said, quietly, 'No secrets.'

And he had to nod, and agree, 'No secrets.'

And that made him feel his stomach twist into knots. No secrets. Except the fact that he was a pervert, who wanted to experience—and, yes, perhaps watch—his wife have sex with another man.

'I love you,' she said, and when he said it back, she smiled sweetly, kissed him again, briefly, on the lips, and then climbed into her car.

———

HE BREATHED OUT, long and slow as he waved his last wave, and her car disappeared out into the road for her journey to the station. He was feeling better, much better. His nerves were much more settled, his fear had been largely doused.

He walked back into the house to find Flo already getting the kids into their home learning, all three of them sitting around the kitchen table, the kids with papers and books in front of them, along with the iPads you just couldn't get away from, even for schoolwork.

Flo looked up, and gave him a warm smile—it seemed like the first smile she'd given him since he'd returned home from his escapade to London. It was a genuine smile, a smile that said she was pleased he had been so forgiving of her daughter, she was grateful that he had turned out to be a caring husband when crisis had struck. Cam gave her a reassuring smile in return—the kind of smile that said it wasn't such a big deal, that he and Marcie had sorted everything out, there was nothing to worry about anymore.

He did wonder what she'd think if she knew, however, that he'd sent Marcie back to London with permission to continue sleeping with her lover. Or worse—if she knew that Cam actively liked the idea of his wife being with someone else.

Well, he didn't need to concern himself with it just now. For now, he felt relief. Relief and a small tremor of hope that things might turn out for the best.

Would Marcie end up sleeping with Michael that night? And how would she cope with their new pledge for no secrets between them?

CHAPTER TWELVE

SHE TEXTED him when she got to the station, telling him that she missed him already. He texted her back that he missed her already too, and he was telling the truth.

He still felt a little nervous, throughout the day, however.

It hurt a little, inside, that she was gone again. Strange, after so many years married. It seemed oddly like it had when they'd only been dating a few weeks or months, when taking her to the airport for a three-day retail industry conference abroad felt like his heart being torn out. Back then, there had been the uncertainty from the fact that they'd only just started seeing each other, and that he hadn't, yet, put a ring on it.

Now, he supposed, he was in a similar time of uncertainty—she'd had an affair, and after she had confessed, he had sent her back to continue sleeping with her lover. There was risk, on both sides, that their relationship could end. Risk from Marcie falling for another man, and risk from Cam changing his mind about wanting to stay with her.

But there was reassurance in her obvious anxiety. It showed Cam that she truly loved him, she genuinely wanted to stay with him. It made her text him every hour or two through the day, asking how he was, letting him know what she was up to, even if it was fairly trivial matters like getting to the station, putting on her face mask to reduce the risk of her getting the coronavirus, hopping onto the train, getting into London.

She took the Tube across town to her office, making sure her mask was on properly. It was still an anxious experience, however. She'd been on the train for a couple of hours, but the carriage had been largely empty—London was a different matter, the Tube was crammed full of people at rush hour, even during lockdown. People had to work, and plenty couldn't work from home.

Her texts really emphasized what a stressful experience it was for her, working in London during the pandemic. But the way things were going for her company, she couldn't work from home, she couldn't even base herself at the apartment—she needed to be at the office.

In the afternoon, Cam was on childcare duty, taking the kids out for a walk, getting some gardening done with them, playing Monopoly. And Marcie was buried in meetings on Zoom, the computer software the entire globe seemed to be using during the pandemic, for virtual meetings of more than two people. It was a little too busy for them to text each other quite so much.

Then evening arrived, supper and bath time and bedtime, and Marcie was still at the office, beavering away. Cam wondered if she was working extra late into the night because she was unsure about what would happen when she got back to the apartment and Michael.

When it got to 9pm, and the kids were in bed—a little later than usual, because Henry and Sarah were disappointed that Mommy had gone back to London for a couple more nights—Cam sent her a text message saying he hoped Marcie wasn't still working.

She replied:

Marcie: Just about to leave the office, honest!

That little nugget of news had Cam's pulse racing all of a sudden. He texted her back, telling her she worked too hard. She replied that she liked her job, that she was very happy he was good with taking on the lion's share of the childcare to let her work as much as she did—whereupon he reminded her that he had help from her mother with the childcare these days.

Then she was on the Tube again, one benefit of her working so late being that there were mercifully few people traveling on the Tube compared to the crush of the morning commute.

Cam was sitting watching TV with Flo when Marcie sent him a text reporting that she was just approaching the apartment. Then tension he'd been feeling all day seemed to swell inside him, and he felt suddenly emotional, confused, and rather uncomfortable.

He knew she wasn't just going to go in the door and shed her clothes and start fucking Michael again—but the butterflies inside his stomach were fluttering like crazy, and he felt a creeping panic beginning to take hold.

'I'm really tired,' he told Flo, pulling himself up from the couch to excuse himself.

'Of course, dear,' Flo said, giving him another one of those reassuring smiles that said he, of all people just then, was allowed to be tired and want to get an early night.

He felt better upstairs, in the safety of his and Marcie's bedroom, sealed away from the rest of the house. He put the little TV on, though he didn't really pay much attention to the 24-hour news channel that was showing—it was just quiet, background noise, a comfort in dispelling the complete silence of the room, though his thoughts were too chaotic to allow him to focus on the broadcast.

What was she doing? What was she saying to Michael?

He lay there staring at his phone, feeling an odd mixture of elation and sadness, all in the same moment. He felt bold for sending his wife back to London with instructions to continue seeing her lover while she was there—and yet, at the same time, he felt stupid, like it was the most idiotic thing a husband could do after his wife had confessed to an affair. He felt excitement and hope that Marcie would do as she wanted with Michael, and that she would want sex—and yet, he felt guilty about his secret, selfish reasons for wanting her to have sex with Michael, and the fact that he had kept those reasons secret from her.

He felt aroused, of course, with his manhood thickening up as he lay there on the bed in his boxer shorts, curled up with his phone, awaiting news. But he also felt a deep sense of shame. This wasn't normal, was it? She was going to discover that he was a little overly interested in the details of her dealings with Michael.

She would know.

Would she be disgusted by him?

A text message made him jump, made his heart rate race, made him sweat and gasp and panic even before he'd read it.

Marcie: Michael's making pasta. He only just got home from the park. He wants to know what we talked about last night.

Cam read, and then re-read her text message, purposefully slowing down his breathing, trying to calm himself down before responding to her text with trembling hands.

Cam: You should probably tell him, then. :-)

He didn't usually use smiley faces, or other emoticons

in his text messages, but one of the women at the gardening magazine he occasionally wrote for always used them in her emails, and though it had never really appealed to his writer's stickling for grammar and proper English, they did seem to brighten up her messages. And he felt he needed to keep his messages to Marcie bright just now.

Marcie: I should tell him you were hurt that I had an affair, but that you want me to keep seeing him, because it was the secrecy that hurt you, the fact that I was seeing him behind your back?

He knew she was getting everything straight in her mind, rather than merely preparing to inform Michael what they had talked about after her admission. But it was reassuring. She wanted to be absolutely clear where they stood, and she was giving him a last chance to change his mind regarding his instructions to her for returning to London and to Michael.

Cam: Yes. You should tell him that it wasn't the sex part of the affair that hurt me. That I actually like the idea of you having fun with him, that he will make you feel good, as well as being a companion while you're in London, so you're not lonely.

He typed the message on his phone, and his finger hovered over the send button, slightly afraid of what would happen if he pressed it. This was what he wanted, wasn't it? But he blushed as he re-read the sentence where he told her he liked the idea of her having fun with him. Was that too close to an admission that he was turned on by her sexual infidelity?

He took another deep breath, trying to steady the nervous, excited shivers coursing through his body.

He pressed the send button.

Was his hard cock making the decisions for him? And yet, though he felt embarrassed by his arousal if he thought about how others might perceive it, he gently stroked his hardness, and it did make him feel a little better, it did ease his anxiety. It made him feel like he was, at least, trying to be honest with Marcie by moving slowly toward telling her everything about how he felt.

Marcie: Okay.

Her reply sent an unexpected jolt of shock—and fear —through him, but the deep breathing helped tamp it down. It was just the final throes of panic sweeping through him, he thought. His body's reaction to his loss of control over the situation after he had given her the clear go-ahead to have sex with Michael as she pleased.

He lay there, waiting, clutching his phone ready to pounce on any message she might send back to him. His paranoia was contained, just barely, but if he let down his guard it could easily leak.

Was he supposed to send a message back after hers? She'd said 'okay', so it sounded like she was going to go talk with Michael, now, so he probably shouldn't respond right now. But it was his turn in the conversation, right? But if he sent something back, it might seem like overkill. Might seem like he was interfering too much.

Deep breaths.

Keep calm.

His gaze even flicked to the TV, and he tried to take in what the presenter was saying—that from the beginning of June, the government was talking about opening up schools to certain year groups, but that social distancing would be observed while kids were back in class.

Looking at the clock in the bottom left-hand corner of the TV screen, thinking, *how long had it been since she'd sent that last text? How long would it take her to talk over everything with Michael?*

But he didn't want to text her back too soon, he didn't want to interrupt any deep and meaningful conversation she was having with her lover. He didn't want to seem like a stalker husband, though he had a stalker's craving for information.

An expert on TV was saying that the most likely scenario was that reception and Year One of primary schools, along with Year Six, who were preparing to move up to secondary school in September, would be among the first year-groups invited back to primary school. So, would that mean Henry going back to school? Sarah was in Year Two, so she wouldn't be.

He noticed that even TV news was apparently using Zoom software for their networking calls. How had that company managed to usurp the entire world's online networking so quickly during the pandemic? They hadn't even advertised anywhere. People had just found out about it from other people they knew. Someday, volumes would be written about the company's incredible word-of-mouth promotion.

Ten minutes. That was long enough for her to explain everything to Michael, wasn't it? Fifteen minutes. But perhaps she was sitting down with him to have dinner. She probably wouldn't want to be seen on her phone, texting her husband, during dinner.

Twenty minutes.

He wondered if she had forgotten about him. But he recognized that that was his paranoia leaking out again. He wondered if his last message to her, giving her a clear green light to continue sexual relations with Michael, would mean she'd simply drop the phone and sidle up to the guy while he cooked pasta for an unusually late supper, her arms slipping around him easily, hands swooping down between his thighs to take hold of his large bulge.

He imagined her saying quietly into Michael's ear something like, *my husband says we can still have sex*.

Michael saying, great, then turning toward her, Marcie

dropping down to her knees, her hands at his crotch, unfastening his pants, retrieving his enormous cock, which was already thickening up to incredible proportions. Gazing up at him with lust and joy on her face as his impressive manhood was exposed and filling her hands. Stretching her lips around its tip.

Michael 'accidentally' dropping a little pasta sauce down, to splash on his shaft, before she sank down on his length, tasting the tomatoes on his flesh. Smiling as she looked up at him and said, 'Needs more salt.'

Cam snapped out of his daze when his phone buzzed, making him jump, shocked at realizing she had sent him another message.

Marcie: I think Michael is kind of impressed with you :-)

Well, that was unexpected.

Cam: Impressed?

Marcie: He says you must really love me :-)

Well, now Marcie was using emoticons with all her texts. But it did convey emotions in a concise way that text messages alone could not. Cam felt his nerves settle a little. He supposed that one of the things he'd been worried about was that Michael would think him a loser for giving his wife free rein to sleep with other men.

Cam: I do really love you :-) I think you'll be happier this way.

She texted him another smiley face. But then she was typing again—his iPhone displaying the three dots that said she was tapping out another message.

Marcie: But do you think YOU will be happier this way?

He smiled. That was an easy question to answer. And one requiring an immediate response, the kind that didn't make it seem to Marcie like he was umming or erring about it.

Cam: I'm sure of it.

Another emoticon response from Marcie:

Marcie: :-)

Even through an emoticon, Marcie's smile made him feel warm and rosy. Lying there in bed, he could picture it as though she was really looking at him, rather than simply typing at him with a smartphone.

But what now? He'd made it clear to her that she could sleep with Michael. And she had promised not to keep secrets from him anymore. She had told Michael that her husband was on board with this affair—except that it wasn't really an affair anymore, because now her husband knew about it—and Michael had responded positively to this development, even managing to compliment him on his love for Marcie. But what now? How did this go?

'No secrets' was great in theory, but in practice did that mean he had to ask her about everything that happened, if he wanted to know about it? Or would she volunteer the information he wanted?

Lying there in bed, his cock was deflating rapidly. What was she doing right now? Still eating dinner? Watching TV? Taking a shower? Or dragging Michael into bed for a bunch of red-hot sex that was now permitted by her loving husband?

As curious as Cam was, he was underpinned by the classic English nature of not wanting to bother other people, not wanting to interfere or interrupt. He didn't want to seem like a stalker. He didn't want to make Marcie groan, in a bad way, every time she received a text from him.

And at the same time, he was embarrassed at this strange new desire of his, the desire for his wife to be unfaithful. He felt a deep sense of shame that he wanted her to have sex with Michael, that he would rather enjoy catching a glimpse of it, overhearing it, grasping some kind of evidence that it actually happened—or at the very least, finding out about it afterward. But if he asked for those details, and pressed her repeatedly about what was going on, she would soon suspect that he had some ulterior motive for knowing what she was up to with Michael.

Would that lessen the goodwill Marcie felt toward him? Would she think, *I know your game, you're not being a kind, sensitive husband at all, you don't care a fig whether I'm lonely in London or not, you just want to get your rocks off treating me as your own personal porn star.*

He felt compelled to wait. He felt he had no choice but to let her come at this at her own pace, in a manner in which she was comfortable. He sighed, took another deep, meditative breath and tried to think about the positives: he knew she was engaged in a sexual relationship with Michael, now; she was ostensibly going to be open about it, and not do anything behind his back; she had clearly stated she did not love him, and would not leave Cam; and occasionally, perhaps he would get some little thrills knowing when she was having sex with him, or finding out some small details after the fact.

Five minutes passed by. Ten. Twenty.

He started wondering if he would hear from her again that night. He hadn't told her to check in every hour, or every two hours, or even before she went to sleep. She could take it as read that she could forget about her phone completely, and go have fun with Michael for the rest of the night without worrying about her husband.

He sighed.

Half an hour ticked by since her last text. He had its timestamp to prove it.

It was ten o'clock—not too early to go to sleep. He started contemplating sending her a 'night-night' text, a simple alert to her that he was tired, he was going to sleep, and that he hoped she had a good night with Michael. He even pondered the possibility that this approach might make it more likely that she would actually have sex with Michael that night—feeling that she didn't have an over-bearing husband breathing down her neck the whole time. And wasn't it his ultimate aim to get her to have sex with the guy? Even if he didn't get to see it, or hear it, or find out about it, better that sex happened between them than it didn't. At least according to Cam's strange new kink.

But he didn't want to go to sleep. He was wide awake. His cock softened, but then he'd start thinking about Marcie hanging out with another man, Marcie seducing another man, and his heart rate started picking up again, and his hardness soon returned.

He wanted there to be half a chance she'd drop some little hint that something was happening with Michael. That would be seriously hot, wouldn't it?

So he waited.

Tick followed tock followed tick followed tock followed tick.

And then it hit 10:15, and Marcie texted him:

Marcie: So, no secrets then. How does that go?

CHAPTER THIRTEEN

THE FIRST THING he felt was a warm little cozy feeling deep inside, that came from the fact that Marcie must have been thinking similar thoughts to him—albeit without the knowledge that her husband was massively turned on by her infidelity.

The second thing was that he felt impressed at her being able to pin down their current dilemma with such a brief text message.

So, no secrets then. How does that go?

The third thing he felt was panic, and fear, and a little excitement, but mostly angst. How did he respond to that? She was putting him on the spot, forcing him to come clean on what he expected for this new reality for their relationship. Did he tell her that she had to text him about every little move made between the two of them? Every glance, every touch, every kiss. Or did he go the other way and play it laissez-faire? Tell her she could do as she pleased, just to maybe keep him in the loop every once in a while. Not hide anything. Answer him honestly if ever he asked her about something going on.

Damn it, it was so unfair, her putting him on the spot like this.

But then, it was he who had said she could go on seeing Michael, only on a no-secrets basis.

He sighed. He didn't like not answering her, he didn't like leaving her hanging. No secrets. He started texting, panic guiding his forefinger.

Cam: To be honest, I'm not sure I thought it all though.

He felt his stomach drop as soon as he sent the message. It made him sound so weak, so pathetic. But there was no way to recall a text message.

Marcie replied fairly quickly:

Marcie: It's okay, I mean, you hardly had any time to really think about it. Some couples separate for months to figure out what they really want.

It was reassuring. The thought that she might be hinting that they could need a period of separation to sort themselves out was disquieting, but he read and re-read her message, and found some confidence that she hadn't meant to suggest separation for them.

After another hesitation on his part, Marcie texted him again:

Marcie: Just tell me what your gut feeling is. When you say 'no secrets', is that you wanting to know every little thing that happens with Michael? Or would you prefer not to know the details, just want to be kept in the loop about what's going on in general?

Marcie's raw intelligence always had impressed him. Right now, she was really hitting the nail on the head as to what he was asking himself. But from her message, he also got the feeling that she wanted to open up as much as she could—she wouldn't have offered it as an option otherwise —and perhaps it was because she wanted to keep close with her husband, she wanted to make sure her marriage was on safe ground at all times.

Maybe he was reading too much into it, but he took it as reassuring.

He texted back:

Cam: My gut feeling... is I'd love to hear as much detail as you'd be comfortable sharing :-)

He was pleased with himself for remembering a smiley face. They did seem to ease the tension that stemmed from it being tricky to convey emotion within simple text messages.

Marcie: Okay then :-) I'll try and share as much detail as I can, while I have my phone in my hands. But you can stop me if I'm sharing too much, okay? If there's things you'd rather not hear... ;-)

He liked the wink emoticon from her. That was hot. He liked her confidence. It had to have something to do with having another man with her, another lover. Men desired her, and she knew it.

Cam: Sounds good :-) I can't think of anything that would make me uncomfortable, though ;-)

Two emotions in one text message. She was going to start thinking he was losing it. But, you know. Two different emotional feelings in the message.

Marcie: Okay... so where do we start... right now I'm chilling out on the sofa with Michael, watching Last Kingdom on Netflix... :-)

So far, so inconsequential.

Cam: Sounds hot ;-)

Marcie: Well, if you must know, he has an arm around my shoulders, and I have a hand on his thigh. Stroking him, gently. :-)

Well, that was something.

Cam: He doesn't mind that you're texting me?

Marcie: He hasn't said anything. I quite often play on my phone while we watch TV. But anyway, I told him about our 'no secrets' thing. He doesn't have a problem with it.

Cam: What are you wearing?

Marcie: Pretty much what I was wearing when I left you this morning. Work stuff.

Cam recalled the elaborate lingerie that had filled her underwear drawer when he'd examined the chest in the bedroom of that apartment. Would she change into something sexy before the two of them had sex? That morning he'd watched her getting dressed, putting on a fairly plain black bra and matching panties. Not something that seemed like the sexy lingerie she kept in London.

Well, she might not have brought anything fancy back home when she'd come here to confess her sins. But surely she wouldn't wear something like that for Michael?

But the question would go unasked. In her eyes, he didn't know she even possessed any of that sexy underwear.

He texted her, saying he wished he could see her.

Two minutes later, she sent through a selfie, a picture showing her all snuggled up on the sofa with Michael, wearing her usual office attire—white button-down shirt, smart skirt, nylons. She smiled up at the camera as she held it out from her to capture the view. Cam felt his heart burn as he saw it. She looked happy, though. Smiley. Beautiful. She looked good with him, although as he peered at the picture for longer—and took in his first real sight of her lover—there was something slightly awkward about the pose.

Michael seemed about Marcie's age—what was she now, 38, 39? He could have been in his late thirties or early forties. Handsome, dark, clean-shaven. He had the square jaw of a superhero, and from what Cam could see, the physique of one, too.

After a moment or two gazing at them, gently strumming his fingers over his stiff cock as he scrutinized this first glimpse of his wife and her lover, he came to the conclusion that the slight awkwardness came from the fact that the two of them both seemed like alpha personalities —extroverts. Jocks, if they were still in school. They looked good together, but they weren't all snuggled up like people who were entirely comfortable with each other.

Lovers, yes, but not *in* love.

That was immensely reassuring to him. The two of them seemed too stiff, sitting there, to be real lovers cozying up together on a couch. Their backs were too straight—their body language spoke of two people trying to impress each other, and maybe to flirt with each other, but they were not melting into each other like long-time lovers would.

They seemed, to Cam, like colleagues who had just started dating because everyone else thought they would make a cute couple—not because they had fallen for each other.

Cam felt quite powerful relief, taking in that picture.

Cam: He's very good looking.

Marcie: He is, isn't he?

Cam: I'm not surprised you were tempted.

Marcie: I shouldn't have. I was weak.

Cam: You were lonely. You don't need to beat yourself up about it anymore.

Marcie: I love you, you know that?

Cam: Sure, I know :-)

All this communication was good for them. No matter that they were going over territory they'd pretty much covered during their big talk the previous night. Every time they went through it, it felt a little more resolved. Every time she declared her love for him, he felt a little more confident with it.

Marcie: Michael already had a suitcase out, ready to pack. He assumed I'd come back today and tell him to leave.

This was very interesting to Cam, because it was more confirmation that the two of them could not be in love. If Michael had assumed that Marcie would come back to London and continue sleeping with him as though nothing had changed, that would be the more worrying development.

Cam: It must be quite stressful, not having a job. Or his own place.

Marcie: He'll get another job soon. He's too good to stay unemployed for long.

Cam: Any update on how long you'll stay at the company?

Marcie: No one knows. We're still pretty far away from securing enough credit to continue, though. It probably won't be too long, then I'll be in Michael's situation, too.

Cam felt his manhood softening again. He liked this new closeness with Marcie—chatting to her while she was in London. They'd fallen out of doing that a long while ago. He'd always assumed she preferred having her own space while she was there in the capital, and he guessed she didn't want to trouble him while he was tired after taking care of the kids.

But the really fun part of this texting between them was when they dipped into erotic territory.

Cam: How long do you guys normally watch TV in the evening?

Marcie: Varies. Sometimes an hour or two. Sometimes hardly at all. Depends if we're tired. Or horny.

Cam: What are you now?

Marcie: I'm not sure. Not particularly tired, though ;-)

That mischievous wink face again. Would she, or wouldn't she?

Cam found the TV remote and switched on Netflix. He was bored with the news, news during the pandemic was just crazy. He wanted something that wouldn't drive him up the wall—because he didn't want to be texting

Marcie every five seconds. He had to pace himself if he was going to continue. He didn't want to scare her away.

A few minutes later, Marcie was the one who texted next.

Marcie: Michael's poured us both a nice glass of red wine. :-)
Cam: That should help get you in the mood ;-)

A moment after that:

Marcie: So I take it you want me to seduce him?

He tried to keep calm. It seemed like she was continually checking him—she couldn't quite comprehend that he wanted her to have fun with Michael, and share details. But at the same time, he had to be sure of it himself. There were no do-overs. If he approved of her having sex with Michael, and then he changed his mind, he wouldn't be able to take it back.

Cam: I think it would be fun, yeah xx

There it was. She couldn't need more permission than that.

A few moments later, to his surprise, she sent another picture. This time, she was snuggled up to Michael in a similar way to the previous pose, except that this time a number of buttons on her shirt were unfastened, and it was pulled open sufficiently to see an expanse of her cleavage and even some of her black bra.

She looked devilishly good. And, surprisingly, that was the bra she'd been wearing that morning.

Michael didn't seem to be paying her much attention, he looked focused on the television.

Cam texted her back:

Cam: I'm not sure how he could possibly resist you right now :-)
Marcie: The TV show is a little overly exciting at the moment. I just have to wait until there's a sexy bit.
Cam: There's sexy bits in this show?
Marcie: It does try too much to be Game of Thrones sometimes.

Michael wants to know if all this means we have an open marriage. Is that it? Do we have an open marriage?

Cam felt the panic in her words, even if it was difficult to convey emotions properly in text messages. It was an interesting question, though. Funny how he hadn't even considered the idea of an open marriage. He hadn't even thought about other women, he certainly hadn't wanted another woman since he'd learned of Marcie's infidelity. If anything, her infidelity had made his sexual fantasies more faithful, not less.

How could he want another woman, when his big turn-on was his wife being unfaithful?

But while he knew how he felt, he could understand why Marcie wouldn't. Logic might suggest that in all fairness, he should be allowed to see other women if she was allowed to see other men. Yet to feel that way would be to entirely miss the point of Cam's newfound desire. Perhaps the problem was that he wasn't being entirely frank about his own feelings regarding Marcie's infidelity.

He wanted to tell her. He just couldn't quite deal with the shame just yet.

Cam: No, we don't have an open marriage. You just have a husband who doesn't want you to be lonely and depressed while you're spending half the week away from home, who doesn't have a problem with you sleeping with other people.

It took a few moments for her to reply to that one. A few moments for his message to sink in.

Then:

Marcie: Wow. But… after what I've done… you're not at all tempted to go on Tinder and start chatting up sexy singletons?

Cam chuckled at that one. He felt a touch of pity for her, though. He could tell she thought it only fair that he'd be able to do that, but he could sense she was mildly terrified that he might do it.

Cam: Not at all tempted.

Marcie: :-)

Marcie: But you don't get lonely being on your own at night, when I'm away?

Cam: I'm not really on my own here.

Marcie: You don't get horny while I'm away?

Her question made him think back to before—before he had discovered her affair. Actually, he hadn't been horny much. He'd always been too exhausted by taking care of the kids to think about sex very often. Perhaps that had helped the sexual bond between them fray.

Cam: I didn't really, before. I was always too tired. But now… I guess I am now that I know you're about to sleep with someone else :-)

There was another long pause before his iPhone told him Marcie was typing another text message. He realized that he'd sort of admitted to finding the thought of her sleeping with Michael a turn-on. In a round-about way.

She replied:

Marcie: Is that what's about to happen?

He was breathing deeply now, his heart rate picking up.

Cam: Don't you want it to be?

Another pause. Was she feeling guilty again? Even though he was telling her it was all right to sleep with Michael?

Marcie: And it would make you horny, to know that I was?

He felt a jolt of fear shoot through his heart. Here it was. Admitting it openly. But he couldn't hold back now.

Cam: It would.

Marcie: Wow.

He blushed, fiercely, even though there was nobody here to see him facing up to his deep sense of shame. Did she think he was a freak? A pervert? Did she think less of him as a man because he had just told her he was turned on by her adultery?

But then she texted again, saying:

Marcie: I think that's the hottest thing I ever heard :-)

He smiled and felt a wave of relief. It also made him feel closer to Marcie, even though they were physically apart. Maybe he could be open about that aspect of her infidelity.

She texted him again, and he could sense her curiosity burning through her words:

Marcie: Will you be okay coping with it while I'm sleeping with Michael?

Her question made him laugh. It also made him hard.

Cam: I think I can cope with being horny. Men have ways of dealing with that kind of thing when we're on our own.

Marcie: So… will you be dealing with it when this episode is over and I drag Michael to bed with me?

Now he was hard as a rock. His stiff cock slipping out through the fly of his boxer shorts, so that he could stroke it.

Cam: I might be.

Marcie: Mmm… I like the thought of that :-)

Cam chuckled. And texted back:

Cam: The thought of dragging Michael to bed with you?

Marcie: The thought of you… dealing with it… while I do. ;-)

Cam: Maybe I'm already starting to deal with it ;-)

Marcie: Wow. :-)

Well, it was out there. He might not have made it clear what a driving force his desire for her to be unfaithful had been to him recently, but at least she might understand a little more about how he was feeling about everything now.

He wrote her a teasing text:

Cam: What if Michael wants to watch another episode after this one?

Her hesitation in replying made him think she was stuck for an answer. But then, after a few moments:

Marcie: I'm pretty sure he won't want that. He has his hand on my thigh right now, and it's creeping up toward interesting places :-)

Cam laughed.

Cam: Interesting places?

Another pause from her end.

Marcie: Mmm… okay… now it's arrived… mmm… I think he's surprised I'm so wet already ;-)

Cam felt his hardness throb in his hand as he read her words. His wife was being touched intimately by another man. She was about to pull him up from the sofa and drag him into the bedroom for sex.

Marcie: I might not be able to text you much longer tonight.

Wow. It was really going to happen, then.

He had absolved her of all guilt, and she was about to have sex with another man with his approval. He was so excited, it felt like he was about to suffer a nuclear meltdown. His breathing was so labored, he was almost panting. His heart was hammering so fast it almost sounded like machine-gun fire. The butterflies were fluttering like crazy in his stomach.

Cam: That's okay… you go have fun… I'll be thinking about you ;-)

Marcie: :-)

Then, after a beat:

Marcie: You're really sure this is all okay with you?

Cam didn't need any time to think about his reply:

Cam: I'm sure. Go have fun. I'm hard as a rock right now :-)

He felt a flush of embarrassment as he texted that to her. It was so revealing, so filthy, so wrong. It felt like the dirtiest thing he'd ever texted her. But her reply came quickly:

Marcie: I love you so much. You're the best husband in the world :-) xxx

Cam: I love you too. Now go! xxx

Marcie: Going xx

And then, as far as he could tell, she had gone.

Cam felt like he was gasping for breath, all of a sudden.

CHAPTER FOURTEEN

HE LAY THERE, awake—of course—his mind reeling at
what was going on hundreds of miles away in London.

It was happening.

Right now.

His wife had gone into a kind of radio silence because
her hands were no longer free to type text messages to
Cam. Her hands were dragging another man to the
bedroom, pulling off her clothes, pulling off his clothes,
grabbing hold of him as she kissed him. Taking hold of
Michael's big cock before he put it in her mouth, or in her
pussy.

Cam lay on the bed, at home in Gloucestershire, his
heart rate pounding inside his chest, sucking in oxygen as
he attempted to breathe enough to keep up with the adrenaline racing around his system. He felt like he was riding a
rollercoaster, clutching the safety bar as it swooped down
impossibly steep dips and roared around ferocious curves
where the G-force was so strong it strained his heart.

He wanted this to happen—had wanted it to happen
from the first moment he'd sent her back to London, with

his consent, to continue sleeping with her lover—and yet now that it was happening, he felt alarmed by it.

The feeling was almost too powerful to bear at first, and despite his belief that he would be prepared for it when it happened, now that it was here, he felt woefully unprepared for it. Now that it was here, it felt like a punch in the gut.

Was it *really* just sex between them?

What if, now that she was more aware of what she was doing, now that she was unencumbered by guilt towards her husband, she suddenly realized she *had* developed feelings for him?

Sure, it wasn't her first time with Michael. It wasn't even the first time she'd slept with Michael since Cam had discovered their affair. But it was the first time she'd done it with her husband's approval. That was big. That was breath-taking.

And the big surprise for Cam was that he wasn't turned on right at that moment. He was excited, sure. He wasn't jealous, as far as he could tell. He wasn't completely terrified, but he was nervous. He lay in bed, not really watching Netflix, thinking about what Marcie was most likely doing in that moment, and his cock wasn't hard, it wasn't even a little bit hard—and he didn't feel like attempting to make it hard.

It was almost as though the realization that she was having sex with another man in that moment was just a little too overwhelming for him to be actively turned on just then.

Was this how it would always be?

Was this him losing sexual interest in Marcie actually having sex with someone else?

Some of his nerves were related to his lack of arousal at such a key moment. He got up from the bed, paced the room. He perched on the end of the bed and scrolled through Netflix titles to see if there was something that might be able to grip his interest strongly enough to distract him.

He picked up his phone and searched through Google for any information about husbands who allowed their wives to sleep with other men.

And, as it turned out, there were plenty of websites offering such information. He even found websites where husbands could share their experiences with other men and women interested in this semi-open form of a relationship. Husbands experiencing their first time having a wife out on a date with another man. Husbands who had discovered their wives had been cheating on them, and had responded to the discovery with arousal, and even joy. Husbands who spent years trying to persuade their wives that their desire for them to sleep with other men wasn't a bad thing, and wouldn't jeopardize their marriages.

Reading it all started to make him feel better about himself, and what he was going through.

He wasn't alone when it came to this strange new obsession of his.

He wasn't a freak.

He was, in fact, very fortunate to have an attractive wife who apparently embraced his enjoyment of her affair, and seemed to be happy to share details about her experiences with another man.

He felt an unexpected sense of relief, an unexpected feeling of reassurance in identifying with these other husbands, even if he didn't really like the way some of them adopted the term 'cuckold' for themselves. Was that what he was? It seemed like such a horribly negative word for the kind of positive feelings he was having about it. But the word did seem to contain a hint of shame, from the way mainstream society—and history—viewed a 'cuckold'. And this hint of shame under the surface resonated with the way Cam felt, deep down, when he considered telling Marcie everything about how turned-on he was by her carnal relations with another man.

Maybe he *was* a cuckold.

But he wasn't harming anyone. As long as he wasn't stupid, this was okay. As long as it didn't spoil his marriage, as long as Marcie didn't fall for another man and decide to move out. As long as he made sure her adventures were consistent with keeping their marriage bond strong.

It was useful to get tips and advice from other husbands who had experienced this kind of thing for, in some cases, many years. Keep the communication channels open. Make sure that her adventures enhance her relationship with you, and that your marriage doesn't become the sideshow. He read, and he calmed down, and he even started to enjoy the strange, nervous butterflies he had knowing that Marcie was currently in the throes of passion with Michael, her lockdown lover.

And after a while, he started getting that familiar warm feeling in his loins. His cock began to thicken up again. He started checking the clock again, trying to figure out how long Michael could possibly have strung out foreplay before he went in for penetration, and working out that even if the guy was some kind of Sting-like tantric master, it had to have happened by now.

There were still nerves, and all the time he did kind of want it to be over, even though he would look back at the whole of this night as one of the most exciting nights of his life. But he was handling it, and that gave him some reassurance, too.

Surely they had to be done by now?

He picked up his phone, disappointed there was no

new message from Marcie. But should he expect one? As far as she knew, she had full approval from her husband to go to bed with Michael. There had been no obligation, or expectation, for her to message him after the deed.

Maybe she was opting for the more traditional sense of the term 'sleep with' somebody; she would have sex with him, and the two of them would drift off to sleep in each other's arms.

CHAPTER FIFTEEN

CAM ONLY REALIZED he'd fallen asleep when his phone buzzed in his hand, jolting him awake.

He'd drifted off to sleep lying on the bed, above the covers, wearing his boxer shorts but his cock still in one hand, phone in the other. He must have been really tired to fall asleep like that.

But now, he peered at his phone and saw a message from Marcie:

Marcie: Hey you! I hope you're not still awake… I had a lovely time with Michael. I know we have no secrets now, but I'm not sure how much you wanted to know about what happened… anyway, I guess this is me wishing you a good night. I love you! Xxx

Cam felt his manhood thickening up as he read her message, even if it was hardly what you'd call explicit. It was confirmation she'd just had sex with another man. She'd had a 'lovely time'. She wasn't sure how much he wanted to know about 'what happened'. That couldn't mean anything less than sex had happened.

Was she telling him she wanted to go to sleep?

He thought she might be. At the same time, he had a

sharp pang in his stomach from missing her, butterflies from his excitement at what she must have just done—and his curiosity to see her after she'd had sex with another man was overpowering.

He couldn't just pretend to be asleep.

He pondered a while, and then decided to text her back:

Cam: Hey gorgeous! I'm awake. Did you have fun? Are you going to sleep now? I miss you, wish I could see you, but no problem if you're tired xxx

For a few moments, he thought, perhaps, she really had gone to sleep. That she'd sent him that message and then had switched off. But just as he was about to switch off himself, he saw the characteristic three dots indicating that she was typing a new message for him.

Marcie: Hey sweetie! Can I call you on FaceTime? xxx

Cam felt his heart nearly stop.

Cam: Of course :-)

He felt a surge of excitement and anxiety. Wondering what she'd look like after she'd just had sex with another man, wondering how he would respond, worried that he would have some kind of change of heart over her infidelity now he saw her fresh from sex, paranoid she would have a change of heart over whether she loved Michael, whether she wanted to leave her husband. Worried that Michael would be there, in on the call, peering at him and trying to figure out how an idiot like him could give up a wife that looked as beautiful as Marcie, and allow her to sleep with other men.

Forcing himself to keep calm, he took a deep breath and hauled his hand out from his underwear, then leaned over to the bedside table to grab hold of his laptop computer. If he was going to talk to her, and see her so soon after she'd slept with Michael. Far better to see her on the bigger screen.

Moments after he opened the laptop, came the familiar tones of the incoming FaceTime call.

At the last moment, he pulled the bedsheet over the huge bulge in his undershorts, so that he might have some kind of dignity when she called. Then he accepted the call with his heart in his throat.

And there she was, on his screen, beaming at him.

'Hey, how *are* you?' she said, cheerfully.

God, she looked incredible. She was clutching a large, white towel around her body, which covered her from upper chest to knees. Her long, blonde hair was down, and apparently still damp, but nevertheless golden and lovely, framing her pretty, brightly-smiling face.

'Hey. Good. How's things?' he said, attempting to smile back as strongly as she was.

Behind her, he could see the living room, the windows looking out onto the street. She must have put her laptop down on the kitchen counter, and was standing there in front of it to talk to him.

There was no sign of Michael, which was a relief to Cam. He wanted privacy with his wife, so that he could deal with everything that was happening without worrying about outside opinions.

'I just got out of the shower,' she said, talking a little more quickly than normal—excited, nervous.

She clutched the towel in front of her as though worried it would fall, and expose herself in front of him. He was just stunned, seeing her. His cock was hard as steel. Here was Marcie, and she had just had sex with someone else.

'I'm sorry,' he said, worried he was interrupting her night. 'I just wanted to see you before I go to sleep.'

Marcie laughed, and in her high, soprano voice, somehow it sounded as beautiful as a fresh, mountain waterfall. 'It's okay,' she said, 'I just really thought you'd be asleep by now. It's nice to see you!'

He smiled again, nervous, though not entirely sure why he was nervous.

'So Michael…?' he asked, without quite knowing how to ask it.

Have you fucked him? Did you ride his big cock? Did he make you come like only another man could?

'He's asleep,' she grinned. 'I just… you know, I like to get clean before I go to sleep…'

Cam felt his cock throbbing, responding to her words —to the fact that for her to need to get clean, she would have to have gotten dirty, and that could only have been from fucking Michael. Under the bedsheets his hand slipped into his underwear to take hold of his hardness.

'…I should probably have put some clothes on before calling you, but I miss you so much,' she added.

'It's okay,' he beamed. 'You don't have to put anything on.'

'No?' She laughed, and clutched the towel more tightly, somewhat self-aware that her husband was seeing her just after she'd slept with someone else.

'I prefer seeing you without any,' he said.

'Really?' Her voice changed, suddenly. Dropping down in pitch. She looked a little surprised at what he'd said, a little stunned.

Well, he didn't usually see her via video call wearing just a towel. In fact, from what he could remember, the two of them had never done anything even slightly risqué over a FaceTime or Skype connection before.

But he wanted to see under her towel. He wanted to see his gorgeous, unfaithful wife.

'You're so beautiful,' he said, not really knowing what to say, how to ask for what he really wanted.

'Oh *honey*...' she said, flattered as hell, and she seemed to try to use the end of her towel to fan herself, except that it made it look as though she was teasing him, giving him a brief flash of a little more skin.

'Yes... take it off...' he said, quietly.

She looked shocked—but, importantly, intrigued.

Without saying anything, she opened the towel, slightly —clutching it tightly to her breasts, but letting him see a stunning portion of her body, the curve of her waist, the sweep of a hip, the smooth skin of her thigh. Just breathtaking.

'So you had fun with him?' he asked her, feeling his heart thumping against his chest cavity.

'Yes, I did,' she said, looking so serious, but in a very seductive kind of way. She was surprised by his question, surprised by his close interest—and yet, underneath it, she was turned on that he was drawing attention to her sex with Michael.

She twisted, slightly, flicking open the towel to give him a brief flash of her bare behind, in all its glory, before she rapidly faced him again and pulled the towel closed. It made her giggle—she was amused at herself for trying to distract from the awkwardness of whether-or-not to mention her sex with Michael by flashing her nudity in front of the webcam.

Then she peered at her laptop, and seemed to notice something.

'Wait, are you *touching yourself*?' she said, quietly.

Cam blushed fiercely, and felt a jolt of acute embarrassment shoot through his chest. But he could hardly deny it. 'Uh... maybe...' he said, frozen in place with the sheet concealing himself from the waist down. He could see from the little preview window in the corner of his screen that what he'd been doing with his hand under the bedsheet was rather obvious.

He heard Marcie gasp at that, and suddenly worried that he'd given away his darkest secret, and that she would think him a freak, that she would be disgusted with him, and if their relationship survived, she would tease him about it for the rest of his life.

But she didn't seem disgusted. Far from it—she seemed overjoyed.

'Should I... lose the towel?' she asked quietly.

Wow. He was stunned.

For some reason, he hadn't thought she'd ever want to strip while FaceTiming with him. It just didn't seem like a very Marcie thing to do. But here she was, offering him the goods—clutching the towel as she swayed on her feet a little, apparently debating with herself whether or not she should dispense with the towel entirely.

'Yes,' he breathed, '*please...*'

She seemed completely taken aback by his interest, but at the same time completely delighted by it.

Then she glanced around herself, as though checking nobody could see, particularly anybody across the street, who might be able to see in through the windows. Then she prised her towel apart, and briefly revealed her full, completely nude form.

Cam caught his breath.

She'd never displayed herself, for him, like this before. She looked absolutely incredible, sensational, divine. Her ample breasts, her trim figure, her shapely legs, her completely bare pussy...

Then she pulled the towel back into place, shocked at herself, but clearly excited underneath the awkward self-consciousness of standing in front of her laptop while her husband watched her through its camera.

'I'm not sure about this…' she said, nervously glancing toward the bedroom, now, as though she was worried about Michael discovering her like this.

'What's the big deal?' Cam chuckled, amused that she might be worried about her lover catching her doing something naughty with her husband.

'I know… you've seen me naked before…' she said, with a little nervous laugh. 'I just… you know… we don't normally…'

We don't normally… Well, 'normally' ended, for us, when I noticed that set of VW car keys sitting on the kitchen counter one night, when you FaceTimed with us, he thought to himself. But it was true, they'd never had the kind of relationship before where either of them would really display themselves in front of the other. Let alone over a FaceTime call.

'I guess it *is* a little… different,' he conceded.

'Different, yes.'

The scene wavered, and he saw that she had picked up her laptop, and was holding it, moving with it, walking to another part of the room while clamping her towel in place with the hand that was not holding the laptop. She got to the sofa, and sat down just in front of it, on the floor, so that she could lean back against the edge of the seat and rest the laptop on the coffee table in front of her.

'That's better,' she said, now toying with her wet hair as it hung down over one of her shoulders, attempting to tease out the tangles.

'Better because nobody can see you through the windows now?' he asked her.

'What?' She giggled. 'I'm not wearing anything under this towel. I don't want somebody else to see me…'

'So you're going to show me some more?'

Another nervous giggle. 'Well... you know... if you're touching yourself... I might as well help you out...'

'You might as well,' he agreed, liking how fixated she was on the sight of him sitting there with his hand between his legs, slowly pumping away under the bedsheet.

Both of her hands were clasping the top of her towel over her chest, now, rather than worrying about her tangled hair. Then she cupped her breasts, gently fondled them a little through the towel.

'You want to see these?' She teased him.

'Uh-huh.'

A giggle. 'Don't I get to see something?' she asked.

He laughed and felt a burst of mild embarrassment before he told himself she'd seen him naked before plenty of times, albeit not on a laptop screen. He cleared his throat, getting up the courage, and then whipped aside the bedsheet to reveal himself.

She gasped and covered her hand with one mouth. He wondered for a moment if he'd gone too far.

But then she smiled and purred. 'Mmm... nice and hard...'

He glanced at the little preview window in the top corner of his screen, showing what Marcie would be seeing on her screen. The angle of the camera made his cock look enormous—he liked that. And he liked that the frame cut off most of his face, showing only from the upper thighs up to his jawline.

'Mmm... you're enjoying this, huh?' she giggled, teasing him, and yet at the same time delighted that he was so hard from watching her.

'Oh yes,' he said.

'I feel a bit silly,' she laughed, clutching the edge of her towel tightly with both hands, edging it down so that almost all of her breasts were visible, her nipples just about covered.

'Don't,' Cam said. 'You look incredible.'

'Mmm…' she giggled and fondled her breasts a little more through her towel.

Then, she let it drop, and for a moment was completely still, her breasts suddenly bare.

After a brief flash, she covered her breasts again, this time with only her hands, and fondled them, quietly giggling in quite a self-conscious way. Cam watched her, and slowly stroked his hard cock so that she could see. That seemed to lend her a little confidence boost. Then she let her hands fall, exposing her breasts once more.

'So… have you been awake this whole time?' she asked him. 'The whole time I've been… with Michael?'

Fucking Michael, he almost heard her say.

'I may have drifted off for a little,' he said.

She smiled, and seemed impressed that he could be relaxed enough about her being with Michael to actually fall asleep. 'I shouldn't have woken you up again,' she laughed.

'I'm glad you did,' he said, feeling a little embarrassed about being turned on by her adulterous sex. Wanting to make it clear to her how he felt, but feeling shame pressuring him to obscure his full reaction to her infidelity. 'I wanted to see you… afterward…'

'*Ohh…*' she said, with that little whine of pity that said *you're so cute*.

She held the towel such that he could see her breasts, as though rewarding him for his devotion. 'Well, here I am.'

'You're so beautiful…' he breathed, and wondered if the microphone even picked up what he said. Her smile seemed to confirm that it did.

He moved his laptop a little closer to him, filling her view with his hard cock as he continued to jack it.

'Mmm… I love it…' she said, as though in awe. Then she said, 'Well, I guess I can try…'

He saw her put her hands back behind her, onto the sofa, and then she was pulling herself up, so she could perch on the edge of the cushion—and as she did so, her legs parted and her bare pussy was completely exposed. He felt his heart do a hop, jump and a skip to lay eyes on it.

Was it a little rosy, from being recently well-used?

'Can you see me?' she asked, shuffling back on the sofa a little, parting her legs so that he could see everything.

'Oh, yes,' he said, pumping his cock a little faster.

'Yeah? It works for you?' She was gazing at his cock, he could tell. He didn't mind. He was just drinking in the sight of her naked, adulterous form. Just gorgeous. Fresh from the shower. Fresh from fucking another man.

She cautiously fondled her breasts, as though not quite knowing how to move in front of the camera. She seemed a little less shy now, though. Less timid. Watching him pumping his hard cock probably reassured her, told her he liked what he was seeing.

'I wish you were here to touch me,' she said softly as she played with her nipples.

'I wish I was,' he agreed.

'I don't know how Michael would feel about you being here as well,' she grinned.

'You think he'd be freaked out?'

She shrugged. 'I don't know. He seems fairly chilled about things. He didn't have a problem tonight… you know, after I told him you knew about us. That you told me I could… sleep with him.'

'He didn't have a problem… getting it up for you?'

Cam asked her, feeling his pulse racing, to discuss her actual sex with another man.

'He didn't have a problem at all,' she said, one hand slipping down between her legs, as though drawn by some magnetic force.

He watched her stroking herself, her fingers caressing either side of her sex, though not, yet, her sensitive folds. Wow. She just looked sensational. Pornography might have softened the shock of seeing a naked woman on his laptop screen—but the fact that it was Marcie, it was his wife, blazed through any sense of complacency he might have had.

'Does he have a big…?' He asked her, not quite getting to the end of his question.

'Why are men always so obsessed by the size of other men's dicks?' She giggled.

'We're just… interested.'

Another giggle. 'Well, I'll tell you he's big enough.'

'Okay. That means he's small?'

'No, it doesn't,' she replied, curtly.

'So he *is* big.'

She gave him a little eye-roll, but its drama was sapped by the fact that she was sitting there, legs parted, stroking her pussy lips.

'In an ideal world,' she said, 'what would you be hoping for, for your wife's lover?'

He grinned. 'In an ideal world… I'd want him to be big,' he said, and saw that she hadn't been expecting him to say that. 'I'd want you to have a good time with him.'

'Mmm…' she said, seeming happy that he would want that for her, as she stroked herself with circular movements of her fingers against her sex. 'Well, then I'll tell you… I always have a *very* good time with him…'

She moaned, and for a few moments, they were both silent, touching themselves while watching each other.

Then she breathed, 'God, I wish you were here…'

He said, 'You should go wake Michael.'

'Right now I want you…' she said, leaning back in the sofa, putting more effort into tending the fires between her legs. 'I want your beautiful, big, hard cock…'

'You're not too tired… after being with Michael?'

'No…' she sighed, her fingers flicking around her pussy, her clit, with expert skill.

'You're not too… sore… after being with him?'

'No… I'm so *wet*…' she changed hands, started stroking herself with her left hand instead, more quickly than before. He could hear her fingers moving within her pussy—he could *hear* how wet she was.

God, she was so sexy. She seemed to have shed her inhibitions, or else her arousal made her simply forget. She also seemed less concerned at somebody catching her—either somebody peeking through the windows from an apartment across the street, or else Michael stumbling out of the bedroom needing a drink or something from the kitchen.

She pulled herself up, so she could kneel on the sofa in front of her laptop, then went back to tracing rapid circles around her sex, and around her clit—either she was combatting pins and needles, or else this position allowed her to stroke her pussy more forcefully, more quickly.

Cam asked her, 'Does he make you come? When you sleep with him? Does he make you come all the time?'

She moaned, and then breathlessly, asked him, 'Would it upset you?'

He laughed, 'Are you kidding me? Do I look upset?'

'He makes me come. A lot.'

'Do I make you come?'

She smiled. 'Of course.'

'No secrets, remember.'

She nodded, and now sat back down on the sofa again, this time with her pussy tilted up a little more, her legs parted wider—he could see everything, she had completely dispensed with any kind of reserve.

'Sometimes… before the lockdown… before Michael… there were times you didn't.'

'There were times?' He probed her, at least verbally.

'Okay… but I don't think it was all your fault,' she said, slowing her masturbation a little, though it still appeared fairly forceful. 'I guess… Michael showed me… I'd been slacking off when I was sleeping with you.'

She whimpered, making it clear that she wasn't slacking off when it came to herself right now, even though her pace had become a little more sedate.

'*Fuck…*' she said, quietly, and the way she trembled a little made it fairly clear she wasn't in the market to fake anything tonight.

He said, 'Does it make you feel good… having two men at your disposal…?'

She smiled, moaned, 'Oh yes…' He liked how she responded to her words.

He said, 'Two hard cocks… sharing you between them through the week…'

'Oh honey…'

He was getting close to his own orgasm, and wanted to slow down, or even bring his own rhythm to a halt—but he could see she was watching his every move, and her own enjoyment was coming at least in part from seeing him stroking himself in response to the sight of her. He didn't want to stop and risk sapping the energy from her own ascent.

'Are you going to come?' she asked him, her voice

sounding increasingly high-pitched, though she was trying to keep the volume down, trying to keep this particular FaceTime call private, unheard by sleeping lovers. 'Are you going to come, honey? Will you come for me?'

'I'm close,' he said. 'I'll come when you do, sweetheart. Come for me.'

'Oh I'm there, I'm there, I'm there…' she said, sounding so urgent, almost afraid of the orgasm that was approaching.

Excitement could resemble fear sometimes. Pleasure could seem like pain in someone's expression. Marcie's face seemed to be tightening, the muscles in her entire body tensing, and as she continued strumming her clit with her fingers, panting for air, letting out little whimpers here and there, her divine form started to shudder and shake.

'Oh God… Oh *God*…' she hissed, trying not to cry out, not to yell loud enough to wake the dead. Her voice was too forceful to be considered a whisper, however.

'Come for me, sweetheart,' he said. 'I'm so hard for you… I can't hold back… you're so beautiful… you're so *incredible*… I love you so much…'

He was just plucking words out of his head—he had no experience, no skills when it came to talking dirty, because it had never been something he did with Marcie before. From her response, however, his words seemed to hit home.

'Oh… oh… oh… *fuck*…'

Then she was shivering for a few moments, like she was seriously *cold*, even though it had been a ridiculously warm spring, and was heading into a beautifully warm summer —and the apartment was fairly well climate-controlled.

'Oh God that felt good…' she murmured, 'God… I can't believe it…'

It seemed like words were just tumbling out of her

mouth without much thought, but at least it was honest, truthful. She came, and he had helped make her come— even after she'd been with Michael, whose ability to make her come was, without doubt, not in question. He felt some sense of achievement in that.

When she opened her eyes again, slowly getting her laptop back into focus, she broke out into a beautiful smile, almost seeming as though she'd had to remind herself that he was there, on the other end of a FaceTime call, jacking his hard cock to the sight of her.

'Come for me, honey,' she said, 'I want to see you come, now.'

She was still touching herself, though it was more as a show for his benefit, now. Stroking herself so he could still see her pussy, stretching her lips open, so he could see where another man had penetrated, spreading her wetness all over her sex so that her pretty petals glistened.

'You make me so wet, honey, so soaking *wet*… I love seeing you pumping your big, hard cock… keep going honey…'

As though he needed it, she sat up on the sofa, and then turned around to show him her delectable rear end— bending away from him so he could imagine fucking her like that. Or he could imagine someone else fucking her like that. Michael.

'…stroke your cock nice and hard for me, honey…'

They reached a moment, as she turned around to face him again, when Cam suddenly started feeling his energy levels going—and he experienced the sudden fear and doubt that came during occasions when he'd slept with Marcie only to lose his hardness halfway through.

But then, suddenly, Marcie smiled brightly, and flaunted her pussy in front of him in a way he would never have imagined she was capable of—and then she said,

'Come for me, honey, come all over me—*just like he did.*'

And that last little tidbit suddenly put a real lead in his pencil—he was instantly rock-hard and leaping for the finishing line, feeling his orgasm welling up inside him before erupting like some powerful volcano.

'Oh God...' he hissed, trying to keep his own voice down.

He came everywhere, shooting spurts of thick, white, cream all over the bed. There would be laundry. But it felt amazing. Better than amazing.

'I'm going to have to take another quick shower,' she said, when he was done.

'I'm going to have to do some laundry,' he joked.

She smiled. 'You need to get some sleep,' she warned him, 'otherwise you're going to be too tired for home learning tomorrow.'

'Oh God,' he laughed, 'don't remind me about the home learning.'

But despite everything, he felt on top of the world.

CHAPTER SIXTEEN

THE NEXT DAY, he woke feeling refreshed, despite the abbreviated sleep he'd had that night. He had adrenaline to get him through the difficult portions of the day—the home-schooling with the kids, who did not want to learn since they were at home, an attitude that seemed to get worse and worse as lockdown continued.

Along with the adrenaline that came as a direct result of his exciting night FaceTiming with Marcie, the thought that his beautiful, wicked wife would be home the following evening also helped Cam to get through the day.

Flo seemed more cheerful than usual. Not that she was usually particularly morose, but throughout the day she gave him the occasional glance that almost seemed affectionate. He got the sense that word had gotten back to his mother-in-law that he had turned out to be a very good son-in-law considering what his wife had done.

Almost as some kind of reward, Flo made one of her legendary beef stews for supper.

And then they were all crowding around the family computer again, because Mommy was calling.

Tonight, Cam sat there with Flo and the kids all through the call, riveted to the image of Marcie on the screen. She was looking gorgeous, of course, tonight with her shoulder-length, golden hair down, framing her pretty face. Her shirt was blue, smart as usual. Nothing unusual about her, as she smiled at the kids and asked them about their day. But Cam saw her differently than before. Or maybe, he thought of her differently.

She just seemed sexier, now that he knew she was sleeping with someone else as well.

He felt like he hadn't really noticed how pretty she was before. How downright sexy she was. He'd been taking her attractiveness completely for granted, perhaps since even before they were married. But now, it was like he'd woken up, and here he was, married to a complete vixen.

Complete adulterous vixen.

Cam had to force himself to calm down. He didn't want anyone else suspecting something was up. He had to try not to think about the fact that, probably, Michael was somewhere else in the apartment right now, waiting for her call to be over. Maybe he was chilling out in the bedroom. And later, he was going to fuck Marcie.

He ran his eyes all over Marcie's face as she talked to the kids, taking in the refined, elegant form of her face—those big, soulful eyes, her high cheekbones, small nose, full lips. He imagined her ending this call and going over to her lover for another, deeper kiss. Dragging him into the bedroom—the bedroom in which Cam had stood just a few days before. Stripping off, pulling out the restraints or the handcuffs from her bedside drawer.

Tossing him over a condom.

After a few minutes, Cam had to stop himself from thinking about it all. Marcie asked how he was doing, unexpectedly in the middle of the call, rather than waiting right until the end for a very cursory inquiry as to his own wellbeing.

'Oh, good, good,' he said, feeling a little flustered that he'd just been thinking about another guy thrusting his big cock into her tight, wet pussy, and now two kids, his wife and mother-in-law were all looking at him as Marcie asked how his day had gone. 'This afternoon while Flo was taking care of the kids, I was just writing up my garden center article…'

'Right, garden centers—they're really suffering from the lockdown, huh?' Marcie said, and the glint in her eyes told Cam that she knew exactly what he was thinking right at that moment, and it wasn't about garden centers. It was about her, and her adulterous sex.

'Yeah, it's normally their peak season,' he nodded, avoiding her eyes, because she was trying to make him laugh, or blush, or something. 'Lot of plants going unsold.'

'And they can't just sell them online?'

'Most of them don't have a clue how,' he said.

'But everyone's out in the gardens during lockdown, right?' She said, and he risked a glance up into her face, and found that she was simply smiling at him, with warm affection.

'Yeah, something like that,' he smiled back, reflecting the warmth from her smile, his tone filled with the love he felt for her—and it seemed stronger than ever, now—and his growing desire for her.

'Well, you guys have been having fun gardening with Daddy, haven't you?' Marcie asked the kids.

'Yeah!' the kids yelled back, cheerfully.

For a split second, Marcie seemed to pause on screen, looking at Cam, giving him another little loving smile, a smile that said she was grateful to him for taking care of the kids, for letting her pursue her career, and because of what was going on with Michael.

Cam got the strangest sense that, in a way, any pleasure Marcie received from Michael from now on was really from him, because he had allowed her to sleep with the guy.

But then Marcie was talking to Flo, asking about grocery deliveries, and whether they all had everything they needed, and Cam was calming down now that the spotlight was no longer on him.

At the end of the call, the kids went up to bed, and Cam was expecting to simply murmur a quick goodbye to Marcie before ending the call, as usual. But she paused until Flo had shepherded the kids out of the room and up the stairs. Then she said, 'I'm sorry I didn't get to text you today.'

Cam looked at her, and realized she felt bad about not texting him all day—and yet he hadn't expected her to. He hadn't even thought she would, particularly.

'It's okay,' he said. 'You don't have to text me all the time, you know. Not even every day. I know you're busy with work.'

'I haven't stopped thinking about you, though,' she said, quietly in case anyone else could hear. 'Can I call you later?'

'Of course,' he smiled.

'Would you… prefer me to call when I'm ready to go to bed… or… after…?'

It was an odd question, but he knew what she was getting at.

Do you want to see me before, or after I have sex with Michael?

'I don't know… whatever you're comfortable with,' he said, and then seeing that she wasn't happy with him leaving the choice to her, he added, 'I guess I'd prefer you to call… you know… last thing. I don't want to delay anything if you and Michael are… in the mood.'

She gave him a naughty—sexy—little grin, and then said, sincerely, 'I love you.'

'I love you, too, honey,' he said, just as sincerely,

'Okay, see you later.'

'See you.'

She even blew him a kiss before ending the call. He sat there for a moment, just letting it all sink in. Was it going to be this way every night she was in London? Sitting here waiting for her to fuck her lover, so he could see her on FaceTime afterward?

His cock twitched.

Perhaps Marcie would give him another sexy little show when she called, fresh from the shower. Perhaps he could persuade her to open up a little more about how Michael liked to fuck her.

God, she was sexy as hell.

CHAPTER SEVENTEEN

THURSDAY WAS ANOTHER BRIGHT, sunny day. This year's spring had been crazy hot, and crazy dry—the driest May for 124 years, as it turned out—allowing Cam and the kids to spend much of the time in the garden, watering things, pulling out weeds, planting out some of the half-hardy annuals he'd been growing from seed since February.

Flo was around to help out with the children, of course. He really couldn't complain about their lot—not everyone could have a grandparent around to help with the childcare after they closed the schools because of the pandemic. Not everyone had a garden, or even outside space, in which to spend time during the lockdown. And then there were single people living on their own during these unprecedented times, who would have to spend so much time alone while the restrictions were in place.

And then you had to feel for those around the world who actually caught the virus themselves—or lost some-body close to the virus. The poor people in the United States who survived COVID-19 and returned home to medical bills in the thousands, or even hundreds of thousands of dollars.

It all put Cam's personal troubles into quite some perspective. When he felt the frustrations of being cooped up in a fairly small cottage with the kids and his mother-in-law, pressured to act as stand-in teacher for his kids when they really didn't want to be taught, he just had to relax and think about how bad it could be for others.

And here he was, with a marriage that was healthy and strong. He couldn't complain about that, either. There were plenty of stories in the newspapers during the pandemic about people suffering significant relationship break-downs—domestic abuse levels were up 20% worldwide, according to the UN. Divorce lawyers had to be rubbing their hands with glee.

Cam waited all day with bated breath for his gorgeous wife to return home.

And then, here at last, was Marcie's little Toyota, pulling into the driveway, the kids running out to greet her, Cam and Flo hovering by the front door to let her enjoy the reunion with Henry and Sarah. Marcie looking delicious as she finished doling out hugs, and now approached the front door.

'Hey, Mom,' she said to Flo.

'Welcome home, lovey,' Flo said, giving her daughter a hug and a kiss on the cheek as the kids ran on by and into the house.

'Hey, you,' Marcie said now to Cam, offering him a warm, affectionate smile, though there was still a hint of caution there, to begin with. He could tell when she looked at him that she was assessing him, trying to determine his state of mind, to ensure he was still in good spirits given that she had recently confessed to an affair and then shared fresh details of her ongoing infidelity over the last few days.

'Hey, honey,' he said, immediately opening his arms for a hug, pulling her in to show her how much she meant to him.

It reminded him how much they'd curtailed even their greetings toward each other over years of marriage. They'd stopped telling each other how much they loved each other, and they'd stopped hugging and kissing when Marcie came home from her commute.

But now, Marcie kissed him, and not only on the cheek —on the mouth, slow and sensual, intensely sweet. Goodness, it seemed like they hadn't kissed properly in years. Had it always been this incredible? It was getting him hard. She kissed him for what was obviously too long considering it was right in front of her mother, he felt her sucking on his bottom lip, as though she was ravenous for more—but it just knocked his socks off.

Could kisses always be like this?

Jesus. Time seemed to slow down. He felt hot and cold all over, all at the same time, like he had a fever. He felt light as a feather. It made him think of the first real kiss a girl had ever given him—Tamara Simmons, a girl he knew at the time would shortly take his virginity, kissing him in the bedroom of a house where they were at some party or other.

Marcie even slipped him a little tongue, and it felt so wicked, so full-on filthy, so saturated with pure raunch, that he had an instant and almost painful hard-on.

Then, just as he was sure Flo was about to make some wry comment about them needing to get a room, Marcie broke the kiss, and stepped back, giving him a little playful smirk, a glint in her eye that seemed to suggest they might explore this a little further once the kids were safely in bed. Then she went inside, leaving him standing on the doorstep, feeling somewhat stunned.

She was horny. He couldn't remember the last time she'd seemed *this* horny in his presence.

Inside, supper for them all seemed fairly normal, except that Marcie seemed to be in a phenomenal mood— all smiles and brightness, cheerful like she'd won the lottery, joking around with the kids, even when Sarah dropped ketchup all over her t-shirt. And in quiet moments, or when Flo was talking with the kids, Marcie kept giving Cam little knowing glances, little secret smiles of love and affection.

He really liked this kind of Marcie. Cheerful Marcie. Flirtatious Marcie.

He felt like she should have had an affair years ago.

Had she even unfastened a few of her shirt buttons? He could see a touch of cleavage, maybe even a hint of a black bra. It was seriously sexy, though subtle enough that her mother, and the kids, would probably notice nothing unusual at all. And was she still wearing her makeup, even though normally she wiped most of it away before she even arrived home? Right now it seemed so crisp, he wondered if she'd re-applied it recently.

God. She was giving him all kinds of signals. He'd never been good at signals. But he could tell what she wanted tonight.

Once food was all done and dusted, Marcie went upstairs to give the kids their bath and put them to bed— getting in some parenting time while she still could that day. Cam cleared away the supper things, and then sat with Flo while she caught up on *Tiger King* on Netflix.

'It's lovely, having her back, isn't it?' Flo said at one point, entirely unsolicited.

'Yes, it is,' he said, echoing his mother-in-law's smile.

It seemed a slightly odd thing for Flo to say. He figured she was subtly checking up on the situation after Marcie had confessed to her affair, and her mother had told her to end it.

'It's such a shame she has to work in London, so far away.'

'Yes, it is. But that's where the work is, right?'

'Well, yes. Can't be helped.'

He wondered if Flo was simply responding, belatedly, to her daughter's little PDA on the front doorstep. Expressing mild delight that they were obviously still into each other, even after several years of marriage and two small children. And one affair.

His thoughts were interrupted by the return of Marcie, who had managed to coerce Henry and Sarah into sleep in record time.

'You still haven't finished *Tiger King*, mum?' She said as she dropped down onto the sofa between her mother and Cam.

'Well, it's very dramatic,' Flo said, defensively. 'I can't watch too much at once, with my blood pressure.'

Cam felt his heart rate picking up just from his sudden proximity to Marcie—his every breath was now scented with her perfume. His thigh was jammed against hers. And he noticed that she was still wearing her work clothes—her smart, rather short skirt, and nylon hose, which just seemed insanely erotic, as though he could just lift up the corner of her skirt a little, and find that they were actually stockings. It struck him as highly unusual—like the fact that her makeup was still immaculate. Usually, she would dress down into sweatpants and a baggy t-shirt as soon as an opportunity arose—even before supper, sometimes, but almost always once everything was done and the kids were asleep.

He felt slightly intimidated by just how sexy she seemed, sitting there wedged against him.

Goodness. How had her infidelity turned him back into a horny teenager?

They watched *Tiger King* for a while, and then some more of the new series of *Ozark*, and Cam was pleased that most of the chat was between Marcie and Flo, because his brain was just about turned to mush by the presence of Marcie's killer legs pressed up against him, he couldn't think straight when his attention was focused on whether Marcie might, or might not, actually be wearing thigh-high stockings for the first time ever in his presence.

After a while, Marcie rested her hand gently on his thigh, affectionately, and he was worried she'd be able to feel how fast his pulse had become. A little later on, her hand started moving higher up his thigh, and he was worried she'd discover his full-blown erection, the result of her sitting beside him like that in her provocative skirt and ludicrously erotic nylons. He was about to suggest he go get them all a glass of wine, with her hand just a hair's breadth away from his raging flagpole—but then Marcie yawned rather theatrically, putting both arms up in the air as she did so, and she claimed she was too tired to stay up any longer.

'It is getting late,' Flo agreed, glancing at the clock by the door to the kitchen.

'Are you coming upstairs?' Marcie said, looking at Cam in a somewhat telling fashion.

Cam looked into her seductive, perfectly lined eyes, and briefly glanced downwards, whereupon he found himself snatching a breathtaking view of her cleavage, and then his focus returned to her eyes, and Marcie smirked mischievously, silently teasing him for being unable to resist ogling her tits. Then she tilted her head slightly, which even he could tell was a signal suggesting they both head on upstairs, and maybe not because she was tired after all.

His erection throbbed.

He had to walk a little like a crab to try and hide the tentpole inside his pants while he went past Flo, following Marcie to the stairs. Thankfully, Flo was too busy flicking through Netflix to find more *Tiger King*.

And now, Cam was following his wife upstairs, his eyes firmly on her fine ass as she walked up just in front of him.

God, she was so sexy.

His unfaithful wife.

CHAPTER EIGHTEEN

THEY REACHED THE BEDROOM, and Marcie paused by the doorway. Then, when Cam was inside, she closed the door quietly but, somehow, very deliberately.

Cam's heart was beating hard.

It seemed possible to cut the tension in the air with a knife, it was so thick. What was she up to?

Cam turned to see Marcie still just standing there with her back to the closed door, waiting for him to face her— and the look on her face was serious, sharp, and ravenous. There were flames in her eyes, but he couldn't quite tell if she was angry, or horny like nothing on this Earth.

He was about to ask whether she was okay.

She said, 'Do you still love me?'

He raised his eyebrows, caught his breath. 'Of course,' he said, and could see her big, blue eyes flickering as they examined his own hazel ones, assessing him for any sign of a lie. 'You know I do.'

She stepped toward him so that she was just inches away—and immediately, he could tell something was up. She looked proud, strong, slightly defensive. This wasn't just Marcie being horny because of their recent expansion into FaceTime sex.

What was going on?

His hard cock throbbed, his heart palpitated. Marcie continued to gaze into his eyes, scoping him out. He could smell her perfume—had she re-applied it?

He couldn't help but glance down, taking in that superlative view of her cleavage. Had she managed to unfasten another couple of buttons on her shirt while he hadn't been looking? Jesus, he could see her bra—black lace. It was one of the ones from her lingerie drawer in the flat in London. Something she would never ordinarily wear for him.

His eyes returned to hers after a fraction of a second, but it was long enough for her to see him look, and to be amused that he'd had to look.

'So you've been writing about your trip to that garden center, huh?' she asked him, reminding him about what he'd told her during the previous night's family FaceTime call.

'Uh… yeah, yeah…'

'After your nice visit on Monday?'

One of her eyebrows rose, inquisitive—or perhaps, more likely, teasingly. She was making fun of his cover story.

She knew. She knew.

'I… uh…' he fumbled, attempting to engage brain to mouth.

'No secrets, right?' she said, knowingly.

Then she was holding up something small, something black. A scrap of black material.

Her panties.

The ones he'd stolen from the London apartment.

'You noticed they were missing?' he said, stunned, and

suddenly very afraid that she was furious with him, that she would hate him for invading her privacy.

She gave him a curt nod. 'I was sorting out our laundry before I left London. And it turned out I was missing one pair of panties.'

She was hiding her emotions. He couldn't tell how she really felt about all this. About his deception. If she was angry, though, she was controlling it well, keeping her cool.

Teasing him.

'And then I came home, and here they were, in the pocket of the jeans you were wearing on Monday,' she said.

'I just… uh…'

He was floundering. He felt so stupid, so shameful.

She knew he'd gone to London to check up on her. To invade her privacy. She knew he'd stolen her panties, for heaven's sake. What a ridiculous thing to do. Why would a man ransack his wife's laundry basket and make off with her dirty underwear?

And yet, now that he looked up at her, she didn't seem to be looking to him for some kind of explanation. He saw her gazing down at her panties, turning them over in her hands, either checking to see whether he'd damaged them, or trying to figure out why he would want to steal them.

Then she looked up at his face again, stern like a schoolteacher.

'So these turned you on?' she asked him, that eyebrow raised again.

He didn't know what to say to that. He just froze.

She knew.

She knew his shame.

She skewered him with her gaze, pinning him to the spot so he couldn't move.

'You liked… how they *smell*…' she said, seeming to

mull the words over as she lifted the black lace up to his face—and gently pressed the material to his nose for a moment or two.

He couldn't help but take in a breath, he couldn't help but inhale that scent, which was still strong enough to seem overwhelming.

There was no point in trying to deny anything. But the detail about him enjoying the way her panties smelled... he was curious about how she knew about that.

She smiled, reading him like a book.

'I had some jewelry stolen from the flat last year,' she said, and before he could ask her why she hadn't told him about that, she smirked, 'I didn't tell you, because I didn't want to worry you. I thought maybe Tony had taken them.'

Tony being the building handyman. The guy who fixed anything that needed fixing.

She smiled, gazing into his eyes as she said, 'So I had secret cameras installed, just in case it ever happened again.'

He gasped, audibly, his eyes widened, his jaw dropping.

Then, as realization set in that she had seen him, she had seen *everything*, Cam blushed, violently. She must have watched him masturbating on the bed with her underwear over his face.

He'd never felt so embarrassed.

But Marcie only smiled at him, warmly. Lovingly.

'When I noticed my underwear had gone missing,' she explained, 'I simply looked at the app on my phone. Checked through some of the video that gets stored auto-matically by my wireless cameras.'

Oh God, the *shame*. He must have looked like a complete idiot, sprawling all over the bed with his dick in one hand, and her panties in the other, rubbing them all over his face.

She glanced down at her panties again, as though there was just a flicker of fear inside her, as though she just needed to remind herself that here in her hands was proof that her husband still wanted her.

She said, 'I watched you searching the flat. I watched you figuring it all out.'

'I'm sorry,' he said, gripped by fear.

Was she going to leave him now? After everything that had happened?

But she shrugged. 'I probably deserved it,' she said. 'I mean… you suspected something was up. So you quietly went all the way to London to find out for yourself.'

'I should have said…' he admitted.

'Yes,' she nodded. '*No secrets*, right?'

He heaved a huge sigh. 'I thought… when I got back, and there you were… that you knew where I'd been. I thought, maybe, Flo had figured out where I'd gone. And then after you started confessing everything… I don't know… it just seemed simpler to skip over the fact I'd been to London.'

She gave a little nod.

Then she stepped toward him, closer still. He tensed up, waiting for her to yell at him. She had every reason to.

'When you got to the flat, you found Michael's things… and my underwear…' she said, her eyes blazing. 'And the first thing you wanted to do was pull out your *big, hard dick*…'

She was standing right in front of him, now, filling his lungs with her perfume, her eyes vibrant with dancing flames—and now he felt her hand on his crotch, pressing against the bulge he had going on down there, her fingers exploring the extent of his erection.

'I didn't realize you had spy cameras all set up,' he said, blushing fiercely, though her fingers caressing his hard-on through his pants felt wonderful. 'So you watched me…?'

'Uh-huh,' she grinned. Victorious. 'I was a little surprised,' she said, touching her hands against his chest now, as though she could, now that the uncertainty between them was beginning to thaw. 'I mean, you looked in all his drawers, you checked out all his things round the whole flat. There wasn't any doubt you'd figured it all out.'

'And I didn't just storm out and call a divorce lawyer.'

'You *didn't*…' she said, her eyes flashing like a catholic schoolgirl who had just witnessed one of the nuns giving head.

She glanced down at her hands again, at the panties she was still holding. She brought them up, to press them up to his nose. Forcing him to take a deep breath full of her adulterous scent.

'It turns you on, doesn't it?' she said, seemingly in awe.

He took a deep breath, but looked into her eyes and blushed furiously.

'It's not just the fact that we've started having seriously good sex again… or that you talked me into getting naked on FaceTime… it genuinely turns you on that I've been sleeping with someone else, doesn't it?'

What could he do, but nod sheepishly?

She'd watched him lying on the bed in their London apartment, overcome with lust after discovering her infidelity. She'd watched him shame himself on that bed, clutching her dirty panties while he'd done so.

So embarrassing.

He said, with some chagrin, 'I don't really know why… it just seemed so… *exciting*… so *sexy*…'

'Me cheating on you?'

He nodded. 'You cheating on me.'

She grinned, full of wickedness, but also of content-ment. It wasn't just that she appeared to have gotten away with her adultery, it wasn't just that she was now fully confident her marriage wasn't about to collapse. Somehow, it was as though her discovery of his weird little kink evened the score between them.

It meant that she no longer had to look at her husband and think about how much she'd made him suffer through her infidelity.

He liked it, for goodness' sake.

It turned him on.

She'd seen how much it turned him on by how he had masturbated furiously right after discovering the incontro-vertible evidence that she had been fucking Michael on the side.

'And does it still turn you on?' she asked him, checking that it hadn't just been some kind of temporary panic response in him. 'The thought of me cheating on you?'

'Yes,' he said earnestly.

Her face brightened still further, if that was possible. She kissed his lips, briefly but with the same kind of unex-pected sweetness as she had earlier, at the front door. Her fingers pressed at his swollen manhood, squeezing him through his jeans.

She said, 'So I suppose you'd probably like me to give you the panties I was wearing last night—the ones I was wearing while Michael pressed me up against the windows and *fucked* me where people across the street might see us?'

His blush might have been fading, but it roared back into full scarlet as his body responded to the thought of Marcie being fucked up against those windows, so exposed…

Then she surprised him by pushing him back onto the bed. She caught him by such surprise, he completely lost his balance and went straight down onto the mattress. And before he could pick himself up, before he could even prop himself up on his elbows, she was on top of him, straddling his hips, moving further up his body until she knelt right over his head.

'Maybe you'd like these ones,' she said, slowly pulling up her skirt to reveal her current panties—sexy, tiny, black and crimson lace, like nothing she'd ever worn for him before. And he was even more surprised to find she really was wearing thigh-high stockings—not pantyhose as he had assumed before.

God, he nearly had a seizure, she looked so incredible.

And he liked this dominant side to her. That was new for them too.

'You don't need me to take them off first, do you?' she teased, slowly lowering herself to his face, so that he could see nothing except the world between her thighs, and every breath he took was saturated by the unmistakable scent of her arousal. Her panties were already drenched.

'No, sweetie,' he said, craning his head a little so he could press his mouth and nose up against her lace-covered sex before she had fully lowered herself onto him.

She smiled as he inhaled a deep breath, clearly enthralled with it, and as he nuzzled into the expensive lace, which was already damp with her excitement. Then she sighed as he kissed her there, as he parted his lips and tasted her through her sodden underwear, clamping his hot mouth to her pussy—

Her adulterous pussy.

She lowered herself further, so that he didn't have to raise his head, so that she was pressing gently down on him, her hips beginning to move so that she started to graze her lace-covered sex over his oh-so-willing face.

'Do you like that?' she asked, peering down at him as best she could.

'Mmm-hmm,' he just about managed to reply, though his mouth was full.

'When I watched you… lying on that bed… it seemed like you might be fantasizing about something like this…'

'Mm-hmm,' he confirmed, and reached around her thigh to slip aside her panties so that he could wedge his mouth directly against her soaking pussy.

Her pussy was so smooth, because she'd shaved it for Michael. So soft, not a hint of fur anywhere. It was just stunning.

She gasped. 'Oh yes, just like *that*,' she said, sounding genuinely taken aback. Cam was guessing Michael didn't do this kind of thing with her. Well, he hadn't done this with her much before, either, in years of marriage. But now he was, he couldn't get enough.

He held onto her hips and pulled her down onto his face, spearing her with his tongue, sucking on her tender folds like a man dying of thirst, caressing her intimately with his entire face, it seemed like, so that he felt her wetness across his cheeks, his jaw, his nose.

Why had they never done it like this before?

He'd just never been so hungry for her before, it seemed. Nor, perhaps, had she been for him. But now she was holding his head with her hands and riding his face, and as her moans became louder and louder—to the point where he worried that she had forgotten about the risk of waking the children—increasingly it was no longer the case that he was lapping at her pussy, but that she was rubbing her pussy against his tongue, and his mouth, and his nose, taking more and more control of the situation.

After a while, she was just using his face to bring herself off.

And he loved every moment.

Thinking about how hot she was, thinking about how sexy she was, inviting another man to stay with her at the apartment in secret. Thinking about her giving in to her lust for him. Thinking about her riding another man's cock, violating her marriage vows, jamming another man into this very pussy.

She came with great shuddering jerks, right on top of his face, and it seemed to come as a complete surprise to her judging by the noises she made. Even beyond how turned on he was right now by having her grinding her exquisite pussy into his face, his head locked between her stocking-clad thighs, knowing that she'd been sleeping with another man, he was given another shot of pure adrenalin from just how powerfully she came.

What an achievement. What a rush.

CHAPTER NINETEEN

WHEN SHE EVENTUALLY MANAGED TO GATHER HER thoughts and calm down, releasing him from her crushing thighs, she said, breathlessly, 'Well, that was *nice…*'

She rolled off him, and he sat up, gazing at her in disbelief as she removed her top and skirt, and then lay back against the pillows like a queen, spreading her legs to expose herself to him.

Stroking her dripping, completely shaven pussy as she told him, 'Why don't you get rid of those clothes?'

He picked himself up off the bed, and peeled off his shirt, gazing at her fingers working her pussy while she watched him strip, enjoying the hunger in her big, blue eyes. She looked just stunning in her black, thigh-high stockings, black lacy bra and the panties she'd pulled aside to stroke her pussy.

'Mmm…' she purred, as he pulled off his jeans, and then, responding to her little nod, his boxer shorts as well, to let his hard cock spring free.

When he was naked, she smiled, and removed her

hands from between her legs, lifting her hips to remove her panties. Then she pointed down at her pussy, and the flames in her eyes told him what she wanted.

He climbed onto the bed, and lay between her thighs, dipping down to gently place his lips up against her sex, breathing in the overwhelming scent of her arousal, opening his mouth to taste her copious juices.

'You like that, don't you?' she said, watching him nuzzle into her pussy, enjoying her tangy flavor.

He moaned gently as he lapped at her pussy, indicating just how much he loved it. Licking her cheating pussy— this shaven pussy that she'd been opening up to another man during the lockdown. This pussy she'd let another man penetrate with his big cock over and over, every night she'd been staying in London for the past few weeks.

It was just thrilling to think she'd been unfaithful with this pussy. He didn't know why, but he was past caring.

'I don't think you've done this for me much,' she said, smiling down at him as he sucked on her pussy lips. 'I guess I should have taken charge a long time ago.'

'Yes, sweetie,' Cam said, glancing up at her.

She nodded, her smile strengthening as she appreciated his devotion.

'Michael showed me how hot it could be, taking what you want,' she said. He felt his hardness throbbing at her mention of her lover.

He looked up at her again, curiosity clear on his face.

She said, 'Oh yes... I mean, I tried not to, if you can believe it. I tried not to cheat on you, when he first moved in.'

She moaned as he stroked between her pussy lips with the tip of his tongue, and then gasped as he put his hands on her, parting her pussy gently with his fingers so that his tongue could reach deeper.

She said, 'At first, I thought I could ignore him. Ignore the fact that while I came home, here, Michael would be sleeping in the bed in our apartment there. I thought I could just go back to London, put the sheets in the wash, and I'd never know there'd been another man in my bed.'

She smiled.

'But you know… I get back to London, work a full day, right through until nine, ten o'clock. And when I get back to the apartment, I'm too tired to do laundry. I just collapse in the bed… and I can smell him all around me—'

She caught her breath as Cam enveloped her clit in his mouth, and gently sucked.

Then she went on, 'His cologne on those sheets… it made me think about him lying out there on the sofa… thinking about his big dick…'

She was thrusting her hips a little, responding to his efforts, breathing hard as he continued to feast on her pussy. He couldn't believe how exhilarating it was, making her feel good like this. It felt like he'd missed out on years of doing this.

She said, 'I started touching myself... God… I tried thinking about you at first… but his scent was all around me… I told myself it was all right, fantasizing about Michael… I mean, I know you look at porn, sometimes… so…'

She gasped as Cam slid a couple of fingers inside her hot, slick pussy, while he peppered her clit with little kisses.

Then after she'd settled again, she said, 'I guess I got a little over-excited, fantasizing about Michael. I was getting a little… loud…'

'What happened?'

She glanced down at her husband, still finding it a little surprising that he wanted to know all the details, that he was really into this, really into her adultery. But there he was, totally absorbed by her cheating pussy.

'The bedroom door opened, and there he was, walking up to me in nothing but a pair of briefs, and I couldn't take my eyes off his enormous package,' she said, grabbing his hair in one hand to pull him firmly against her pussy as she began to squeeze her hips, grinding her sex against his mouth.

It was a moment or two before she was able to continue: 'God… I was too far gone by then to refuse… he walked up to the bed and I just had to have that thing inside me…'

She broke off to moan as her devoted husband flicked his tongue all over her dripping pussy lips—his mouth on her sex was too distracting for her.

But then after a moment, she pushed him away, asking him, 'Are you still hard for me?'

A moment later, he was lying on his back on the bed, and she was kneeling between his splayed thighs, brushing the back of her hand down his chest, around his hard dick, amused at how his erection stirred as she touched him, at how he responded to her while she avoided touching his cock.

'Michael has such a big cock,' she said, leaning forward to kiss his mouth briefly, before sitting back on her haunches again, her hand skimming tantalizingly over his dick this time. She said, 'That first night, when he came into the bedroom and gave it to me… I couldn't believe how it felt.'

She wrapped her hand around his cock, now, and he had to make an effort not to simply explode in her hand.

She started slowly stroking it, squeezing it, rolling her hand around its length, driving him crazy by the feel of her soft fingers against his sensitive shaft. She was obviously enjoying how he responded to her words, to the explicit details about her affair.

'You know, I thought I'd never feel another man inside me. Not after we got married. A couple of my friends have had affairs over the years, but I always resisted…'

She laughed, squeezing his cock.

'I felt so guilty after that first time,' she said. 'I've felt guilty a lot, recently. And here you are, after finding out… harder than I've ever seen you.'

She let go of him, and just gazed at his cock for a moment or two. Then she reached behind her back to unfasten the catch on her bra.

'Jesus. I mean, it's immense,' she said. 'Did you take a hit of Viagra or something, after the kids went to sleep?'

'No, I didn't,' he said.

She removed her bra, teased him a little with it before fully exposing her stunning breasts. She seemed thrilled at how he was looking at her—paying full attention to her, for once. Now that he knew she'd been with another man.

'All this time,' she said, 'I could have cheated on you, and come home to this?'

He said, 'I don't know…'

She nodded, knowing that he couldn't say if he'd have reacted this way a year, or five years, or ten years ago. She said, 'Well, we know now, don't we?'

He nodded as she took his hard cock in her hands again.

Marcie leaned over and kissed the tip of his cock, as though it was something she'd never come across before, something she needed to sample.

'You know, when I checked that security footage, it was a huge surprise seeing you go into the flat,' she said.

'You were surprised I found out?' He asked her.

She smiled, 'I thought we'd been so clever.'

She kissed the side of his cock, and took a slow, deep breath as though savoring the smell. He wondered if she was comparing him to her lover. He thought maybe he needed to start wearing cologne again to keep up.

She went on, 'I couldn't believe it. I'd been so terrified when I first told you about Michael. It felt certain you'd want to leave me. It was like my world was collapsing around me. But you were okay about it all along.'

'Well, I wasn't exactly keen on the thought of you lying to me. Or doing things behind my back.'

She nodded in agreement. 'But when you found Michael's things in the drawers. You didn't pull everything out, throw it out the window. You didn't take a pair of scissors to his suits. You weren't angry at all.'

'No, I wasn't,' he agreed.

She gave him an affectionate smile. 'And then you just lay down on the bed, and—'

'Embarrassing,' he said, blushing, even though she wasn't teasing him about it.

'Sexy,' she said, flicking her tongue around the tip of his cock before glancing up at him to flash him a wicked smile. 'Sexy as hell.'

'You must think I'm a complete pervert.'

'I *love* that you're a complete pervert,' she smirked, and took the whole upper part of his cock into her gloriously hot mouth for a moment or two. Then she said, 'I was thinking about that video footage my whole drive up here today.'

'Seriously?' Cam said, blushing deep red. There was something deeply humiliating about being caught masturbating, even by your wife.

'I had to stop at Beaconsfield Services to watch it again,' she said, stroking his cock. 'I had to be sure.'

'Sure?'

'Sure about how you felt about me. About us. I mean, at first I thought you might be in shock, you were so calm about everything… But I watched you take off your clothes… and you were so *hard*… and the way you used my underwear…'

'So humiliating…'

'So *genuine*…' she said, still just amazed by it. She ducked down to kiss the tip of his manhood again. 'You were so *thrilled*, it looked like, so excited. I played that clip back again and again—when you came into the apartment, when you first looked into those drawers and found Michael's stuff… it was like a huge relief to you. You smiled like someone just told you that you won the lottery.'

Cam admitted, 'It was… pretty hot, finding out.'

'And you didn't look like you hated me for what I'd done—even though I would have totally deserved that,' she said. 'You looked as though you loved me. The way you looked at my things, the way you used my panties to get yourself off…'

'Uh-huh,' he smiled, somewhat sheepishly.

She laughed, squeezed his dick like it belonged to her. 'I love you,' she said. 'You know that, don't you?'

'Uh-huh.'

'And I'm serious when I tell you, with Michael, it's only *ever* been about the sex.'

His hardness throbbed at her words, and to his surprise, since her fingers were squeezing him at the time, she seemed to notice it—it seemed to startle her, and then made her smile. 'It really does turn you on like crazy, doesn't it?' She said, peering at his cock, still trying to process it all. 'Finding out about me… *cheating*.'

'You think I'm a freak?' he asked her.

She shook her head. 'There are a lot of guys out there who fantasize about their wives sleeping with someone else,' she said, then when he raised an eyebrow at how she might know such a thing, she laughed. 'After I discovered my panties were missing, after I checked that security video of you… I did some Googling at work, to figure out if you really could have been *turned on* by my cheating, rather than angry about it.'

'You did research on me?' he laughed.

'Only a little. But it turns out you're not a freak at all.'

'That's good news.'

'You're a cuckold,' she said, tapping his cock against her lips.

'I suppose so.'

The word felt odd on her lips, odd out in the open. Odd that it was a label for him. But it did make him feel less of a freak, that it was common enough that there was a term for it, for men like him. And Marcie seemed entirely unconcerned that he might be one.

'It was interesting, finding out,' she said, using both hands to stroke his dick, right in front of her face. 'A lot of different kinds of men enjoy it when their wives sleep with other people. Some of them seem to prefer the term 'stag'. I guess 'cuckold' has a certain derogatory nature to it…'

She was looking at his dick like it was some kind of miracle. That he could be this hard for this long.

She said, 'A lot of guys seem to like it when their wives take control. Not all of them, of course… but when I watched you touching yourself while you pressed my panties to your face…'

She grinned, as though victory was hers, and squeezed his cock a touch too hard, as though challenging him to tell her he wasn't turned on by the thought of her taking charge.

He didn't know what to say. His cock just throbbed in

her hands, as though speaking for him. It amused her, but it also excited her.

Hungry for it, she sank down on his hardness, taking him deeper than he ever thought possible.

It felt just phenomenal.

She'd come up for air, peppering his cock with sensual kisses, lashing him with her talented tongue. Jesus. Fellatio, one of those other parts of sex that had long since fallen by the wayside in their marriage. But seriously. Had she been *this* good back when they'd still done it?

Then she lifted up, her hand still on his cock, pumping him.

'You like being a cuckold?' she asked him.

'I… yes…' he said, as she tugged hard on his manhood.

'You like being my sex slave?'

'Uh-huh,' he said, trying to sit up, his muscle memory wanting him to go on top, to make love to her in the missionary position, as they had always used to do.

She pushed him back down on the mattress. Then she knelt up, lifted one leg over his thigh, and then the other leg so that she straddled his waist.

'You want my pussy?' She asked him. 'You want my *cheating* pussy?'

'Yes… please…' he said.

'Will you do anything I say to get my pussy?'

'Anything.'

She grinned, kneeling over him so that his cock was inches away from her pussy, but not yet allowing him to put it inside her. She said, 'You have to stop looking at pornography.'

'Okay.'

'Promise me.'

She rocked back and forth over him, so the tip of his

cock rubbed against her pussy.

'I promise.'

'And you can only come when I say you can,' she said, and he looked genuinely startled by that, but she gave him a serious look that said he didn't have a choice in this.

'Okay,' he agreed.

'Good.'

She lifted herself up a few inches, her hand diving between her thighs to take hold of his cock and guide it to her entrance. Then she eased herself very slowly down, and he felt her searing-hot pussy touch against the tip of his manhood—then gradually envelop it.

'Fuck…' he moaned.

'Yeah?' she smiled as she reveled in his response to her taking him inside her. 'You like being inside my *pussy*?'

'Uh-huh,' he groaned.

'You know, this time last night, I had Michael's big cock inside me.'

She giggled as she felt his manhood throbbing within her pussy.

Then she closed her eyes, responding to the sensation of his cock moving inside her, moaning, 'Uh…' as she began to slowly ride him, placing her hands on his chest as she started to gyrate her hips and gently rock back and forth on top of him. After a few moments, she opened her eyes again and looked down at him, flashing him a mischievous smile. 'You like thinking about someone else fucking me?' she asked him, and the way he responded to her words was the only reply she needed. 'His big cock squeezed inside of my slutty pussy…'

She increased the speed and the power of her movement, riding him harder and harder for a while, until he nearly came inside her.

Then she slowed down again, and lowered her shoulders enough that he could reach up and kiss one of her breasts, and take her nipple in his mouth.

'Mmm…' she moaned as he sucked on her. 'That feels nice,' she said, dipping down a little more to make it easier for him to suck on her breasts. She said, 'You know, sometimes Michael likes putting his cock between my breasts… sliding it between them… it feels so *naughty*…'

Cam couldn't help but be thrilled by the thought of another man fucking his wife's tits… it seemed so wrong… but it stirred Cam's desire even more, his body reacting to the thought of another man infringing on his territory by making sure he was in a good state to claim her back. He rubbed his face against her breasts, kissing them, sucking on them, taking her nipples inside his mouth.

And then he very nearly came early again, when she said: 'And last night, when he was done, he pulled out of my pussy and took his condom off—then he came all over my breasts…'

He had to work hard to try and rid his mind of the thought of another guy coming all over these beautiful breasts in order to avoid coming, when she hadn't told him he could.

He had to take his face away from her tits.

It didn't help for long, because after that she went back to riding him, hard and fast, panting and gasping, rocking the whole bed. Moaning loudly, until she remembered they had to be careful not to wake the kids—and not to scare Flo.

She sat up and bounced on him, her magnificent breasts jiggling as she rode him.

But then as her orgasm approached, she pulled his cock out of her pussy, and instead pressed her sex against his shaft, grinding down on his full, hard length, without him actually penetrating her.

She gasped and cried, stifling her noise as best she could, until she was right at her peak.

Then she lifted up, picked up his dick and then plunged down onto him, filling herself with his hardness again just as her powerful climax hit.

'Oh God… oh God… oh God…' she whimpered, and he'd never seen her quite like this.

But she hadn't yet allowed him to come. He felt like he was going to burst soon.

As she recovered, slowly rising and falling on top of him, her gorgeous breasts rising and falling as she inhaled deep chestfuls of oxygen, her pretty lips curled into a smile as she realized how desperate he was getting to come.

She lifted off him, just long enough for his cock to withdraw from her pussy. Then turning to glance over her shoulder, she took his shaft in her hand, and started a slow bounce on top of him again, this time pressing his hard cock between her buttocks as she rode him.

'God, you're still so hard,' she said. 'Are you sure you haven't taken something?'

'No, I haven't,' he smiled.

'Mmm…' she purred, squeezing his cock in her hand.

But she knew he didn't have long, now. She pulled off him, ushered him up so she could turn around, sit facing him, opening her stocking-clad legs so he could see her exquisite shaven pussy, saying to him, 'You want me to let you come?'

'Yes, please.'

She smiled, stroking her pussy herself as she lay back, and spread her knees for him, exposing herself fully. 'You want to come inside your slutty, cheating wife?' she asked him.

'Yes, please,' he said, getting into the swing of submitting to her.

'Even though I had another guy fucking me like this, only yesterday?'

'Yes please.'

She spread her pussy lips with her fingers, and as with a lot of what she'd done this evening, it really struck Cam as something she would have never done with him before. That maybe she'd been told to do it by Michael during her affair—that he had changed the way she fucked.

'You have to ask nicely,' she teased him, masturbating right in front of him as he held his hard cock poised and ready to enter her.

'Please can I fuck you, my sweetness?' he said, amused but still kind of into it.

She laughed. 'Very well..' And took hold of his cock to guide it into her entrance.

Now he was inside her, thrusting into her slowly, but steadily gaining force. Just in awe at how different it was, even though he'd been sleeping with this woman, and only this woman, for ten years. She was changed, in his mind, and it wasn't only because Michael had clearly taught her new ways of fucking.

Just thinking about her as being the kind of woman who would have an affair changed her in his mind.

Just thinking about her giving her body to another man.

Just thinking about another man fucking her, like this, or from behind, or from beneath her, on the bed, in the shower, on the floor, on the sofa, on the kitchen counter… it changed her in his mind.

Just thinking about her wanting to dominate him in bed, perhaps as Michael dominated her, changed her in Cam's mind.

She stroked her clit as he gripped her thighs and thrust into her again and again, fucking her, reclaiming her, feeling alive like he hadn't for so very long. Fucking her as she told him how incredible it felt, how amazing, even though he didn't stretch her pussy quite as much as Michael did with his colossal dick.

As she told him how much she loved him.

As she told him how much it turned her on to have two men fucking her.

As she told him how sexy it would be if Cam could watch Michael fucking her.

Then, finally, she said, 'Come now… you can come now, my sweet… come inside me…'

With that, he just let go, releasing the pressure inside him, tearing down the mental blocks he'd put up to prevent himself from coming before she told him she could. And he felt himself just explode, the heat and energy bursting through his hard cock as it started to buck and jerk inside her, shooting off jet after jet of thick, hot cream.

She seemed fascinated, watching him come. Watching the mind-blowing orgasm sweep through him.

Maybe he was changed in her mind, too.

Maybe he wasn't quite the husband she'd thought he was.

Turned on by her adultery.

Turned on by her taking control in bed.

Turned on so much he became a Titan in bed. Albeit, a somewhat submissive Titan.

Afterward, he could only collapse on the bed, gasping for breath. Marcie pulled herself up, and headed into their en suite, and he heard her switching on the shower. Well, she always liked to be clean and tidy.

Completely drained, he was asleep before she came back to bed.

CHAPTER TWENTY

IN THE MORNING, Cam let Marcie sleep late. He went downstairs with the kids when they woke up at the usual ungodly hour, and fetched them breakfast, and helped them get dressed, and kept them from arguing, and got them started on their schoolwork in the little dining room next to the kitchen. They were in lockdown, but it was still Friday, still a school day. The school published worksheets for each class on their website that he could print off each day to guide them through various lessons and activities.

When Marcie emerged from upstairs after a nice, long, lie-in, she looked radiant, as though she was at peace with the whole world, enlightened, free of all stresses and strains.

After the way she'd taken charge of him in the bedroom, Cam almost assumed that she'd carry on her new attitude into the daytime—perhaps bossing him about more than usual, even putting him in his place. He was almost embarrassed that she might do that in front of other people, in front of the children. But she wasn't like that at all. She was all smiles, full of sweetness and tenderness and laughter. She didn't make demands, she didn't treat him mean, she didn't do anything to humiliate him.

She seemed like the perfect wife, the perfect mother.

And yet, at the same time, occasionally he'd share little intimate smiles with her, hidden from the others, that acknowledged and celebrated the rekindled bond between them, reminding each other throughout the day how hot it had been the previous night between them.

There was a glow about her all day—and it wasn't just the sexual satisfaction that gave her a settled air of powerful contentment. It seemed like a whole load of stress had evaporated from her life, a whole load of guilt.

She'd been feeling the strain of continuing a secret affair behind her husband's back. But now, everything was out in the open.

And her husband had demonstrated how much he enjoyed her having an affair.

Marcie took over the home-schooling mid-morning, so that he could slip up to the little study to get a couple of hours of work done. She even seemed happy to be taking the kids through their learning, even though Cam knew how tough it was trying to get the home schooling done when the kids really didn't want to have school in the home environment.

At lunch time, Cam noticed Marcie checking her phone, and felt a strange mix of excitement and uncertainty. Had she been texting Michael? It was strangely sexy to think that she might be connecting with him right now. But despite the fact that he trusted Marcie, there was still a hint of fear deep down. Paranoia, perhaps. That she might come to feel something stronger toward Michael than just the need for sex with someone different.

But he figured he had to trust her. The guy had already moved in with her, even if it was temporary. If it was more than just sex between them, then making her feel she had to continue hiding that side of her life from him was not going to help prevent some deeper emotional connection build between her and Michael.

That afternoon, when it was his turn to take over the home-schooling duties, he saw Marcie head out into the garden wearing sunglasses, a light skirt and a thin shawl, carrying a towel, and to his delight she laid the towel down on one of the sun loungers on the patio, peeled off her skirt and shawl, and indulged in some sunbathing wearing a little blue bikini. That gave him something nice to look at whenever he had a quiet moment overseeing the kids doing their arts and crafts. She looked sensational in her swimsuit.

And as he secretly spied on her through the dining room window, he saw her looking at her phone, smiling as she gazed at the screen, as though she was chatting with someone, rather than reading something amusing. Cam felt butterflies in his stomach—nervous, that he might be taking a risk, but excited, that she was engaging with her other lover, right in front of him.

Later, when he and the kids were out in the garden, planting lettuce seedlings in the vegetable patch, Cam looked back at the patio and saw his pretty wife texting some more. Her eyes flicked up as she realized someone else might catch her texting with her boyfriend, and a hint of fear even flashed in her face as she saw that, sure enough, her husband had seen her doing it. But he smiled at her, and while no one else might hear, he wandered over to her, asked her, 'How's he doing?'

'Good,' she grinned. 'He says I seem happier, now everything's out in the open.'

He felt a little flush of mild embarrassment. '*Everything's* out in the open?'

She glanced over, to see that nobody was paying attention to them. Flo was with the kids now, filling a watering can so they could water in their lettuce seedlings. Then she said, 'I'm sorry, but you know Michael does have access to the security cameras, too…'

Cam's embarrassment deepened to think that Michael knew about how he had responded to discovering an apartment full of evidence of Marcie's infidelity.

'What did he say about it?'

She shrugged. 'He didn't seem fazed by it. Said he has some friends who are professional footballers who really like to party. And they're kind of into the whole… you know… *sharing* women.'

'Wow. Sharing?'

She grinned, 'He said it's all normal nowadays. Like that married woman who's also banging the journalist from *Girl With A Dragon Tattoo*.'

Well, there you go. Thank you, Stig Larsson. Sweden— normalizing unconventional sex since the Second World War.

'He said maybe some time you could try… watching us.'

Cam's heart stopped for a couple of beats.

'Watching?'

'Would that… freak you out?'

He breathed. His heart rebooted.

He said, cautiously, 'Wouldn't he be freaked out about it?'

Marcie laughed. 'I told you, didn't I? He totally gets off on the thought that people are watching. He likes doing it up against the windows…'

She flashed her eyes, reveling in her wickedness.

'You know, you ought to be careful you don't get arrested for that,' Cam said.

But then the kids needed help with something, pulling him away from her as she smirked and blew him a kiss.

CHAPTER TWENTY-ONE

MONDAY MORNING, Cam was awake even before Marcie got up early to get ready for work. When she was heading into London, she always set her alarm for 5am. It was a long commute, so she always tried to be out of the door by 6.30am, usually just about managing to say goodbye to Henry and Sarah as they were waking.

This morning, though, Cam was awake before her, watching her rise from the bed, and slowly peel off her sleepwear so she could take a shower.

She turned to check on him while she undressed, and smiled to find him awake.

'Excited to see Michael again, tonight?' he asked her, watching her peeling off her little, white tank top.

'Uh-huh,' she said, enjoying his response as she revealed her bare breasts to him. 'And are *you* excited I'll see him again, tonight?'

He returned her smile. 'I guess so…'

She slowly drew her panties down her legs, before holding them up to show him, joking, 'I suppose you'll be wanting these?'

He laughed, but she threw them to him, and he made a show of holding them up to his face, and breathing in her scent.

He drifted back into half-sleep while she showered, but then roused again to watch her dress, donning a sexy blue satin thong and matching bra before putting on a crisp, white shirt and her smart suit. He wasn't really thinking as he watched her sit in front of her dressing table to apply her makeup. He just felt the arousal between his legs, and brought up the little scrap of white cotton to his face so that he could breathe in that subtle but delightful scent of her pussy while he thought about her getting to the London apartment, where Michael would be waiting for her.

Only when she suddenly stood up, and stepped over to him, did he realize she'd been able to see him through the mirror on her dressing table, gently stroking himself under the sheet while he breathed in the smell from her panties.

'Hey,' she said, and peeled back the sheet that had been covering him from the chest down.

He felt some embarrassment, but there was clear delight plastered all over Marcie's face as she laid her eyes on the full erection he was sporting.

'Mmm…' she purred, before surprising him by kneeling down beside the bed, leaning over to take his hardness in her hands, before slipping the tip into her divine mouth.

After a few moments, she withdrew from his cock and grinned, saying, 'You have to remember—you promised not to come unless I tell you that you can.'

He looked down at her, surprised.

But he had promised, that much was true.

She laughed, then said, 'You *can* come now, if you like.'

Then she went back to her unexpected blow job,

relishing how rock hard he was—it was still a marvel after so many years having sex with him while he was less than fully hard.

He knew she didn't have time for this, though it felt just wonderful. But with all the thoughts of her going to London to hang out in their little pied-à-terre with a secret lover, it was next to no time before he was letting out a quiet groan and coming hard in her mouth. She swallowed it all eagerly, and then stood up as casually as if she'd simply dropped an earring on the floor, and stooped to pick it up. Flashing him a mischievous grin, she licked her lips, before perching on the stool by her dressing table to begin applying her makeup.

'I set that app up on your phone,' she said, as he lay there in a state of quiet bliss.

'You set it up?'

'You'll be able to watch me with Michael tonight—you know, if you've got nothing better to do.' She smiled, giving him a knowing glance via her mirror.

Cam felt his manhood thickening, inexplicably soon after she'd just made him come. But the thought of *watching* her with Michael while they were in the apartment together… it was just crazy hot.

'You really think Michael wouldn't mind me looking in when you two…?' he asked her.

She giggled. 'He won't mind. I told you, He has a thing about people watching.'

'And if he isn't happy with it?'

She shrugged. 'Then maybe I'd have to find a boyfriend who is.'

CHAPTER TWENTY-TWO

THE EXCITEMENT just continued to build once Marcie had gone back to London. All day Monday, Cam was thinking, are they really going to let me *watch them*?

Will I actually get to see her being unfaithful?

All day, he knew he had to try to keep calm, and make it seem like it was just another, ordinary day for the kids. Focusing on home-schooling when it was his shift, making lunch for everybody, getting a little work done in the afternoon, while Flo played with the kids in the garden.

He tried to compartmentalize his clean, daytime thoughts from his sinful, night-time thoughts.

It wasn't easy when Marcie kept sending him little texts about how her day was going. He liked that, though. He liked her keeping in touch, occasionally teasing him by asking him things, like whether he was looking forward to tonight, whether he was thinking about getting to watch her with Michael.

At lunchtime, she even sent him a selfie, taken in the women's restroom at her office building, in which she gave him a superb view up her skirt. He had to hide away in the bathroom to fully appreciate it, whereupon she persuaded him to send her a dick pic, which she seemed to enjoy very much, rewarding him with a more explicit selfie in which she was tugging aside her panties.

God. This was all very unlike the Marcie he believed he'd been married to all these years. He wondered if it was some kind of mid-life crisis for her. Did women get those? Only, instead of going out to get a Porsche, she'd found a lover.

As usual, just before the kids' bedtime, they had their usual FaceTime call with Marcie, and just seeing her made it almost impossible for Cam to stop thinking about dirty things. After a while, he had to make some excuse about having to get the laundry done, leaving Flo to sit with the kids while they talked with their mother, so that he could disappear and hide an embarrassing erection.

Marcie texted him later to ask if everything was okay, since she'd noticed he'd disappeared early on in the Face-Time call. While giving the kids their bath, he'd texted back to tell her that seeing her in that apartment—where she'd be soon sleeping with Michael again—had been a little too exciting for him.

She'd texted back a smiley face to that, and then said Michael would probably be home a little late that night because he always did extended hours on a Monday with his delivery job. But she added that she couldn't wait to play with his big cock, so that Cam would be able to watch on her security cameras.

With that, Cam had to put his phone away and ignore it until the kids were safely in bed.

And then once the kids were in bed, he had to try not to take his phone out while he chilled on the couch watching Netflix with Flo—until it was at least 9:30pm, and he could safely go to bed without Flo thinking something was wrong.

Then it was going on ten o'clock, and he was safely in their bedroom, pulling out his phone, seeing Marcie's texts:

Marcie: He's on his way back to the apartment.

Marcie: Let me know when you're watching, sweetheart. I want to know.

Marcie: I haven't stopped thinking about how hard you get, thinking about me and Michael.

Marcie: I bet you're nice and hard now he's going to come fuck me, any moment.

Marcie: Are you still watching TV with Mom? Lol. Trying to ignore your phone so you don't get a boner in front of her ;-)

Marcie: Here's a picture of my wet pussy just before it gets stuffed with Michael's big cock xxx

She'd sent him a picture of her sitting on the sofa in the apartment, still wearing her work clothes, but with one foot resting on the cushion so he could see up her skirt, see her thigh-high stockings, and her panties tugged aside to expose her glistening pussy.

He texted her back to tell her he was in the bedroom now, ready to watch her. Hard as a rock after she'd sent him that picture.

Naturally she demanded he take a picture of his hard-on so she could see how hard she was making him as he waited for Michael to come and fuck her. Cam pulled off his clothes and did as she demanded, receiving a text full of smiley faces and love-hearts in return.

Then came the message:

Marcie: He's on his way up. Are you watching? Remember, no coming unless I tell you that you can. Xxx

Cam exited the messenger app and found the security camera app. He switched out the lights and made himself comfortable in the bed, clutching his phone.

Jesus.

His heart was pounding.

Cam flicked through the views available from the cameras, and found one showing the front door. He was taken aback by the quality of the high-definition cameras as he watched Marcie approach the front door, then open it to welcome the tall, dark, younger man.

Michael.

Cam felt himself shiver, his cock thickening in his hand.

No wonder she'd fallen into temptation. Michael closed the front door and put a hand behind Marcie, on the small of her back, pulling her in for a kiss. She melted into him, and for a moment or two Cam couldn't quite believe he was witnessing this.

Cam felt a hint of panic under the surface—it was just his subconscious, really. His body feeling that it was obliged to feel threatened by another man moving in on his woman. His heart was pounding, he was getting short of breath. Feeling the hint of fear that Marcie might have feelings for this other man, that there was a chance she might choose him instead. That Cam had thrown everything away.

And at the same time, that fear, that risk, just seemed to spice everything up.

He was panting, watching them. As they turned so that he could see them kissing with tongues.

Michael, strong, athletic, picking up Marcie like she was made of feathers, her arms around his neck as he carried her, like she just adored him. But watching him putting her down onto the sofa, switching to another camera pointed toward their new position, Cam was still rock hard. He tried to ignore the fears, and embrace the voyeuristic excitement.

He watched Marcie sitting on the sofa, wrestling with Michael's belt, pulling open his fly as he unfastened the buttons on his shirt, peeled it off to reveal the kind of ripped physique that any woman would kill for. The guy looked so powerful. In peak condition. And now Cam watched his wife tug down her lover's pants to reveal a huge cock.

She took it in her hands, gazing up at him with adoring eyes, and he put a hand on the back of her neck as she started to lick that thing, as she touched the tip to her lips.

Jesus.

This was Marcie, who'd seemed so disinterested by sex for so very long, her lips wrapped around a colossal dick, hands clamped around its base, bobbing down on it so that more and more of it disappeared into her mouth each time.

Dear Lord.

Cam was riven by angst, but he couldn't get over how sexy it was watching her touching this guy's big dick, stroking it all over her soft cheeks, flicking her tongue around its tip, sinking it into her mouth. His stomach was squirming with butterflies, but seeing her like this made him want her more than ever. He wanted to take her back, kiss her, suck on her pretty face, after she'd been so intimate with that obscenely large cock.

Marcie slipped off the sofa onto the floor, kneeling under her lover to kiss the base of his cock, and lash his balls with her tongue, while squeezing his immense shaft in one hand.

Michael didn't look like a finance guy. He looked like a guy who spent his life in a gym. Cam watched Marcie working on his cock, appearing delighted to get her hands on this man's body. Cam imagined how it must have been when she'd first let him stay at the apartment—perhaps things had been friendly between them, but not inappropriate. Then she'd started stealing glimpses of him at night, or when he slipped into the bathroom to take a shower. Glimpses of him with nothing but a towel wrapped around his waist. Her eyes taking in his muscular form.

Her pussy moistening up to take in the sight of him.

There had probably been more than one night where she'd lain in bed, quietly stroking her sex as she imagined giving in to temptation. Thinking about going to him, pleading for him to take her. Thinking about him pulling out his dick while he lay on the sofa, masturbating to thoughts of her while she masturbated to thoughts of him.

Thinking about him throwing caution to the wind, coming into the bedroom wearing nothing but a tiny pair of briefs straining to contain his monumental bulge. Demanding sex from her.

Had Michael heard her touching herself, bringing herself to orgasm in the night?

He'd seen her looking at him, he'd seen the way her eyes lit up as she 'accidentally' caught glimpses of him wearing next to nothing on the way to, or from, the shower. He knew she wanted him.

And here she was now, sucking on his cock like it was providing her life-saving sustenance.

Standing up, reaching under her skirt to pull down her panties. Falling back onto the couch, her legs spreading wide, her bare pussy exposed to him. Letting him kneel down in front of her, directing that massive dick to the glistening pink folds of her hairless sex.

Cam gasped as he realized they weren't using condoms. He'd been assuming they had been—there had been a box in Marcie's bedside table, after all. They must have used them to begin with.

But here they were now: tall, dark, handsome Michael

directing his bare cock to Marcie's pussy, touching its tip to her open lips, squeezing it into her so that it slowly disappeared inside her, her copious wetness glistening on his stiff shaft as he then withdrew, only to plunge it back inside her while he gripped one of her knees in his other hand.

As her lover began to thrust into her again and again, Cam caught sight of Marcie glancing up into the camera, and it nearly made him come prematurely. She knew exactly where the camera was, she was looking over at it hoping her husband was watching her. She was lying on the couch, propped up on her elbows, in the best possible angle for the camera to capture the sight of Michael entering her like this. She'd worked it all out in advance. She was getting off on Cam watching all this.

Cam watched her gasping for air as that huge dick seemed to push it all out of her with each thrust. Michael grabbing hold of her shirt, tearing it open so the buttons popped off, exposing her bra, and then her breasts, so he could fondle them while he fucked her.

He watched the guy fucking his wife, and Cam felt such a buzz, he couldn't believe it.

Marcie was so beautiful, a goddess.

And now she had the attention she deserved—from a buff, athletic lover, and also now from a husband who had woken up from his daze to appreciate what he really had. A husband who craved the chance to worship her sexy, wicked, promiscuous sex as soon as he saw her again.

He watched Michael now stand and reach for Marcie's hand, to pull her up from the sofa. He watched as he tore off the rest of her clothes, other than her black, thigh-high stockings, and then led her over to the windows.

He watched as he made her stand facing the floor-to-ceiling glass, to let anyone across the street who happened to be watching from their own lockdown containment see the full-on naked beauty of Marcie, Cam's very own wife.

The whole street could see her place her hands on the glass, arch her back, and expose herself while her powerful lover stood behind her, and slid his big cock back inside her from behind.

Cam switched to another camera—of course there was another camera, lined up perfectly to see this very sight—to see Michael's muscles tense as he thrust his great dick back into Cam's wife. Marcie flinching, and then groaning in ecstasy as he filled her completely, stretching her pussy with his outsized manhood.

Cam watched him, the sweat already glistened on his skin, fucking Marcie like he hoped the whole world could see. Triumphantly.

And Cam thought that maybe the two of them had placed the car keys on the kitchen counter on purpose, that night. Maybe they'd even left clues in the FaceTime call before, wondering whether Cam would see. It seemed like Michael wanted nothing more than for Cam to see him taking his wife. Had they guessed that Cam would approve of Marcie having an affair? How could they have possibly known that it would turn him on?

Maybe Marcie had just been hopeful that once the affair was out in the open, Cam would accept it. Maybe they'd just struck lucky that Cam was actually turned on by the thought of the two of them secretly fucking while Marcie was in London.

Maybe it was more common than he thought that husbands enjoyed watching their wives being unfaithful.

Maybe Cam was just reaching for explanations.

He watched them go into the bedroom, Marcie climbing on top of Michael, but as he jammed that big dick back inside her, it was Michael still doing most of the work. Pounding into her, making her wail and scream as he filled her with that thing—there was no sound for Cam to hear, but from the images it was clear that she wasn't making any attempt to stifle her cries, and he wondered if anyone in the other apartments around could hear Marcie cheating on her husband like this.

Marcie turned around, to face the camera as she straddled Michael, reverse-cowgirl, her stocking-clad legs spread so that Cam could see absolutely everything, the guy's huge shaft disappearing inside her as she rode him. Marcie was getting a thin, glistening sheen of perspiration all over her body by now, and her hair was damp with sweat. Somehow, it made it all seem more real to Cam. This wasn't pornography—these two were real people, really turned on by each other, fucking right now while Cam watched them. It was seriously athletic sex—a full workout— and Cam wanted her more and more with every moment that he witnessed.

Then she was on her back, propped up on her elbows, her knees raised, as Michael penetrated her while holding onto her ankles. Rocking the whole bed as he pounded into her. Michael was no slouch, that was for sure. Even after a full day performing a valuable service to society, he could come home and pound Marcie like he was training for the Olympics.

Cam started wondering if this, rather than Marcie's regular lunchtime visits to the gym before lockdown, had got her in such great shape recently. The Infidelity Workout. At the very least, it had helped keep her in amazing shape since her normal gym was unavailable.

Cam was so close to coming, but he had Marcie's orders running through his mind: *You have to remember—you promised not to come unless I tell you that you can.*

It seemed like an impossible task at times, especially

when Michael was done, and Marcie slid off the bed to kneel on the floor in front of him—conspicuously in front of the camera—as the big guy jacked off his colossal dick a few more times, before spraying his thick, white cream all over her pretty face, her soft neck, her gorgeous tits.

Cam had to stop pumping his own cock, he was so close to coming himself at the searing-hot sight of another man shooting jet after jet of come all over his sweet wife's face and breasts.

He sat up, just breathing, calming himself down.

He didn't want Marcie to call and force him to admit that he'd come already. That he'd been too weak to refrain. But the need inside him was just pulsating.

Cam wondered what Marcie's ultimate plan was—would she refuse to let him come all week, until he saw her again on Thursday? That might prove intolerable if she was going to have sex—in front of the cameras—with Michael each night. There was no way he was going to be able to hold it that long.

Somehow, he managed to avoid coming this time.

Perhaps in the future, he'd have to try to watch her without touching himself. Save up his response until she was back with him on a Thursday night.

CHAPTER TWENTY-THREE

BY WEDNESDAY NIGHT, he didn't even have to watch them on the security cameras.

Tuesday night, Marcie was texting him videos of herself kissing Michael, pointing her phone at them as they sucked on each other's lips, selfie-style. Showing herself groping in his lap, saying she could tell how big he was, just from the bulge.

Later that night, she sent a video of herself going down on Michael's big, fat cock, moaning as she stretched her lips around it, the biggest cock Cam had ever seen. Looking into her phone's camera lens as she stroked it with her hand, as she flicked her tongue around its tip, as she opened her mouth and bobbed down on it.

And Michael was even helping her shoot those video clips.

Michael liked fucking her against the windows.

Michael liked other people watching.

Wednesday night, Marcie called him while she was in the bathroom getting ready to go out and fuck him. He gazed, stunned at her as she posed for him on the Face-

Time app, showing him her tiny white g-string, and matching bra, telling him how excited she was that Michael was going to take her to heaven and back with that huge great dick.

Telling her husband how wet she was at the prospect of him watching them fuck.

Saying things like, 'Have you seen his cock, though? Isn't it huge?'

While she re-applied her lipstick.

Telling Cam to take out his own cock and show her how hard he was already, to let her see him starting to stroke it while he watched her getting ready for another man.

Telling him not to come until she said so, while she turned around and showed him just how tiny that g-string was, just how little of her gorgeous derriere that it covered.

Then she was still on the FaceTime call as she went back out into the bedroom, holding the phone up so that Cam could see her walking back out there, saying 'hey' to Michael in the bedroom, posing up against him as he took hold of her, pulled her against his bare chest, her breasts crushing up against his ripped muscles.

Giggling before tilting her head up to kiss him.

Kneeling down to reveal that Michael wasn't just bare-chested, he was bare everything, and his dick was already Smith & Wesson hard in her hands—then moments later, in her mouth.

They weren't humiliating Cam, but Michael was standing tall as the alpha male, not caring that the husband was watching it all, as he took hold of Marcie's head and started gently fucking her pretty face right in front of that phone she still held. His cock occasionally slipping out of her mouth so he could slide it all over her face, rub it against her cheeks, as though marking her as his territory.

Marcie pausing part-way through to tell Cam to his face that this was the biggest cock she'd ever had, the most beautiful cock she'd ever put in her mouth.

Panting and moaning as he used her mouth, as though it was just sublime.

Cam watching as she propped up her phone on the bedside table, so Michael could lie on the bed and she could direct all her attention to worshipping his unbelievably large manhood. Michael holding her blonde locks out of her face while she sucked on him, like some kind of public service act for her husband's benefit.

Cam soon got over the shame of being on a FaceTime call as this other man got lucky with his wife. Knowing that they could see him there, beating his meat while he watched them.

It wasn't ideal, he wouldn't have chosen to be on the call. But Marcie had decided. Michael didn't seem even remotely bothered. So, after a while, Cam wasn't bothered, either.

He watched her telling him, 'I want you to put it inside me right now.'

Michael telling her to take off her clothes, and then Marcie was kneeling up, reaching behind herself to remove her bra, with two men stroking their cocks while they watched her. Marcie turning around to show him her beautiful ass as she peeled down her g-string, and then that was gone, and she was naked, straddling him, moaning even before she had that great thing squeezed inside her.

Tonight, Cam could *hear* her as another man entered her, he could hear her sigh and moan as she sank down on him, as that huge thing filled her up completely. As she began to ride him.

She looked like some kind of professional as she fucked him.

Cam couldn't exactly see everything, with the phone pointed at this angle, but he could see enough. And more than that, he was there. On the call. Hearing everything. Getting every nuance of her pleasure as she bounced on top of him.

She sucked his cock again after that, even though it was glistening with her juices.

Then she was on all fours, and he was kneeling up behind her, sliding back into her, doggy-style, only he was one hell of a doggy. A Great Dane, perhaps. Marcie screwing up her face as she took all of that thing inside, as it stretched her pussy to its limits.

He fucked her, and she turned so she was facing her phone, facing her husband as he watched this beast driving his huge cock into her again and again from behind.

So sexy, seeing her face as she was fucked by another man. Registering the ecstasy in her expressions.

Her skin getting a little shiny from perspiration, her hair getting a little damp.

Marcie and her lover—and it was so clearly all about the sex, it felt so reassuring to Cam to be part of the experience. Michael might be the strong man, but he was the husband.

After a while, Marcie was on her back, and Michael was sliding into her holding her furthest knee high, so that Cam could see everything, Cam could see that big dick entering his wife's pretty, pink pussy. Marcie stroking her clit while her lover thrust into her again and again, rocking her entire body each time he entered her. Then after a while it got too delicious for them both again, and Michael lay forward on top of her, going for it, his hips firing like a piston as he hammered into her over and over and over again, draped all over her like she was his.

And Marcie was going crazy, thrashing about, yelling

and crying as he fucked her—no longer needing to care about children who might hear them. Cam had to turn the volume down as he watched, but then he had to tone down his stroking as he heard her telling Michael to come inside her, that she wanted to feel him filling her with his hot seed.

Jesus.

Cam saw Michael slow, kneel up again so that he could see all the details as that enormous cock pierced his wife's beautifully wet pussy. Then Cam nearly lost it as he watched the man's glistening column begin to jerk and pulse—and he knew this man was coming inside Marcie, pumping her full of his thick cream.

Marcie making contented little mewing noises as her lover came inside her.

Then Michael pulled back, and she continued stroking her clit, her legs parted so that Cam could see her freshly-fucked pussy, see how wet she was—and, after a moment, see a hint of white come leaking out of her.

'Oh, God, honey, that felt so incredible,' she breathed, dipping a finger into her sex to coat its tip in her lover's come, before bringing it up to her mouth to taste it. 'He came *so much* inside me.'

But this time, as Michael disappeared to hit the shower, she looked into the phone and her eyes connected with her husband's, and she smiled wickedly, saying, 'I don't want you to come right now, honey. I want you to wait.'

Cam groaned, but felt a strange little buzz from the challenge she was setting.

'Don't touch it anymore,' she ordered him. 'Save it for me, okay? Save it for when I come home tomorrow.'

She smiled affectionately as she lay there, stroking her pussy and spreading the other man's come all over her sex. Teasing her husband a little, but enjoying his attention.

Then she told him to go take a cold shower, and she blew him a kiss, telling him she'd see him the next day.

And Cam watched the call end, before doing as his wife asked, though his cock was stiff to bursting, desperate to come.

CHAPTER TWENTY-FOUR

SHE WAS late home from London the next day. She even had to call the kids from the car—while she was on her way home, stopped at a service station en route—to wish them a good night via FaceTime.

If Cam was excited about her return, it was as nothing compared to when Marcie sent him a text message, after the kids were asleep, telling him to go to bed, that she wanted to fuck him as soon as she got home.

He went downstairs only to get a drink and tell Flo he was feeling very tired after a long day of home-schooling, that he was going to get an early night.

He went back upstairs and stripped off before taking a quick shower in the en suite.

Then he slipped under the covers, lying in the middle of their large bed with only the bedside lamps switched on, offering a low, warm light as he waited, reading a Kindle book on his phone.

It wasn't a long wait.

He could hear her car pull up on the gravel driveway outside, the closing of her car door as she exited the vehicle. His heart rate quickened as he imagined her saying hello to her mother on her way in, telling Flo not to get up from the couch, where she was watching some particularly violent episode of Peaky Blinders on Netflix. Then he heard her footsteps on the stairs on her way up.

'Where's my sweet husband?' she cooed as she came into the bedroom, and Cam felt flames flare up inside his chest as she swept through the door.

'Hey, honey. Good day at work?'

'Mmm…' she smiled, closing the door behind her as he ran his eyes over the tight lines of her suit, and the way her pencil skirt squeezed the full roundness of her behind. 'I hope you've got that beautiful cock out for me.'

He grinned, his facial expression offering himself to her as she stood in front of him, at the foot of the bed, and slipped the catch on her skirt, allowing it to drop to the ground.

She enjoyed his attention, his gaze taking in her little black panties as she reached behind herself to brush her hair back over her shoulder and out of her face.

Then she leaned forward to peel the bedsheet off him, revealing his bare legs, and then the rest of him, her eyes lighting up as she confirmed that he wasn't wearing a thing under that sheet, and finally he was completely on display to her, and his cock was at full attention already.

'Mmmm…' she moaned, flames dancing in her eyes as she climbed onto the bed, kneeling between his legs, her hair tumbling down to brush against his bare thighs as she brought her pretty face close to his exposed manhood.

She breathed him in, almost purring as she said, 'Freshly showered, huh?' Then her eyes flicked up to meet his, and she added, 'I'm sorry I'm late.'

'It's okay,' Cam said quietly, his hardness stirring as she

touched her lips to its base, and then slowly ran the tip of her tongue up its full length.

She flashed him a wicked smile, looking up at him as she said, 'I had to stop off at the apartment on my way home. Michael was there, of course.'

Cam felt his hardness throbbing as she stroked it with her soft cheek, his heart pounding inside his chest.

'You…?' he said, barely

She nodded. 'Two hours ago, he was inside me.' Then she sucked the first few inches of his cock into her mouth.

Cam nearly came right then and there.

He only just escaped since she was going so slow, really savoring how hard he was, indulging in the feeling of her second cock of the evening in her hands and in her mouth.

She had only just fucked Michael.

She still had her white shirt on, but as she swirled her tongue around his cock, she thrust her hips up, and he could see her exquisite behind, covered by her tiny black thong, and he could consider the fact that just before she'd driven up from London, her other man had fucked her, maybe even as she lay on the bed like this.

'How…?' he said, just stunned at her.

She smiled wickedly.

'It was only quick,' she said, squeezing his cock hard as she pumped it. 'We didn't even make it into the bedroom.'

He moaned, noticing her gently smeared makeup, and the way her hair seemed slightly unkempt, frayed at the edges, as though she'd had a good workout but had not showered afterward.

She'd fucked him and had come straight here.

'He was sitting on the sofa when I got there,' she grinned. 'I don't think he was expecting me. I went down in front of him and sucked his cock, right there and then.'

She gazed down at Cam's manhood, amused at how it

jerked and bucked in her hand as he responded to her words.

'Then he had me kneel on the sofa, and he just hiked up my skirt and pulled aside my panties—and slid that beautiful, big cock inside me from behind. He must have like the surprise visit, because after he made me come, he pulled out and came all over my breasts.'

She let go of her husband, knelt up to unfasten the buttons of her white shirt, and then shimmy out of it. Her bra went, too, leaving her in a pair of tiny black thong panties.

'Are you glad I drove right on up here afterward?' she asked him, kneeling up to flaunt her almost bare body, those gorgeous breasts full out in front of him.

'Very glad,' he said, but she only had to look at how his raging hard-on stood proud to tell how turned on he was.

She tugged on the waistband of her panties with both hands, adjusting them, pulling them tight against her cheating pussy.

'I could smell him on me all the way up the motorway,' she said, pulling her hair back out of her face, over her shoulder. 'All the way from London, I was driving, I could smell his cologne on me. Smell his come on me.'

She put her hand on Cam's thighs, pulled on him to encourage him to shift down on the mattress a little way. Then she climbed onto him, straddling his hips—but she didn't settle there. She shuffled up his chest, so that now he could detect her lingering perfume—and maybe, her lover's lingering cologne on her stunning body.

She paused there, her knees tucked under his armpits, letting him take in that incredible sight up her body.

It was so unlike Marcie to do any kind of exercise and not want to shower afterward. And here she was, freshly fucked by another man. Cam nearly came right there.

'He had me lie on the sofa on my front,' she said, again playing with her hair, pulling it back, tying it up, letting him feast his eyes on her sublime, adulterous form. 'Then he squeezed that big dick inside me, really filled me up… it felt so good…'

She lifted one knee, over his shoulder, sliding herself forward so her warm thigh brushed his chest, and her sex —covered by that tiny triangle of black cotton and lace— eased close to his face, close enough that he detected the scent of her arousal, and of her recent sexual liaison.

He moaned and breathed her in, shivers of pleasure sweeping over him as he inhaled the powerful evidence of her infidelity.

She lifted her other knee, and now she filled his face with those little black panties, pressing herself down on his mouth and nose, overwhelming him with that dark, spicy aroma.

'Mmm….' She purred as she settled over him, leaning back a little so she could see him nuzzling up to her pussy, breathing her in like a man addicted.

He tugged at the waistband of her panties, and she helped him slide them over her hips, down her thighs. She lifted a leg to remove them, and then she was kneeling over him, her pussy bare and glistening, just an inch above his lips.

'Does it still turn you on?' she asked him. 'Thinking about me cheating on you?'

'Uh-huh,' he said, just in awe of her, captivated by her sweet pussy.

'Does it turn you on that he was fucking me, just a couple of hours ago?'

'Yes, it does.'

She grinned. 'He bent me over the sofa, shoved his huge cock inside this little pussy of mine…'

She stroked her fingers over her pussy, from bottom to top, right over him, and it only seemed to strengthen the scent of sex between her thighs. Then, at last, she eased downward, and he could reach up to kiss her there, to run the tip of his tongue along her silky, slippery groove.

'Oh *yeah*…' she breathed, and he loved the sounds of her breathing deepening, the way she responded to his touch, the way she settled down lower, parting her legs further, opening herself up to him, her jaw dropping as he pulled her down on his face, as he kissed her deeply there, sucking on her pussy.

Her nipples were so hard on her full breasts, it felt like an achievement for Cam. He lapped at her pussy, indulging in the unusual savory flavor of her abundant wetness, the thought never quite straying from the center of his mind that another man's cock had been here not so long ago, squeezing in past these pussy lips, making her wet, making her scream. And she gasped and sighed, taking great, deep breaths as he pleasured her with his eager mouth, as he connected in the most intimate way with this unfaithful pussy.

He loved how surprised she seemed at how much pleasure he could give her this way. He loved impressing her. He loved making her feel good.

She leaned back, supporting herself with her hands on his stomach, and he reached up, to take hold of her breasts in his hands, manhandling them, reveling in their shape, and in how she responded to his fondling of them. The stiffness of her nipples against his fingers. As he stroked and squeezed her breasts, her sighs became moans, and she was unable to stop herself from moving her hips, starting to press herself down a little harder over his face, gently rubbing her sex over his mouth.

He continued to worship her pussy, but let her steadily

take control, so that she was carefully thrusting herself over him, fucking his face, grinding her sweet sex against him so that her wetness covered him, cheek to cheek. She reached behind herself, briefly, and he felt her take hold of his hard cock—but it was more like she was gauging how he felt about all this, making sure he was still having fun as well.

His hardness in her hands seemed to reassure her, and he didn't mind that she let it go, forsaking it as she sat up on his face, using him as a toy, crushing her soaking pussy against him as she thrust it back and forth. He let her ride his mouth, but while she did so, he could grip his own cock, and stroke it for himself, while taking care never to quite let himself get close to orgasm.

She came, though. Clamping his head tight between her thighs, shuddering and shivering over him, quite clearly trying to stop herself from crying out, to prevent others in the house from hearing her, as her burning-hot, oily pussy nearly smothered him.

After that, he felt like he'd completed a masterpiece.

She eventually pulled herself off him, breathless, and climbed off the bed to slip into the en suite, to find a towel for him. She dabbed at him, her expression apologetic for leaving his face in such a state. He didn't mind. He gave her an ear-to-ear smile, just buzzing to have her wetness all over his face, her come making his cheeks and his jaw feel cool as it evaporated from his skin.

She lay with him, beside him but also half on him, one smooth-skinned leg slid over his, her hand closing around his hard cock.

'You're amazing, you know that?' she said, completely out of the blue.

'I don't know about that,' he chuckled bashfully.

But she looked at him, seriously. 'Most men would have run a mile if they discovered their wives were having an affair. Maybe some would have stayed home, but they'd be twisted by anger…'

Cam shrugged. 'You still love me, don't you?' He asked her.

'Of course. More than ever.'

'Well, then. Why should we have a problem?'

She smiled. Stroked his cock a few times. Then she said, 'But this is more than just you 'coping' with me having an affair, isn't it?'

'How do you mean?'

She glanced down, taking in the sight of his bulging erection in her hand. 'You haven't been this interested in sex for a while,' she said, and she didn't sound angry about it, just matter-of-fact.

'No, I suppose not.'

'And now… you can't get enough.'

Cam gave a little nod. 'I guess it's woken me up. I've realized how lazy I got. Taking you for granted.'

She said, 'But it's more than that, isn't it? This is a thing for you. I mean, having me sleeping with someone else. It's not just something you're handling, because you don't want to lose me. It's something that really gets you going.'

'Yes, it does.'

'Like, if I wasn't going to see Michael anymore… you'd want me to see someone else.'

'I would. Whoever you wanted.' He said it without even really thinking about it. Her hand squeezing his shaft may have prompted him, but once it was out of his mouth, they both just seemed to stare into each other's eyes and really *thought* about it.

Eventually, he said, 'I just think… we've got to that stage in our lives… in our *marriage*… where it's no longer enough to just strip off and have sex. We've done all that.

For us to just keep to ourselves… it's just going through the motions over and over again.'

'Uh-huh,' she nodded, and he could see her thinking through what he was saying.

'I love you,' he said, 'you know that I do. And I realize I've been overlooking how… *gorgeous* you are…'

She blushed faintly at that, but at the same time appreciated it.

'…but… I don't know… if it's just us… I think it would go back to the way it was again.'

'Yes, maybe.'

'We'd just have sex when we got a little horny, just to release that tension. And we'd go back to doing it quickly, cutting corners.'

'Probably,' she nodded.

'This way… you get to explore with other people… and when you come home to me, I get to explore you. You remind me how sexy you are, you remind me to appreciate you properly, to take my time…'

She climbed onto him, straddling him so that her sex pressed against his shaft, though he didn't penetrate her. 'What about you?' She said. 'Does that mean I should be letting you out, too? Letting you break lockdown? Or at least, the lockdown of our marriage.'

He smiled. 'I don't need anyone else,' he said.

'But do you think, someday, you might?'

'I don't know,' he said, honestly. He sensed that she wasn't quite like him. That although she recognized that it was potentially unfair of her to want to prevent him from seeing other women if she was going to see other men herself, that she might not be able to handle that.

He said, 'For me, this whole thing is about you.' She smiled. He continued, 'I know it's not exactly normal… but you're my wife, and it turns me on that you're unfaithful. Ever since I discovered your affair… it's always been about you. I think about other women… I see them on TV… I can see that they might be attractive, but whenever I feel horny… it's about you. I think about you. There in London, with Michael, or here with me, after you've been with Michael.'

'And what would happen if I ended things with Michael?' she asked him, adding, 'Not that I'm planning to, yet.'

He shrugged. 'I don't know. Maybe you could try Tinder, or something.'

That made her laugh. But then she looked at his face, and how serious he was—and, taking in the fact that he hadn't been joking, one of her eyebrows rose on her face, indicating curiosity.

'You'd want me to start dating again?' She asked him.

He smiled. 'It might be fun, don't you think?'

'God,' she laughed, 'what if I've forgotten how to do the whole dating thing?'

Then she added, 'What if they've changed the rules since we were dating ourselves?'

'You'd just have to work it out as you go along,' he said. 'But then, dating always was working it out as you go along.'

She raised her hips, and now jostled herself over him, and then moments later he was inside her, his cock enveloped by her unfaithful pussy, and it just felt incredible.

CHAPTER TWENTY-FIVE

THINGS SEEMED to settle down into a new routine for a while. It was still difficult, tiring, frustrating, to be confined to the house all the time, and to get through all the home-schooling—or at least, enough to assuage the guilt of the kids missing school. Even with Flo helping out with the home-schooling, it was still difficult to get through.

But at least there were the evenings to look forward to.

Cam had lots of early nights, though Flo seemed to believe it was just that he wanted to get as much sleep as possible, to stay healthy. The thing was, even when Marcie wasn't actively having sex with Michael, Cam found that he wanted to watch them together on the security cameras, steadily building the sexual tension within him as he watched them together, hanging out, flirting more than a little, gradually getting into the mood to fuck.

Later, Marcie might send him a few text messages, making sure he was in the mood to watch her with Michael, maybe prod him in the right direction with some teasing pictures of herself. Further on down the road, she started sending little video clips of herself teasing him, flashing him while she was in the bathroom. A couple of weeks on, and she was calling him while she was getting ready to have sex with Michael. The whole deal seemed more of an event. She would strip off, shower, and get herself dressed in sexy lingerie while Cam watched and even talked with her.

Then he'd watch the main event, like it was some kind of live sex show on the Internet, only it happened to feature his wife as the star, cheating with another man.

When Thursdays came along, the new routine saw her late home from work most weeks, though made later still because she came home via the London flat, via a quick fuck by Michael.

Home late, then she was soon rubbing her cheating pussy in her husband's face.

Taking his cock deep in her creamy, well-used sex.

Cam felt vaguely guilty about breaking the rules of lockdown, since Marcie was essentially flicking between households. But she kept countering him by saying Michael was essentially in their household. It was just that the household was split between the Cotswolds and London.

CHAPTER TWENTY-SIX

THERE WAS something deeply sexy about watching her doing things with Michael that she would never do with him.

There were some things that Cam felt certain he could never do with her. It just wasn't in his nature. And yet, witnessing it between her and Michael—it was seriously hot.

And he never knew quite what was going to happen when she fucked him.

Watching her slowly getting ready for her latest tryst, stripping off her work attire, taking a quick rinse in the shower, drying off, slipping on a pair of black, thigh-high stockings, a garter belt, a sheer g-string that hardly covered anything at all. The matching bra.

Marcie telling him she was feeling a little nervous, a little flustered, at the prospect of what was about to happen. It made Cam feel nervous, flustered. But also hard as a rock.

'You're going to have to watch us on the cameras tonight,' she said, checking her makeup in the mirror. She was wearing way too much lurid red lipstick—it made her seem cheap, slutty, and yet it was highly erotic for some reason.

It made Cam think about how she was planning to smear that lipstick all over Michael's cock.

'I'm not going to be able to deal with this phone.'

'Yes, sweetie. No problem,' Cam replied.

'How do I look?'

'Amazing.'

'Okay. Get that beautiful cock of yours going, darling. Come on, show me.'

He showed her. She liked to see him in position, fired up and ready to go.

'But no coming tonight,' she declared. It disappointed him, and yet he knew by now that it always seemed to improve things when Thursday came around again. It seemed to give him extra energy to handle her when she came back from London craving his devotion.

'Okay, love you,' she said, and then the phone was off.

Cam switched to the camera in the bedroom, watched his wife emerge from the en suite wearing her sexy black lingerie. Michael wearing a black shirt, black jeans, stepping over to her, putting something on her—a necklace? He kissed her, briefly, on the lips, and then she knelt down at her feet.

And Cam saw there was a black studded collar around her neck, and Michael was holding a thin, black leather leash that was connected to the collar.

Jesus.

He watched Michael walking her around the bedroom —around the apartment—like she was his pet. She just looked incredible in those stockings, the garters, that g-string hardly there. She followed him obediently on the end of the leash. He had her sit, like a trained hound, in the middle of the living room floor while he slowly walked around her, inspecting her.

Prodding her.

Squeezing her.

Touching her.

He sat in the armchair, and had her come to him, turn slowly around, lower her behind so that she could rub the bulge in his jeans with her pussy. Then he ordered her to kneel, and when she complied, he kissed her overly-painted lips, and had her remove his jeans entirely.

Cam watched, transfixed, as his wife was confronted with this other man's enormous cock, stiff and pointing aloft. She brushed her hair out of her face, and he gently pulled her to him by the leash until her pretty face was above that obscene object. Then she parted her lips, and sank onto it, taking a surprising amount of it into her mouth.

Sitting in the middle of their marital bed, his phone in hand, manhood in the other, Cam watched Marcie sucking on this other man, her eyes uplifted to make sure she was doing as Michael wanted at all times. Pulling away from time to time to stroke his length in her hands, just as he directed her.

For a powerful woman, she seemed to like giving up control to him.

But this wasn't something she could do with her husband, he was sure of it.

And that was fine. She would have other men for that.

Cam watched her sucking on her lover's cock until the man was done with it, at which point he had her stand, so he could slip down her g-string, and then turn to face away from him. He directed his huge cock to her entrance as she lowered herself onto his lap.

And then he was inside her, making Cam wonder how

she could fit that colossal thing within her. Anatomically, it was somewhat astounding. The human body is a wondrous thing. Cam watched Michael wrap his arms around her, holding her tight, pulling her back further onto his lap. Cam could see between her legs, he could see Michael's cock buried in her gorgeous pussy.

Then Michael's hand covered her there, pressing at her sex as he thrust into her from beneath, pressing at her clit to get her going.

Marcie was so submissive, it seemed completely against her usual nature. And yet, as Michael directed her up, using that leash to lead her where he wanted her—onto the sofa, her legs splayed—Cam could tell that this was a thrill for Marcie. She was experiencing something outside her normal experience. This was not something Cam would be able to give her—and yet, if you looked at it another way, indirectly he was essentially gifting her this experience, by letting her do this with Michael.

Cam felt his heart burn with fear and excitement as Michael knelt on the edge of the sofa, and then directed his big cock to her open pussy. Stabbing her with it. Claiming her with it. Using her with it. He thrust into her, fucking her, again and again, as she gazed up at him, taking it obediently.

A few moments later, Michael stopped, and led her by the leash through to the bedroom. She walked on all fours like an animal, like a pet. Then her lover had her stand up in the doorway of the bedroom, again directing her movement using the leash attached to the collar around her neck. Not something Cam would do, but it was something Marcie was responding to.

Michael fetched something from the drawer in Marcie's bedside table. Cam saw the glint of steel—the handcuffs—and caught his breath.

Now he watched the tall, dark Michael click the handcuffs around one of Marcie's wrists, and order her to raise her hands above her head. She complied, of course, and he handcuffed her wrists together like that. As she stood like that, shackled, he took a step back from her for a moment, examining her, inspecting her. Then he had his hands on her, groping her, caressing her, pawing at her breasts—and then her pussy.

He was making her feel her place. Making her see that she was just a toy for him.

He shoved her back against the bedroom door and fingered her pussy, pulling her bra away from one breast so that he could forcefully suck on it. But she was moaning, she was enjoying it.

At last, he had her move to the bed, lie on it on her back.

He leaned over her, kissed her mouth.

He spanked her with the leash—not hard, and she seemed to like the teasing. Rapping that thing against her exposed pussy, brushing it and tapping it against her delicate flesh. Again, it was not something Cam would have wanted to do to his wife. But he enjoyed seeing how she responded to it.

And then he was standing over her, pulling her to him, so that her butt was lined up with the edge of the mattress. Shoving her handcuffed wrists up over her head, again, so that she was completely exposed to him. Pulling off his shirt so that his muscle-bound form was fully revealed. Placing that crazy-big, hard cock down against the pink, glistening folds of her pussy.

He gripped the leash tight in one hand as he thrust his hips and slid the tip of his cock along the slippery folds of her sex. Cam saw her gasp, he saw her breathing deepen as she felt his huge tool coursing through her pussy lips,

stroking up against her sensitive pussy without yet penetrating it. He held her by the leash as he kept driving the
tip of his cock against her, up and down, and now he was
getting her to beg him to fuck her—which, she eagerly did.

Then, at last, he directed it downward, into her, and he
was inside her, filling her up, making her gasp with the
sensation of being stretched by him, taking a monster
inside her. Michael thrust his hips, hard. He fucked her,
hard. He held her by the leash and rocked her body as he
pounded into her again and again, his muscles rippling
while he worked that enormous manhood inside her.

Cam nearly exploded as he watched the man fucking
his wife. He had to let go of his own cock, calm down,
though he couldn't take his eyes off her as the man fucked
her so royally.

He watched as Michael forced her up, so he could lie
on the bed himself. Then she was straddling him, riding
him, while he continued to direct her and hold her by the
leash. It made Cam think of Princess Leia wearing her
gold bikini in Return of the Jedi, chained up to Jabba the
Hut. She rode him a while, her skin flushing pink, shining
as she worked up a sweat.

He had her suck his cock some more.

Then she was on all fours, only for him to force her
face down on the mattress, pulling her arms behind her
back, holding her by the handcuffed wrists as he pounded
into her from behind, her deliciously rounded buttocks
shivering and shaking as his body slammed into hers again
and again.

Did she come? She must have, though it was disguised
by the forceful way in which he powered that huge cock
into her again and again.

She seemed so very satisfied when he pulled away from
her. Allowing her to lie there, splayed out on the bed on

her back, relaxed except that he presented his cock for her to lick, and she then did so—sucking on him from time to time, smiles plastered all over her face—until he was reaching his own climax, spurting thick ropes of his come all over her pretty face, her ample breasts, her smooth, flawless skin.

CHAPTER TWENTY-SEVEN

HE LIKED it when they used her phone to capture the details, close up.

It was great watching them on the cameras Marcie had set up in each room of the apartment, but when the phone was there, and they were filming themselves, it got Cam going like nothing else.

It seemed more as though he was there, with them.

It was more intimate, somehow, more personal. And he felt more involved, rather than some distant witness, catching what was going on from a camera hidden up on a tall bookshelf, or somewhere like that.

It almost felt as though they were doing it for him.

They could have been shooting a personal sex-tape, something each of them could watch later, during the quiet moments when they weren't together. But it seemed to Cam like Marcie was looking into her husband's eyes when she gazed at the camera while kneeling between her boyfriend's thighs, flicking her tongue around the end of her boyfriend's cock.

Michael wasn't shy. They weren't doing this kind of

thing to humiliate Cam, as some husbands seemed to enjoy in pornography, but Michael was definitely showing off his ability to fuck Cam's wife. And he knew Cam was watching this.

Here she was one night, on all fours on the bed, and Michael was holding the camera, pointing it down to get a superb view of her hindquarters as he lined up behind her. She was wearing a pair of fairly plain white panties, nothing special. But the way Michael was filming her was special. The way she reached back to stretch and tug her panties aside to show the camera her intimate parts. The way Michael stroked her soaking pussy, smearing her wetness everywhere, all over her pert derriere.

He propped up the camera by the TV and Marcie removed her panties. Cam found himself gazing up his wife's fabulous legs at her gloriously bare pussy and her peach of a behind she lay there on the mattress on her front.

Now Michael returned to the frame, rubbing his hands together like he was washing them. When he put them on Marcie's body, Cam could see they were covered in oil, which he now rubbed over her skin, focusing on her buttocks, her upper thighs, and between her legs.

She moaned, and arched her back, lifting her hips off the bed a little, pushing her butt upwards so that when Michael's hands moved away, Cam could see her exquisite little pink pussy—and even her exposed anus. It felt like he'd never caught such an intimate view of his wife before, he'd never seen her quite this exposed.

The shock factor only made it seem more erotic.

'You okay?' Cam heard Michael asking her, as he delved a hand right between her upper thighs, right over her sex.

'Uh-huh,' she sighed, sounding very relaxed.

Michael slowly glided his hands around her pussy, squeezing her inner thighs, sliding the edge of his forefingers right up against her pussy lips, his thumbs slipping over her rear entrance. Marcie moaned, and Cam actually felt envious of his other man, that he was giving her such an intimate, personal massage.

She wiggled her hips, just a little at first, but then noticeably, and Michael seemed to respond by pressing a thumb to her pussy, stroking her inner lips, tracing circles around her clit. She was getting so wet. Cam almost wondered if they'd needed massage oil at all.

Michael slid a finger inside her pink pussy, and she groaned, low and loud, gyrating her hips as he withdrew his finger again and stroked her with his thumb, then thrust his finger back inside.

Cam was a little surprised how much time Michael was taking, how much attention he was spending to touching and stroking her pussy before squeezing his big cock inside it. But it was certainly having its effect—she was unable to keep still, he was driving her crazy.

And then while he continued to stroke her pussy with one hand, Cam saw Michael run his other thumb between her buttocks, over her anus. He was stroking her there, too. Her husband had never seen such a thing. Shocking. Strangely hot.

Marcie gasped, and gradually Michael was paying more and more attention to her ass, stroking her there, slipping the tip of a finger inside her, delving his thumb into her tight hole. He interspersed a little anal penetration with his finger with a stroking of her entire rear, keeping her relaxed, opening her up to this new treatment, coating his fingers in oil again each time he slid one inside her ass.

Cam was transfixed to the screen. Of course he knew people did this kind of thing. But he'd never felt the urge to try anything like this with anyone. Marcie had never expressed interest.

It was bold, it was startling, but that was part of the fascination and the eroticism.

Michael was going where no man had gone before.

Marcie shuffled back a little, and opened her legs wider, and it only gave Cam an even closer view of her intimate area, as Michael massaged her ass, and penetrated her anus. Marcie's own fingers reached between her thighs to begin stroking her pussy while her lover explored her other hole, but she stopped after a few moments as though the combination was just too intense.

Was it making her feel good, all this attention around her ass? Michael gave her a little light spank, as though to reassure her, to tell her she was doing well. Then he reached behind him for something, and when he brought back his hand, Cam saw he was holding something metallic, something very shiny, silver.

A vibrator?

But as he watched Michael touch the tip of the thing to Marcie's little pink hole, Cam caught his breath as he recognized what it was. A butt plug. This was getting serious.

With its tip pressed against her rear entrance, Michael twisted it, this way and that, and Cam could see it had a large faux gemstone on the end facing away from Marcie. Very bling. Michael was coating it in oil and very gently pressing it into her hole again and again, each time thrusting it very slightly further inside her.

She was panting, and letting out little moans, and reaching behind her legs to stroke her pussy while Michael eased it incrementally inside her ass. As the thickest part of the bulbous thing squeezed inside her, she was gasping, moaning a little louder. But then it was in her, and there

Michael left it. He stroked her buttocks some more, as though returning to his role as masseur, but he no longer touched the bejeweled plug.

It just stayed there, as though someone had censored Cam's view of his wife's anus with a large, sparkling purple gemstone.

Michael stroked her pussy some more, and then Cam watched him slide his big dick deep inside her sex, and slowly fuck her until they both came hard.

But the plug stayed inside her the whole time.

Them Michael withdrew, leaving Marcie lying on the bed, gasping for breath, looking as though someone had just connected her to a car battery and given her a big jolt —she rolled around the bed, moaning, to the point that Cam worried she'd actually been hurt.

But then, when Michael went into the bathroom to take a shower, and Marcie went out into the living room to talk to her husband on FaceTime, she seemed fine. Better than fine, actually—she had the broadest smile on her face.

'You're okay?' was the first thing he asked her.

'Oh yes,' she said, and then gave him a mischievous smirk that looked almost as though she'd been caught by a teacher smoking a spliff, but she knew he wasn't the kind of teacher who'd do anything about it.

'You looked like you were in pain.'

She laughed. 'God, that was incredible. With that thing in me… and then Michael inside my *pussy*…'

She perched on the edge of the sofa, her laptop resting on the coffee table in front, and parted her legs, her bathrobe opening to show Cam everything. She couldn't keep her hands away from her sex.

'I guess I understand so much more about it, already,' she said, reaching down to toy with the strange thing protruding from her ass. 'You know... why anyone would want to do it...'

'So it felt good?'

'So *intense*.'

'You're just going to leave it in there tonight?' Cam asked her.

'I'm supposed to leave it in for 24 hours,' she said, as though it were a medical prescription, rather than orders from her dominant lover.

'All day tomorrow?'

She nodded. 'It's so *big*,' she said, and seemed a little breathless as she sat on the sofa, having to wiggle her hips and re-angle her entire body so that she could sit there comfortably.

'Aren't people gong to think... you know... you're sitting funny in meetings?' He asked her.

She giggled. 'Maybe. Do you think they'll be able to tell?'

He was taken aback at her attitude. That she might risk discovery by wearing such a thing under her clothes at work.

'How does it feel?'

'Weird,' she said, as though a little out of breath, her voice tighter than usual, higher pitched. 'I feel so... full... but... I guess it's hot, knowing what it's for.'

Like she was desperate to go to the restroom.

She was sitting there, touching herself, and goodness, if she didn't seem like she was going to hit orgasm again very soon.

'What happens in 24 hours?' He asked her. 'What happens at the end of all this.'

She said, 'Tomorrow night... he's going to fuck me in the ass. Oh honey, are you going to watch me? I've never done it before...'

He told her he would. He told her he could hardly believe she was doing this, particular with a man of Michael's size. But that he would watch.

He watched her frantically stroking her pussy, and he pumped his cock, and it all seemed like some strange, slightly surreal dream.

When he wished her good night, he briefly asked her if she'd take it out while she slept. She shook her head and flashed him a nervous smile.

'I'll be okay,' she said.

He could hardly sleep that night. Thinking, was she really going to go through with this?

In the morning, he went about his usual routine for a weekday, and things were busy enough that there wasn't even time to think about what had happened the previous night.

Then Flo took over, leading the morning's home-schooling, and Cam had space to think as he pottered around in the garden, tending to a little weeding, a little watering, before settling down to do some work. Only then did he think back to Marcie's night with Michael—and only then did he remember what she was supposed to be doing today.

He texted her:

Cam: So are you still wearing it? ;-)

He didn't even expect her to respond particularly quickly—but then she did, almost instantly.

Marcie: Oh, yes.

It made him hard, thinking of her going about her daily schedule in the office, wearing that the whole time. It wasn't only the way it must be making her feel all day, while she was supposed to be concentrating on her work, reminding her every moment that she was going to experience anal sex that night, for the first time ever. It was also the sheer commitment she was giving to this, to doing what her lover told her. Doing something her husband would never have asked her to do.

Normally, he didn't like to bother at work, but today, he couldn't stop himself.

Cam: How is it at work? Do you notice it at all?

She didn't seem annoyed that he was disturbing her.

Marcie: Oh, I notice it. All the time. Last night, I kept waking up, feeling it there. Today… I'm intensely aware of it—all the time.

Cam: Is it unpleasant?

She hesitated at that one. He supposed it wasn't quite as easy as saying it was pleasant or unpleasant.

Marcie: Sometimes, I really don't want it to be there. When I'm walking. When I'm sitting on certain chairs. Other times, though, it just keeps me thinking about Michael. About what he did to me last night. About what he's going to do to me tonight.

Later, just after he'd made lunch for everyone, he texted her again for an update. Asking whether it was still in there. Answer: yes, it was. And, to his surprise, she sent him a picture—a close-up, obviously. A selfie. It showed her pink, hairless pussy and half of the plug covering her rear entrance, the purple faux gemstone and its round, silver frame glinting in the light from her iPhone flash. He could see a little of her upper thighs, but nothing else.

He noticed that her pussy lips were glistening.

Cam: You think you'll last the day?

Marcie: I'm doing my best!

❖

CAM DID the lunch time slot taking care of the kids, with Flo taking over mid-afternoon, and then when Cam started work, he couldn't resist the temptation to fire over a little text message to Marcie asking how she was doing with the plug.

Her text message made him smile:

Marcie: It's insane. I'm trying so hard to keep calm, I'm like a zen master. But I had to go out at lunch to buy fresh underwear.

Cam laughed at that.

Cam: I thought all the clothes stores were shut?

Marcie: I found a little place on Bond Street that's doing a Click 'n' Collect service. Bought five pairs—seriously expensive, but best I could get at short notice.

At that point, Cam received a selfie looking up Marcie's skirt, showing a pair of expensive-looking blue satin and white lace panties with a rather large wet spot where they covered her pussy. The picture appeared to show her sitting in a restroom stall, though there wasn't much visible beyond her upper thighs and crotch.

Marcie: And you know what happened when I got back to the office?

Cam: What happened?

Now he received another picture. It was the same as before, except now she was holding something in front of her wet panties—another butt plug. It was almost the same as the one Michael had put inside her, except that the faux gemstone in the hilt was turquoise instead of purple.

Marcie: He couriered it over to my office at lunch time!

Cam chuckled. Michael had sent her another butt plug?

Cam: Why does he want you to have a different one?

Marcie: Because this one's bigger. Much bigger.

Now she sent him another picture, this time similar to the selfie she'd sent him at lunch time, except that now the faux gemstone peeking out from between her cheeks was turquoise.

It made him hard as a rock.

Marcie: I only have two dry pairs of underwear left—I hope I make it through the rest of the day!

Cam: lol. Good luck! xx

He liked thinking of her spending all day with that thing inside her, unable to keep her pussy from constantly soaking her underwear. It helped time to fly by while he was taking care of the kids, getting them to bed.

And then he was tired, excusing himself from a night of watching TV with Flo, to disappear up to bed early, only to sit there peering at his laptop, watching the feed from Marcie's security cameras.

Michael was there, waiting. Watching TV.

Marcie arrived home, looking flustered, red-faced, a little sweaty, hair not quite as perfect as normal. Grabbing a quick bite to eat in the kitchen while Michael continued watching TV. Slipping out into the bedroom to undress.

She was looking at the camera as she undressed, and Cam thought it hot that she was performing for him, displaying herself for him. She even picked up her phone, texted him to make sure he was there.

Marcie: You watching?

Cam: Oh yes. You bet.

Naked now, she smiled at him, and bent over the bed, showing him the large turquoise gemstone that seemed to cover up her rear entrance, until you realized it was actually protruding from it.

Then she padded out into the bathroom, where he could not see her. He assumed she was taking a shower. Getting herself ready for Michael.

More waiting.

Michael looking so calm, watching TV, wearing a smart shirt and pants, but seeming so relaxed he could have been expecting nothing but an evening of soap operas and delivery pizza.

Then, here at last was a beautiful naked goddess stepping out of the bathroom, dripping wet but looking perfectly fresh and pure. Cam watched her drying off with a towel, then taking a hair dryer to finish off her long, golden hair. He watched her step in front of her chest of drawers to select some sexy underwear for her special evening. And after she'd perused everything she had, she put on nothing but a pair of white, lace-top thigh-high stockings. Hold-ups, which didn't even need a garter belt.

He watched her drift to her closet and select a fairly simple, but elegant black dress that hung off her shoulders by the thinnest of straps. No bra. No panties. She sat at her dressing table to put on her makeup—lipstick, a little mascara, eye-liner; she didn't need foundation or anything like that. A spritz or two of perfume—on her neck, her wrist, her inner thighs

It was like date night, except that she only had to step out of her bedroom door to meet up with her date.

There she was, looking up at the camera, smiling at her husband. Picking up her phone from the bedside table, texting him:

Marcie: You ready, sweetie?

Cam stunned that he was going to watch this. That she would involve him in it. Texting her back:

Cam: I'm ready, honey. You look absolutely stunning. Are you ready? You don't have to do this if you don't want to. Even now.

Marcie: I'm ready. I want to do this. I want you to watch. I can't believe how much it turns me on that you'll be watching.

Another smile for him once he'd read her message. She blew him a kiss.

Then her focus was on another man.

CHAPTER TWENTY-EIGHT

HE STOOD AS SHE APPROACHED. Cam could not hear them, but he hardly needed to, to work out what was going on. He was drinking in the sight of her in that dress, looking so perfect, just delicious under the dimmed lights.

She was looking serious, and so was he. Cam could tell that Michael was asking her if she was sure about this. It was reassuring that he would.

Marcie was certain.

She slipped one of the thin straps of her dress off her shoulder, revealing one of her pert breasts, a stiff, pink nipple. And then the other. She pushed the dress down her body, revealing her trim curves, her stomach, her hips, her bare mound, her sex. Down it came, to her thighs, and only then as she revealed her virgin-white lace-topped stockings, was she unveiled as not entirely naked.

And there she stood, exposed except for stockings that emblazoned her need for sex.

Michael was impressed, but was containing his emotions. She touched his chest, took a step closer to him, guided his hands to her rear, as though to emphasize what she was giving him.

She kissed him, and Cam could tell he was touching her in such a way that he could tell she had her plug in place. She'd done her prep work. He kissed her back, there were tongues. The two of them were perfect, sexually for each other. Cam felt envious. A little jealous, even. But it all underscored his arousal for this moment. For his wife to have an experience she could not have with him.

The kiss dissipated, and Michael pulled off his shirt. He missed one of the buttons, and it popped off as he tore at the garment, making them both laugh for a moment or two.

Then the moment of levity was passed, and the two of them were back at each other, sucking on each other's lips with passion, with hunger. Marcie worked at Michael's belt, pulling open his fly. She stooped as she pulled down his pants, sank down until she was kneeling in front of him as his giant member was revealed.

Was she really going to take that thing in her ass?

Cam sat cross-legged in the middle of his bed, watching them on his laptop computer, his own diamond-hard manhood in his hands, just gazing at the sight of them through Marcie's security cameras.

She brushed her flowing, golden hair back over her shoulders with both hands, and then took hold of the man's colossal penis at the base, before enveloping its end in her mouth. She seemed so familiar with it, now. It was no longer such a stretch to get her lips around it.

She sucked on it, licked it, gazing up at him with adoring, worshipful eyes.

But then he took a step back, sat on the couch. He needed only a look to invite her onto his lap. She draped herself over him, along the couch, her behind a little raised, in perfect position for his hand to come down on her beautifully rounded behind.

He gave her a little swat on one of her cheeks, and her mouth opened wide. Another, slightly harder spank, and her pale behind gained a flush of pink, shivering from the impact.

Marcie moaned, though her husband couldn't hear her. She moaned, and closed her eyes tight, and Michael sat primly like a school principal in some bygone era, disciplining a naughty girl.

After a few spanks, Marcie's open mouth turned into a broad smile. She tilted her hips slightly, and Cam could see something glinting from between her buttocks—the faux gemstone in the hilt of her plug. Michael spanked her, her entire body moving with the impact, and Marcie bit her lip. Cam could tell she was warming up quickly. That was the point.

Her peach of a behind was taking on a rosy glow in both cheeks, and Marcie looked as though she was in ecstasy.

Cam smiled. She was so much more kinky than he ever knew.

But now, Michael's spanking came to an end. He grasped her pink-flushed cheeks and parted them, examining her. He took hold of the hilt of her plug and partially withdrew it from her pink hole, rolling its bulbous end around, stretching her, testing her.

Cam could see her breathing change, deepening, as she felt him stretching her there.

On his laptop, he flicked between the two cameras set up in the living room. Through one view, he could see a good view of Michael toying with that silver plug, clutching her buttock with one hand as he played at penetrating her with that thing, slowly, carefully, gently.

Through the other view, he could see Marcie's face expressing her reactions to his touching her there.

She was smiling, nervously, as though she was lining up to go on a famously extreme rollercoaster. Excited. A little scared. Brave. A little reckless. Breathing consciously, as though someone had told her to focus on her breathing.

Doing the 'ooo' face as he dipped that huge plug into her anus.

Gasping when it filled her.

Closing her eyes and moaning as she thought about him replacing that thing with his big, hard cock.

Then Michael gave her one more swat on her behind, and she pulled herself off his lap. Cam watched her kneel down on the floor in front of the sofa, bending over the low coffee table, facing toward the camera so that he could see her pretty face. She was smiling, waiting. Nervous. Her heart had to be thumping hard. The butterflies fluttering in her stomach.

Michael returned to the picture. He was holding something, something small and black.

Cam's phone started buzzing. He had to dive on it to stop the raucous noise of its bleeping alarm.

A FaceTime call, from Marcie.

He accepted the call, and here was a live video feed showing the view from Marcie's phone, which Michael was holding. Cam watched, amazed, as the sight of his wife's exposed ass filled the screen of his phone.

Cam could see her face on his computer, her rear on his phone.

He saw her smile as Michael's hard cock touched down between her cheeks, just resting there, as though warning her that it was on its way. Stroking her a little. She opened her eyes and looked at the camera, seeming to gaze into her husband's eyes, that little sparkle of anxiety in her own eyes suggesting she could hardly believe this was happening.

Michael stroked her a little with his cock. Then, with the hand that wasn't clutching that phone, he was squirting something on her. Clear liquid. Lube, Cam supposed. Lots of it.

'Oh…' Marcie cried out, and flinched, quite clearly, from the coldness of the liquid splashing down between her buttocks. Cam could hear her through the phone, now.

He watched as Michael slowly removed her plug once again, and used the rounded silver object to coax lubricant into her tight aperture, getting her fully prepared.

And now, the moment was at hand.

Marcie was reaching behind herself, her hands on her buttocks, parting them as though to it might give him just a fraction more room when he entered her. On his phone, Cam watched the glistening tip of Michael's enormous cock approach Marcie's rear entrance. On his laptop screen, he saw her close her eyes as the tip touched against her hole.

She suddenly opened her eyes, looked straight at her husband. So beautiful. She breathed out, slowly through pursed lips, and Michael eased ever-so slowly forward, his tip sinking inside her ass.

'Oh…'

Marcie's eyes narrowed, her lips made the unmistakable 'ooo' sound again as she felt that foreign object slip just inside her ass.

Then her mouth opened again in a gasp as Michael slipped a fraction more of his cock inside her. She seemed surprised by it.

Michael withdrew, giving her time. Marcie smiled, brightly, somehow amused at what she was putting herself through, perhaps feeling taken aback at the level of emotion she was going through. Then she jerked a little, and Cam saw that Michael had slipped the tip of his cock back inside her ass, and slid a touch more length inside her.

Marcie bit her lip, then gasped a little more dramatically as he slid a half-inch more inside her.

'*Uh…*'

Cam could see her raising herself up a little off the coffee table as though ready to do push-ups.

Another gasp, a long moan as Michael eased more of his substantial shaft inside her.

'Hmm…hmmm…'

Marcie brushed a few strands of her hair back behind her ear, over her shoulder, and breathed harder through her pursed lips, giving the full 'ooo' face to the camera as Michael's cock, dripping with lube, gently thrust its top few inches within her ass.

Cam was panting almost as much as Marcie was by now. Was she okay? Was she in pain? Or was she experiencing intense pleasure? It was difficult to read her entirely. She jerked a little more as Michael fed a little more of his length into her, and let out a somewhat startling groan.

'Uhhh…*uhhhh…*'

Another gasp, a cry.

Cam couldn't believe how dramatic this was. He was giving them the benefit of the doubt, but he felt poised, in case he started sensing that she really was in pain, that she really wasn't enjoying this, that she was in some distress. He was ready to grab hold of his phone and order Michael to stop.

But then she brushed her hair back over her shoulder again, and amid pantings, flashed a bright smile at the camera in front of her—and Cam was reassured.

She was enjoying this, then. Perhaps that was too simple a word for this complex experience.

Breathing hard, she pressed her lips together each time Michael entered her, to try to contain her cries—and yet at the same time, she had a clear look of exhilaration on her face as her lover filled more and more of her ass.

Cam heard Michael ask her, 'You okay?'

She nodded. Moaned like she really was enjoying this.

Michael started thrusting a little more into her ass, properly fucking her now, albeit gently, tenderly, going easy on her. She was panting, and groaning, and crying out while trying to keep a lid on her full volume—as though worried she'd wake others in the house while Cam watched her, even though Cam could turn the volume down on the phone if things did get too loud.

'Uhh…. Uh…. Hmmm… uh…'

Michael kept the camera of Marcie's phone directed downward to show her husband his big, glistening dick disappearing into her ass again and again, her pert buttocks either side of her opening, the whole thing looking strange, wrong somehow. And so raw.

Marcie's first-ever time like this.

'Uh… uh… uh…'

Crying, so breathlessly. Was it normally like this? Cam had no real reference to go from. He'd seen anal scenes in pornography, occasionally, but they were all so staged, so fake, making it look as though the man could just grab hold of a woman off a street corner and slot his cock straight inside her ass with no warning, no preparation— and then she would be quietly taking it, looking as though it was as easy as a walk in the park.

Marcie wasn't exactly starting from the ground level, here. Perhaps she'd been a little too ambitious. She could have found someone with a smaller cock for her first lesson in anal sex.

But she seemed to be coping, now, she seemed to be settling. She was still moaning, breathing hard, clamping her mouth shut from time to time as he pushed into her again and again, but she no longer seemed to be in shock, no longer jerked and spasmed with the surprise of him moving inside her.

He started to properly fuck her, and she was smiling a little, when she could. Closing her eyes to take it, panting even harder as he started to pound into her hard enough to make her buttocks quiver.

'Oh… oh… oh my *God*…'

Gasping, moaning, wailing as Michael leaned over her, pressing himself against her back as he piled into her ass again and again. Marcie flushed and shiny with perspiration as the big man fucked her ass for the first ever time.

Cam lost the view from the phone as Michael let it fall to the floor, his focus on fucking her, now—fucking her ass.

At least she was smiling a little more, now. Exhilarated, this experience just taking her breath away. She was in the closing act of the rollercoaster, now—she'd been through some of the worst drops, some of the most ferocious loops, she knew what she was doing, now, she was coping with the barrage, she was braced for the g-forces, she was no longer the downy innocent not sure what she was up against.

And then it was Michael who was panting, gasping and —yes—jerking over her.

Michael, coming in her ass.

And the moment was so powerful, so intense, Cam couldn't stop himself either. He sprayed forth from the middle of the bed, spurting his cream all over the sheets, and only just managing to keep it from splashing over his laptop.

'Oh… oh God… oh wow…'

Had Marcie come as well? It was difficult to tell. She'd sounded as though the experience had been one long orgasm.

Wow.

Cam could hardly believe what he'd just witnessed.

Was that what anal sex was usually like? He felt like he understood it a little more, now. Understood what people might see in it. He smiled—it still wasn't really something he wanted to do himself. But he understood it more than he had.

It had certainly turned him on to watch Marcie doing it with a man who had the experience, who knew what he was doing.

And now Michael leaned in to gently kiss her cheek before picking himself up, gathering his clothes, and heading into the bedroom for his post-coital shower.

Marcie just stayed there for a while, breathing, recovering.

Eventually, she was able to peel herself up off the coffee table, and glance around for the phone Michael had dropped.

'You still there, sweetie?'

'Yeah, I'm here,' he replied into his own phone. 'You okay, honey?'

'Oh, yes,' she said, still out of breath. 'Oh my *God*…'

She smiled as she looked at him through the FaceTime call. Shocked, but exhilarated. Euphoric. Like she'd just climbed a high mountain, and was now being presented with the most incredible view.

'Are you… you need me to…?' she asked.

He gave her a bashful smile, flushing as he shook his head. 'I… I kind of finished, too…'

She grinned. 'You made a mess?'

'Pretty much.'

She giggled, but seemed delighted. Her husband's pleasure was part and parcel of this, for her. Her affair, when it had been a simple affair, had been selfish. But now it was out in the open, it was more selfless than being focused purely on her own desires, her own needs, her own pleasures.

This was for her husband, too.

'Was it… okay?' he asked her.

She grinned again, nodded. 'I… it was just unbelievable. I mean…' She couldn't find the words. She couldn't find the oxygen.

He said, 'But you did… *enjoy* it. I mean, it gave you… pleasure?'

She smiled brightly. 'When it started… it was just *strange*. A little… painful. At first. But I was so turned on already… and after a full day of that thing lodged in my ass… Wow. I mean, it was so *intense*… and he was moving inside me… and…'

She was sitting on the coffee table by now, clutching the phone. She looked so beautiful, her pretty face flushed and glistening with sweat.

'He made you come?'

She looked uncertain, but then, after a beat, nodded. 'Yeah. I mean, it wasn't like normal… it was different. Different places… I never felt anything like it.'

'You'd do it again?'

She grinned. 'Yeah… I would… but maybe not for a while…'

He let her go. There were smiles and blown kisses and professions of love all around, but she started to look tired as the adrenaline faded, and he could tell she was ready to drop.

He wished he could hold her, but at least there would be someone there to do it for him.

The call ended, and he was on his own, and he couldn't wait to see her. It wasn't so long until Thursday would be here again, and then he'd get to have her himself. And now he'd watched her do that with Michael, it only seemed to add to her mystique, to her attraction.

PART III

CHAPTER TWENTY-NINE

THE SUMMER ARRIVED, cold and strangely rainy after the hottest, driest spring. June rolled on, and it became more and more frustrating to be locked inside one's home —even if you had a house, a garden, enough food and Disney Plus to keep the kids entertained.

But Cam had his beautiful wife to keep him motivated.

Her adventures in London. Her returns to the country-side and his own, warm bed.

One Thursday night she brought her handcuffs home with her, back to the house in the Cotswolds.

She was home *really* late, that night. When she phoned the kids just before bedtime, she was still at work. Meetings running late into the evening. Cam knew full well it was because her company was now in the process of filing for bankruptcy—despite applying for government bailout funds, money to cover salaries of staff put on furlough because of the virus, the absence of retail sales was really cutting into the business. Investors were already fleeing.

Cam was worried about her, but she seemed to be taking everything in her stride.

'We have savings that'll cover us for a while,' she'd say.

Or sometimes, 'I'll get another job, as soon as the lock-down ends. With my experience.'

At least she could distract herself from it all with her nightly workouts on Michael's cock—or, when she was home, her nightly workouts on her husband's face.

That particular Thursday night, though, she was home so late that Cam was almost asleep when she arrived back. After her FaceTime call with the kids, it was 8pm and she was still at the office. He made the assumption that she would most probably spend the night at the apartment in London, before making her way back to the Cotswolds and home.

But then it was midnight, and he was stirred from his semi-slumber by the sound of her car pulling up in the driveway outside.

Still sleepy, he hauled himself out of bed and found a t-shirt to put on, in case she needed him to go downstairs to make something for her if she'd not managed to grab anything for dinner. But he was moving so slowly, he didn't get out of the room before she was there in the doorway, looking gorgeous in a little black dress and what he assumed were black, thigh-high stockings.

She didn't even seem tired.

What she did seem was very, very horny.

'Hey,' she said, kissing him briefly on the lips as though tasting him.

'Hey…' he said, breathing her in as he enjoyed her kiss. Her perfume filled his chest, but he couldn't detect the tantalizing hint of sex on her body, or another man on her breath. Had she been unable to see Michael before her journey home? No wonder she was feeling horny…

'I've got something for you,' she said, a twinkle in her big, blue eyes.

'What is it?' He grinned, not expecting anything from her, of course.

She smirked and put her hands over, then behind his head. Then he felt her slipping something over his scalp, positioning it so that it covered his eyes—a blindfold.

'What?' He laughed.

He'd been enjoying their gradual move away from purely vanilla sex since she'd come clean about her affair with Michael, knowing that he had Michael to thank for her gaining the confidence to try new things in the bedroom. But they'd never tried a blindfold.

'Trust me,' she whispered into his ear, and he found even the thought of what she might be up to exhilarating.

He heard her, and to some degree felt her, step past him into the bedroom. Then she grabbed one of his arms and pulled it behind his back—and as he let her do it, he felt her slip something cold and hard around his wrist. Handcuffs. Then, she was taking his other arm back, handcuffing him so that his hands were behind his back.

Kinky.

He heard the bedroom door close, which was something of a relief. But then there were a few moments where he couldn't hear her, couldn't feel her, couldn't smell her perfume—he couldn't tell where she was. It was a little intimidating, though he hung on her command to trust her. After a moment or two, he heard her breathing, and felt her hands on his shackled wrists, pulling on him, encouraging him to take a step back.

'Sit,' she said, and he did as he was told.

He sat, and found that she'd put a little wooden chair behind him—the one she used when she was sitting at her dressing table, putting on her makeup. He had to lift his arms, and put them over the back of the chair so that he could sit on it properly.

Then she was in front of him, he could hear her heavy, excited breathing, and he could smell her perfume. It was a real thrill—it made him wonder why they'd never thought to try using a simple blindfold before. Somehow, depriving him of sight really did seem to boost his other senses—his hearing, smell, touch. What was she planning on doing with him?

His heart was thumping, his entire body fizzing with apprehensive excitement. His cock was thickening rapidly.

He felt her hands on his knees, then on his thighs, and the smell of her perfume intensified as she came close, leaning forward over him so that her face closed in on his.

'You sit there, and don't move unless I let you,' she said, so close to him that he could feel the heat radiating from her face.

'Yes, my darling.'

Now he felt her straddle his thighs, standing so that his face pressed up against her stomach, her breasts jammed against the top of his head, albeit contained within her dress. Then she sat on his lap, and he felt her weight on his thighs, the heat of her body pressing at the bulge in his pants.

'Mmm…' she moaned quietly, pleased to see how hard he was for her already.

He felt her hands encircle his head, her fingers combing through his hair, and then she was pulling his head to her chest, so that his face was buried between her breasts, so that he felt the smooth, soft skin of her cleavage just above the low neckline of her dress.

He kissed her there, and breathed deeply, trying to detect any hint that she'd recently been with another man.

Had she fucked Michael before coming home from London? She was so late, there might have been time.

'You trust me?' She asked him, releasing him from her

cleavage, though her hands now clutched his head firm, keeping him exactly where she wanted him.

'Yes, my sweet,' he said.

'Good,' she replied, and he could tell from her tone that she was smiling, enjoying the power she had over him.

He felt her face come close to his again, and though her hands fell away from his head, she remained there, close. He felt the tip of her nose gently touch the tip of his. He felt her fingers gently touch his chin, his lips, examining him. Then he felt her tongue on his mouth, licking his lips, wet and warm.

'Mmm…' she moaned, pressing herself down against his hardness, rocking her hips gently to stir herself against it.

Was she wearing stockings? He could hear the sound of the nylon rubbing against his sweatpants as she ground herself on his erection. It was like he had Spidey senses.

'Do you like this?' She said, almost purring. 'Do you like being in my complete control?'

'Yes, my darling.'

'Oh yes, you certainly do,' she said, pressing down on his hard cock almost to prove how much he liked her dominance.

She licked his lips again, and it felt so dirty, her tongue on his mouth like that.

'Now, you're going to be a good boy and sit there for me,' she said, embracing him, her cheek sliding against his so she could talk into his ear. 'You're not going to move until I tell you that you can. No matter what happens. You clear?'

'I'm clear.'

Now she pulled away, off his lap. It actually felt cold, once she was away.

But then he felt something press against the bulge in his

sweatpants, and stroke him there. It was her face. Her mouth. She was kneeling on the floor between his legs, exploring his bulge with her lips.

'Mmm…. You're so hard for me…' she breathed, and he felt her pull up his t-shirt, and then her lips on his bare stomach, kissing her way up. She pulled his t-shirt up over his head, though she didn't try to take it off him, since he was handcuffed. The t-shirt remained there, along the back of his shoulders, feeling like it was also being used to tie him to the chair.

He felt her fondling his chest, kissing him there. He felt the tip of her tongue flick around his nipples.

Then she was up, kissing his mouth again, licking his lips like she owned him, like she could do whatever she wanted with him, like he was her toy. Well, that was true enough.

'I have a surprise for you,' she said, her mouth close to his ear again so that he could feel his breath on his skin there.

'What is it?' He asked her, feeling a little uncertain for the first time, since he'd thought when she said she had something for him that she'd been referring to the blindfold, or if not the blindfold then the handcuffs and the chair.

She laughed softly, like a Bond villain holding 007 captive and about to reveal her full masterplan for taking over the world. 'You have to promise to be a good boy,' she said.

'I promise,' he said.

'You have to promise to be a good boy and not move from this chair. No matter what happens.'

He wasn't sure about that part.

Jesus.

He remembered watching some of the encounters

between Marcie and Michael. Some of the kinkier occasions. When the handcuffs had been involved, that dog
collar, the leash. The Basic Instinct re-enactment, when
Michael had had anal sex with Marcie again, only this
time as she pretended to be Jeannie Tripplehorn taken over
a sofa.

Michael liked to dominate Marcie in London, and
when she got home Marcie liked to dominate Cam.

Now he was suddenly nervous that Marcie had it in her
head that her husband might like it if she took *him* anally.
Some kind of scary strap-on. Now Cam was getting very,
very nervous.

He liked it when Marcie was dominant. But he did not
want her to violate him. Not in that way.

'Promise,' she demanded.

He felt no option but to reply, quietly, 'I promise.'

Nervous, he told himself she wouldn't have had him sit
on a chair if she was planning on fucking him with a strap-
on. He told himself that if she'd wanted to do that, she
would have had him lie on the bed, probably on his front,
giving her full access to his rear.

He breathed, trying to keep calm.

She loved him, didn't she? She wouldn't do something
to cause him pain.

Oh, but she had *cheated* on him. In the beginning.

Even so. This was the age of #MeToo. Surely she
wouldn't do *that* sort of thing without his explicit
consent?

Her hand gently swept down his face, down his chest,
as though it was a signal to tell him that he'd done well, he
was a good boy for doing as he was supposed to do. He
heard her kneeling down again between his thighs. Those
Spidey senses again—it was crazy, he almost came to forget
that he couldn't see a thing. His other senses compensated.

He could almost follow everything Marcie was up to, so long as she stayed close to him.

Her hands went to the waistband of his sweatpants. She pulled them down, and he lifted his hips on that chair so that she could pull them off him.

She surprised him a little, then, by shoving her face back between his legs, clamping his stiff shaft in her mouth, though it was covered by the cotton of his boxer shorts. She stroked him, she fondled his hardness, exploring the fullness of his member through his underwear as though teasing herself with how hard he was.

'So hard…' she whispered. 'I love it…'

Then she pulled on his boxer shorts, yanked the material so that his erection sprang free.

He felt her hot breath on the sensitive flesh of his manhood, he could tell she was right there, close, staring at it, gazing at it, examining it. A moment or two later, it was in her mouth, her lips stretched around it, enveloping it in the hot wetness that felt just exquisite.

Was this the surprise she had for him? A blowjob?

But she wasn't giving him a blowjob. She wasn't sucking on him, she wasn't fucking him with her mouth. She was touching him, she was feeling him, she was fondling him, she was squeezing him, but it was for her benefit. She kissed him there, licked him, she tasted him, but she wasn't trying to make him feel good—she was savoring him, she was experiencing him, she was enjoying how hard he was for her.

She was teasing him.

She even gently bit his shaft, scraped her teeth along it, tested how stiff he was by clamping him tight in her vice-like jaws.

She grabbed hold of him, and she pumped his shaft a few times—but she wasn't trying to get him off. She turned around and pressed his hard cock between her buttocks, like a stripper giving him a lap dance. But she wasn't pleasuring him, she was taking pleasure from him.

She was having her fun with him, and making sure he was hard.

Then she was on her feet again, leaning over him, kissing him so that he could taste his own dick on her lips for a moment or two. She broke away from the kiss to murmur in his ear: 'Remember that I love you. Only you. Remember that.'

And then she was gone, and he felt cold because the heat of her body was no longer there.

One-one-thousand.

Two-one-thousand.

Three-one-thousand.

Where was she?

What was she doing?

He sat there, waiting patiently, his arms shackled behind his back, his underwear yanked down so that his hard cock stood up proud, waggling in the air-conditioned air.

He was getting nervous again.

Telling himself she was just teasing him, she was probably lying on the bed, touching herself, getting off on her sense of power, because her husband was tied to a chair, doing exactly as she told him to do, waiting for her to do whatever she wanted with him.

She wasn't putting on a strap-on, he told himself. She wasn't going to fuck him in the ass.

Ten-one-thousand.

Eleven-one-thousand.

Twelve-one-thousand.

CHAPTER THIRTY

DARKNESS.

Silence.

Then he heard the bedroom door open. Was she leaving the room?

Now he was getting a little frustrated. He'd been enjoying Marcie's take-charge attitude in the bedroom, he'd been enjoying the feeling of letting go and just worshipping her like some kind of besotted fan, adoring her new sexy persona of sin and infidelity. He loved that she could bring him into the bedroom and tell him exactly what she wanted him to do to give her pleasure—no more guessing, no more trying to work out the signals.

But he wasn't the kind of guy who really went for the full humiliating horror of the dominatrix thing.

He didn't want her to belittle him, degrade him, embarrass him. He didn't want her to make him suffer, not in the true sense of the word. You type 'dominatrix' into Pornhub, and you get all kinds of scary stuff. The gimp masks, the torture, the pegging, the verbal abuse. A man could enjoy a powerful, independent woman without all that nonsense. A man could appreciate a promiscuous, self-confident wife without all that kitschy absurdity.

Now he was worried that she had the wrong idea of what got him going. That she'd tied him up and blindfolded him, and now she was going to leave him like this for a long while, believing he'd enjoy the hardship.

He sighed, but the frustration was getting to him. It suddenly felt uncomfortable, sitting there with his hands cuffed behind his back. He could just about get off the chair, he'd be able to lie on the bed to wait for her, but he wasn't going to be able to get out of those cuffs, and he was no gymnast capable of contorting his body to get his hands in front of him so that he could use them for anything.

He was thinking, maybe he'd even call out for her. To hell with the fact that everyone else in the house was asleep. This was unacceptable.

He wondered if she might be using the bathroom. Maybe it was worth waiting a few minutes, just in case she was indisposed.

Then he heard something that froze him in his seat. Soft footsteps on carpet, and Marcie's quiet voice, saying brightly, 'Yeah.'

A little giggle.

Was she on the phone? Had she called Michael, to make her boyfriend watch her tease and humiliate her bound husband? Cam recoiled in horror at such a thought.

The door closed. Cam tensed up.

Little footsteps coming into the bedroom, along with the very soft sounds of breathing. The bedroom door closed. He could smell her perfume now, faint, but there again. He could tell she was there. His Spidey senses were jangling. His manhood thickening, despite his fear.

Another little giggle, almost imperceptible. Not for his benefit. Flirty, girly. The kind of giggle she'd make for a guy she was dating, not for a husband she'd been with for ten years.

He wondered if she was simply going to have some kind of phone sex with Michael in front of him, while Cam was bound to the chair and forced to listen. That would be okay. That would be kind of sexy, actually. So long as she didn't feel the need to humiliate Cam by showing Michael how he was all tied up, with his cock exposed, helpless before her.

But then Cam froze again, caught his breath.

He heard a wet sound, and a soft little moan, and some more wet sounds that could not be mistaken for anything else whatsoever.

Two people kissing.

Cam's thoughts started racing. At first, he scratched for the least shocking explanation for these sounds. Was Marcie watching pornography on her phone, or on her laptop, while she made herself comfortable on the bed, to masturbate in front of her husband? She wasn't on the bed yet, he could hear that. But was she preparing to bring herself off while watching porn?

But the sounds were too real. Too three-dimensional.

Not coming from a phone, or a laptop.

After a moment or two, Cam was certain she couldn't even be FaceTiming with Michael.

He could smell something more than just Marcie's date perfume. He could detect the disturbing, woody sweetness of a man's cologne in the air.

She was quietly moaning and gently kissing a man in the bedroom, right there in front of her blindfolded husband.

Was it Michael? It had to be.

Cam was shocked.

And yet his cock had never been harder.

There were a few little quiet moans from a guy, and Cam was certain that Marcie had, somehow, brought Michael back with her from London. He felt himself blushing fiercely, brutally embarrassed that another man was there in the bedroom, while he was blindfolded and cuffed on his chair.

He heard Marcie break off from a kiss and murmur softly, 'I've been waiting for this all night.'

They were breathing deeply now, as they kissed. It wasn't subtle anymore. There were tongues involved, they were truly sucking face. Cam could hear the silky sounds of hands sweeping all over naked bodies. Had they taken off their clothes?

Marcie sighed, and mewed, and moaned flirtatiously, 'Oh my God…' and Cam heard Michael chuckle quietly.

Cam's Spidey senses were working on overdrive. He could sense that she'd got her hands on the man's huge cock, and she was just loving how big, and how hard it was for her. She was moaning, kissing him, but now her husband could detect the quiet repetitive beat of her hand stroking her boyfriend's mighty cock.

Cam had his ears pricked. He could take in and analyze the most subtle sounds in this room. He surprised himself by how aware he was able to be of what was going on. He heard their quiet moans and deep breathing shift, and the mattress quietly creak, and he could tell that Michael was sitting down on the end of the bed, with Marcie kneeling down in front of him.

He heard Marcie's breathing change as she licked the man's cock, just a few feet away from her bound husband.

He heard the wet sounds of her stretching her lips around his tip, taking his cock inside her mouth. The sounds of her bobbing down, and up, and down again on his shaft, moaning in her contentment at doing this here, right in front of Cam.

Michael's deep voice, quietly in awe: 'Fuck, that's good…'

After a few moments, there was no subtlety to it. Marcie was even doing it louder than normal, exaggerating her performance so she could be sure her husband could garner every possible detail from listening to them. Cam knew how she sounded when she went down on him, and recently he'd come to know how she sounded when she went down on Michael—this was an enhanced presentation, for the benefit of the audience.

She said, 'It's so fucking big, I love it,' and Michael chuckled again quietly.

Cam couldn't believe this was happening.

His wife was having sex with another man, right in front of him.

How had she got him here from London? This was breaking all kinds of lockdown rules. And what if Flo, or even worse, one of the children, had seen her sneaking him into the house?

Jesus.

She had her hands around the base of his big, fat dick.

She had his cock wedged in her mouth.

She was panting and moaning and sucking and licking and rubbing that huge cock all over her pretty face.

Cam heard the mattress creak again, sensed that Michael was moving—standing up? But Marcie was still there. Her moans were more like gasps, her rhythm slower but more deliberate. Michael was standing up and holding her head, fucking her face. The alpha male taking what he wanted from her.

Then Marcie confirmed it, saying, 'I love it when you fuck my mouth…'

Michael saying, 'Fuck, yeah...' as he did so, driving that huge thing into her mouth.

Cam breathing deeply as he heard it, his hardness throbbing, his sense of shame and humiliation evaporating. Michael sounded as though he hardly even knew that Cam was there. Ignoring him as he fucked his wife's face. Certainly, he was way past amusement at her husband being there, half-naked, shackled to a chair.

They were way past the point of being self-conscious about Cam being there while Marcie had sex with Michael.

Cam's main wish, now, was that his hands were free so he could touch himself while he heard Marcie fucking her boyfriend. It was even more of a priority desire for him than being able to actually see them fucking.

After all, his Spidey senses were getting better all the time.

He heard it when Michael stopped fucking her face, and she stood up. When they were kissing each other again, mouth-to-mouth, and she was squeezing and stroking his stiff cock in one hand.

He heard it when Michael shoved her onto the bed, and playfully slapped her buttock as she got on all fours.

He heard it when Michael bent down over the end of the bed, tugged aside her panties, and tasted her soaking pussy. Marcie's deepening breath, her sighs quickly turning to panting again, as the man ate her out from behind.

Her breathless, 'Oh my God...' and her whimpering moans as he clamped his mouth over her sex and sucked on her slippery folds. Her little breathy cries, her 'God that feels so *good*...'

Cam sat there and shivered as he smelled his wife's arousal in the air, and knew that she wasn't faking anything, although she was certainly playing up her audible responses for the excitement of the captive audience. Gasping cries as he took her with his mouth, making her husband intensely envious.

'Oh my God…'

Signaling what was going on so that Cam could have no doubt.

'Oh yes… I'm ready for that cock… please… that big, fucking cock…'

The sound of Michael getting up, kneeling on the bed, lining himself up behind Marcie made him tremble. Was he really going to fuck her, right there on the bed, right there in front of Cam, just a few feet away?

This was just incredible.

And sure enough, there was a high-pitched little groan from Marcie, and the quiet—but audible—sound of Michael stroking the tip of his cock against the wet lips of her pussy.

Jesus.

'Oh… oh… *oh*…'

The rising pitch of Marcie's little cries signaling to her husband that Michael was entering her pussy, and filling her inch by inch.

'Oh God, your cock is so huge,' she said, as though Cam couldn't tell that already. 'It's so fucking *thick*.'

Michael groaning, almost growling as he began to slowly stir his manhood inside her, murmuring, 'You're so tight…'

Marcie's cries, her panting, her whimpers giving her husband full coverage of that big dick squeezing inside her, Michael beginning to pump his hips, to thrust that thing into her. And as his pace accelerated, underneath her breathless panting, Cam was beginning to hear the unmistakable wet sounds of the man's cock sliding into and out of her sex.

'My pussy's so *wet*,' she said, providing a commentary for her husband.

Michael just moaning as he thrust into her again and again.

Then for the first time, Cam was shocked as Marcie spoke directly to him, saying, 'His cock is so big, honey. He's really stretching my pussy as he's fucking me…'

Cam nearly came, right there and then, without even touching himself.

Michael didn't seem bothered that she was talking to her husband while he fucked her.

'Oh God… can you hear him fucking me, honey? Can you hear that thing squeezing into me?'

But then he was upping his game, and her cries became louder, and shriller, to the point where Cam was worried that it might wake others in the household. After a moment or two, she seemed to remember that, too, and put a dampener on her decibels—but she was still moaning intensely, and Michael was gearing up until he was really pounding her, Cam hearing the impact of his body each time it collided with Marcie's rear end.

Michael moaning, Marcie hyperventilating as he slammed into her again and again and again, drilling her like a jackhammer.

After a few moments, she seemed to collapse on the bed, she must have been lying stretched out on her front, from the sound of it, but Michael was still on top of her, pounding away as she gasped and cried beneath him.

'Oh my God… oh my God…'

And then the storm seemed to suddenly break, the pounding slowed dramatically, their moans turned quiet, low, as the energy levels suddenly dropped. He was just sliding that thing leisurely into and out of her for a few moments, letting them both get their breaths back, and to keep himself from hitting orgasm too soon.

Cam heard them disengage, and at least one of them climb off the bed.

He detected a stronger waft of his wife's perfume—and, he was sure he wasn't imagining it, but her arousal, too.

Then she said, 'Are you having fun, honey?' And she was suddenly very close to him, making him jump.

'Uh-huh,' he said.

He heard the sound of something sliding down her body—the snap of elastic and the movement of the sound confirming that she was standing in front of him and pulling down her panties.

Getting closer to him again, she said, 'He's making me so wet, fucking me with that big cock…'

She kissed her husband on the lips, briefly, then she said, 'Here, see how wet he makes me…'

He felt something on his cheek. He smelled the strong scent of her arousal, the smell of sex. She moved whatever it was she was pressing to his cheek, and he realized it was her panties. She was caressing his face, his jaw, his chin, his cheeks, his lips, his nose with her sodden underwear.

It was absolutely drenched.

She held it to his nose and the scent was almost overwhelming.

The smell of adultery.

The smell of his beautiful, golden-haired wife fucking another man right there in front of him.

She slowly spread her wetness over his face, and then she giggled, and spread her wetness all over his stiff cock.

Then she kissed her husband's forehead and leaned in to whisper in his ear, 'Now he's going to make me come again with that big, beautiful cock.'

CHAPTER THIRTY-ONE

AT THE END OF IT, Cam heard them murmuring to each other as they lay on the bed, and though he'd just heard another man making his wife come like crazy right in front of him, he found that his paranoia wasn't yet done feeding him fear.

What if they lay there together, whispering sweet nothings to each other as they recovered from their energetic sex—and they drifted off to sleep, forgetting that Cam was still there, handcuffed to the chair?

Well, actually, he wasn't handcuffed *to* the chair. He would be able to get up from the chair, just about. He might even be able to stagger down to the living room and collapse on the couch, although it would be difficult with his pants and underwear around his ankles, and he'd have to pray that neither Flo nor the kids would need to go downstairs for a drink in the middle of the night.

But even then, he'd still have his hands cuffed behind his back.

He really didn't like the thought of having to wake

Marcie up later, to help him get the cuffs off if she went to sleep.

They were lying there, murmuring whatever. Marcie even giggling a little, quietly. Sounding very, very content. Satisfied. Then there was movement, the mattress creaking a little as one, or both, of them clambered off. Cam felt relief, feeling certain that she would free him soon.

Then, there she was. Her voice, suddenly close: 'You okay, honey?'

'Good,' he chirped up, his voice dry, cracked.

She kissed his mouth, and at first he was surprised, and somewhat overwhelmed by the contact. His senses were suddenly saturated by her—her warm, sweet-and-salty lips crushing against his, the heat of her face as she pressed it against his, and that heavy, dark, earthy scent of sex that surrounded her, making him tremble as he breathed it in. And then she slipped off his blindfold, and he was startled by the bright light flooding his eyes, even though when he grew accustomed to it, he saw that it wasn't all that bright in there at all, with just the bedside lamps on.

Here she was, leaning over him, now wearing a white tank top, a pair of tight, blue gym shorts, though her body was still flushed from the effort of so much sex, and her skin still shiny with perspiration, her golden hair hanging damp around her pretty face, framing her dazzling smile.

Michael was nowhere to be seen. Cam was a little relieved about that, although the guy had been there for quite a while to see him sitting, exposed, in the chair while he fucked Marcie. He wasn't feeling particularly rational just now. More emotional.

'Did you enjoy your surprise?' She asked him, as she now moved around him, behind him, so she could unlock his handcuffs.

'God…' he breathed, then, 'Yeah…'

She giggled. He felt her hands fiddling with the cuffs around his wrist. Then there was a click, and one wrist was free.

'I don't think Michael would have a problem with you watching us,' she said. 'But I thought it would be so hot, if you couldn't see what was happening, this first time.'

Click, his other wrist was free. He pulled off the t-shirt that had been half off already, and brought his hands around in front of him, wincing at the aches in his muscles, particularly around his shoulders. Nursed the parts of his wrist where the cuffs had pulled at his flesh.

'What's he doing here?' he asked her.

She perched on the corner of the bed, just in front of him. Giving him a little space, it seemed, to get his head around what had just happened.

'I thought it would be fun,' she said. 'Sneaking him here for a night.'

He grinned, 'Well, you were right. Where is he now?'

'Downstairs, having a bite to eat. He said he can sleep on the couch tonight.'

'What if someone sees him?'

She shrugged, 'Flo's fast asleep. The kids, too.'

He nodded. Chances were small that anyone would venture downstairs at this time of night.

'And in the morning?'

'I can drop him at the station for the first train, before anyone gets up.'

She raised a knee onto the mattress beside her, and started gently stroking herself through her gym shorts. Was she still horny? He hoped so.

She said, a touch melancholy, 'I don't think I'll get to see Michael for too much longer.'

'Really?'

She smiled regretfully. 'We filed for bankruptcy,'

He nodded, knowing it had been coming.

'Everyone's been given notice—the company's being wound up,' she said, slipping her hands under her thighs as she explained. 'I don't need to go into London for work anymore. Not unless I somehow luck out on another job.'

Cam asked her, 'So we'll give notice on the flat?'

She nodded. This had always been the plan, if her job finally dried up with the coronavirus. They had a good amount of savings, and Cam had a little income coming in from his freelance work, but there was no way they could keep renting a flat in London if Marcie was no longer in employment.

'Michael can stay there during the notice period,' she said. 'But then he's going to go up north—he has an aunt up there. Newcastle, I think. He has a couple of interviews, a second interview. He'll probably get something around there, then he can get a place of his own again.'

Cam nodded. 'It'll be a shame to see him go. He seems like a nice guy.'

Funny to talk of his wife's boyfriend like that. How sad was she? Had she been developing feelings for him?

But she shrugged, said, 'Yeah, he is a nice guy. We'll stay in touch. You know. Maybe I'll visit Newcastle sometime.'

Cam smiled. Always good to have options.

Marcie stood up, stepped over to him again, and leaned down to kiss him. This time, he kissed her back more fully, sucking on her lips, delving into her mouth with his tongue, as she delved into his with hers. Tasting the other man on her, so fresh, the realization that she'd been sucking on his cock with these lips, this tongue, making him feel more than a little strange, but adding to the thrill.

'Why don't you go run us a nice, hot bath?' she said to

him quietly, her hand dropping down to find that his manhood was still stiff as a board.

'Sure.'

'I have to go make sure Michael has everything he needs downstairs.'

'Don't be too long,' he said, and she blew him a kiss before she disappeared out into the hallway.

When he slipped into the gloriously hot water, he was still hard. His wife's infidelity was like the strongest hit of Viagra. He'd never been able to get, never mind sustain, erections like this before discovering her wicked secret.

The heat of the water felt good, particularly as it reached his aching muscles. He breathed in the calming lavender of the bath oil, and tried to relax.

Where was she?

Perhaps she'd been tempted into a little more than just making sure Michael had the blankets and pillows he needed to spend the night on the couch.

He lay back, breathed deeply, relaxed.

He started touching himself under the water, gently, stroking the big piece of meat between his thighs. She hadn't let him, but then she'd given him the impression she would be back right away, so he felt like being a little disobedient.

He imagined her with Michael in the living room, kissing him. Feeling the man's big cock thickening up again. Maybe dropping to her knees in front of him…

'You still in the bath?'

He heard her voice, and let go of his cock.

She entered the bathroom, and he was just stunned at how beautiful she was.

'Sorry, I got talking with him, and then… well, let's just say his recovery time is quite *extraordinary*…'

She stepped in front of the bath, and he could see she was loving the expression on his face, the reaction to knowing she'd just gone and had another quickie with her lover before coming back to him.

'I hope you're not too tired…' she said, doing a sexy little dance in front of him to flaunt herself—stirring her hips, dragging the hem of her tank top upward to reveal her taut stomach, and a little of her breasts.

'Uh… no…' he said, transfixed.

'We could always wait until morning…' she teased, showing him her bare breasts, fondling them with her top shoved up to her armpits.

'Can *you* wait until morning?' he asked her.

'No,' she admitted with a grin, and made him think she was going to peel off her tank top completely—only to slip it back down, to cover up her breasts.

'You're only half done, aren't you?' He said, laughing. 'Even though you just had sex with him *again*, and you've come what, three times tonight?'

She turned around, still moving like she was dancing for him, a stripper in a gentleman's club. Peeled down her gym shorts to reveal her gorgeous ass, covered by the tiniest little white thong.

'I need my honey,' she said, beaming as she stepped out of her gym shorts, and then turned to face him, taking his breath away as she toyed with the string-like waistband of her thong, stretching it, making it seem like she was deciding whether or not to take it off.

'You're *still* horny,' he chuckled.

'Well, that's your fault,' she said, reaching up to brush her hair back out of her face—and then deciding to tie it up into a ponytail with the hairband that was on her wrist. 'Sitting there with that big hard-on the whole time I was with Michael…'

She lifted one leg, slipped a foot up onto the edge of the bath. He could see that her panties were already wet, the moisture turning the white material semi-translucent so that he could see a hint of her pussy through it.

'And that was *your* fault,' he said, making her smile as she climbed into the bath, standing over him still wearing that white tank top and her thong.

'I hope we're not going to argue about who's at fault,' she joked, being careful not to slip as she put her feet between his thighs, enjoying the look on his face as he sat up and put his hands on her hips, amazed at the sight of her.

He slid his hand up her stomach, feeling the clammy sheen on her skin from her recent sexual encounter, breathing in the strong scent of sex from between her legs, just enthralled with her.

Was there something wrong with him, being so turned on by her infidelity?

Was he genuinely going crazy because of lockdown, because of being cooped up in the cottage with the kids and his mother-in-law so long?

He didn't care. He was only led by his feelings. He craved her, and her adultery was driving his craving, so he was going to embrace it. She was his wife, and he adored her. She was his goddess, and he worshipped her.

He was just stunned by her beauty, and it was her infidelity that had opened his eyes to that.

'Are you going to let me take a bath first?' she said

quietly, as he held her hips in his hands, and nudged his face up against the damp, little triangle of white cotton covering her pussy, inhaling the wicked aroma of sex.

'You do as you want,' he said, gazing up her sensational body. 'Isn't that the deal?'

She smiled, but she still stood there, over him. Letting him indulge in the sight of her, the feel of her body as he swept his hands all over her.

Letting him slip her thong aside so that he could kiss her between her legs.

Letting him slide the tip of his tongue inside her, grinding his face against her clit.

Letting him caress her smooth stomach as he sucked on her unfaithful pussy.

She moaned and ran her hands through his long-uncut hair as he worshipped her with his mouth.

'Can you smell him on me?' She asked him, as he gently sucked on her clit, breathing so deeply he was in danger of hyperventilating.

'Mmm…' he said, or moaned, and she shivered from the vibrations of his deep voice as he pressed his mouth against her sensitive little button.

He loved the sweet sounds of her responding to his mouth, little gasps and sighs, the silent, silky song of her breathing as she gazed down upon him, her hands pushing up her tank top to stroke and squeeze her bare breasts. He loved how it became too intense for her to leave it up to him, so that she ended up taking hold of his head in her hands, carefully thrusting her hips to graze her soaking pussy over his face.

Her cheating pussy.

She'd taken another man here, just moments before.

Cam was intoxicated with her.

But she wasn't just going to use his face. She took his

hands from her hips, urged him up, out of the water, so he was standing with her, her eyes gazing down at his ridiculously stiff cock, just enchanted at how hard he was for her.

'I get the idea you don't want me to clean off at all,' she grinned, kissing him breathlessly as they stood there.

'What would be the point?' he laughed, kissing her back, indulging in the wrongness of how her lips tasted, so soon after she'd been with another man.

'I never knew you were so kinky,' she joked.

'I never knew you were such a bad girl,' he responded, making her smirk.

He peeled off her tank top, and she helped him pull it up over her head. And then he luxuriated in the feel of his hands over her bare chest, feeling the stickiness over her smooth skin, taking in the crazy, sexy thought that another man had sprayed his thick come all over her, just before she'd returned to him.

She slipped off her panties, but then she surprised him by stepping out of the bath. She turned back only to curl one hand around his stiff cock, and give him come hither eyes. He climbed out of the bath, too, and then her hand was back on his manhood, squeezing him, directing him. She led him by the cock out into the bedroom, giggling at being able to use his manhood as some kind of leash.

But then she climbed onto the bed, and he climbed onto her, lying between her legs, pressing his hard cock against her well-used pussy, kissing her mouth, her cheek, her neck, sliding down her body to kiss and lick his way over her chest, her breasts, her stomach, taking in the enormity of her adultery until he was feasting ravenously on her pussy again, completely addicted.

'Are you going to fuck me?' she said softly, making herself clear. It wasn't really a request.

'Of course,' he said, moving back up her body, to kiss her mouth.

'You have to make me yours again, don't you?' She smiled.

He knelt up, and planted a hand upon one of her splayed thighs. He directed the tip of his cock to her rosy-red, glistening pussy lips, and dipped it inside. She was so wet, he just glided inside her.

She gasped as he entered her, and it struck him that she was reacting to having two different cocks inside her sex in the space of just a matter of minutes.

His had been bigger, maybe. But she only got the experience of having a second cock inside her now that her husband was penetrating her.

He thrust into her, her pussy still tight around him, despite being stretched by another man. She was so wet, he was able to slide fully into her, at the first attempt. She groaned, long and low, closed her eyes and turned her head to the side as he filled her up. Then she was breathing deep and hard as he began to thrust into her.

It wasn't exactly the powerful pounding she'd gotten from Michael. But she seemed to respond to it, taking pleasure from it in a different way. She'd had her raw meat, her massive chunk of rare steak—and now she was enjoying a glass of aged Bordeaux afterward, just as pleasurable, but different. And combining well.

After a while, she turned onto all fours, and had him fuck her from behind. It was never going to be as dramatic as her adventures with Michael, and yet she gripped the mattress and he thrust into her, and she wasn't faking anything.

But she didn't come until she was on top of him, straddling his hips, taking control and riding him like a rodeo bull. She could direct his cock inside her to exactly where she needed it to be. He held onto her hips and she held onto his knees, and he had a magnificent view of his cock disappearing into her exquisite pussy again and again until she hit her peak, leaned forward, and collapsed onto him, taking his head between both her hands, kissing him hard on the mouth as her entire body shook like somebody had jabbed a jump wire to her hips and connected her up to a car battery.

When she eventually came up for air, there was a look of surprise on her face.

'You didn't come?' She said, confused that he hadn't taken the plunge with her.

He replied, 'You didn't tell me I could.'

She smiled, laughed, and pulled herself back from him. 'Okay…' she said, moving down to kneel between his legs, taking his slick cock in her hands. 'You can come now. Come in my mouth.'

Then she was licking him, sucking gently on his balls. Holding her fair hair back out of her face as she dragged her tongue up the full length of his shaft. Taking his manhood inside her gloriously hot mouth, even if it was slick with her own wetness. Grabbing his hardness in her hand and pumping him until there was no way he could hold back.

He came in her mouth, he came on her face. She played with him as it spurted out of him, reveling in her ability to make him come, indulging in the unmistakable proof that she had made him feel sensational. This ordinarily prim and clean and ultra-tidy wife smearing his cream over her cheeks, her forehead, giggling at her wickedness, amused at her naughtiness, energized by having two lovers under the same roof, making love to two men in the same night.

Making two men come within the same hour.

CHAPTER THIRTY-TWO

IN THE MORNING, Cam awoke to the sound of the bedroom door closing. When he first opened his eyes, he was surprised to see Marcie's side of the bed empty.

But then he felt the mattress move, and he breathed in a fresh hit of her perfume, and then Marcie was lying beside him, spooning up against him, putting her arms round him, lodging her chin over his shoulder so she could murmur in his ear.

'Morning my sweet!'

'Hmmm?' he was still sleepy, but the feeling of her naked body pressing up against his back was enough to rouse him.

'We got away with it,' she whispered, sounding triumphant.

'We got away with it?'

'I just drove Michael to the station. And the kids aren't awake yet.'

'Hmm…'

She appeared to be moving her hips—circling them. Slowly humping his hip, in fact. Was she horny again? He turned a little more toward her, so that he was lying on his back. Her hand swept over his stomach, and down between his legs, seeking out his thickening cock.

'What are you doing…?' he said, his voice slow and languid with remaining drowsiness.

'What do you think I'm doing?' He could hear the amusement in her voice as her fingers curled around his stiff shaft, and started to pump it.

'Aren't you tired?'

She giggled. 'I told you. I already took Michael to the station. And now I'm back.'

She nuzzled into his cheek, kissed him, continuing to dry-hump his side as she jacked his cock. He took a long, deep breath, inhaling in her scent. Was he imagining it, or did she have a faint hint of Michael about her.

'You just woke up and took him to the station?' He asked her.

'I might have let him fuck me, just before we left,' she whispered into his ear. Then she giggled as she felt his cock throbbing in her hands.

'What?'

She grinned. 'We got there a little early. He'd only have had to wait on the platform.'

He turned his head so he could look in her eyes. 'He fucked you at the station?'

She shrugged. 'There wasn't anyone else around. I told you—it's still early.'

She enjoyed shocking him. And actually, he enjoyed being shocked. She kissed his cheek again, and then picked herself up, climbed onto him, straddling his chest.

'I take it you enjoyed it,' he said, gazing up at her. A glance downward told him she was still wearing panties— pink and gray, fairy ordinary cotton, but in a sexy, girly, Victoria's Secret kind of way.

'Uh-huh,' she said, beaming from ear-to-ear.

'So what did he do?'

She leaned down, lowering her breasts to his face, stroking them over his mouth, his nose. Her skin was so soft, so smooth.

She said, 'We parked, and got out of the car, and I told him how early we were. So he came around to my side of the car, and…'

'You did it in the parking lot?'

She giggled as he took one of her nipples in his mouth. 'I know, I should have taken you with me. You could have watched. But you were sleeping…'

He wasn't actually annoyed he'd missed it. It was hot enough that it had happened at all, and that she'd come straight back here to tell him about it, still horny as a vixen.

'So he just… fucked you?'

'We were making out a little,' she said, sitting up on his chest, gazing down at him, looking just stunning, her pert breasts poised, her stiff nipples jutting out. 'Then he had his hand up my skirt…'

'You wore a skirt to take him to the station?' he said, dryly.

'I did,' she laughed.

'And then?'

'He lifted up one of my legs, pressed me up against the car… and slid inside me.'

'Wow.'

But that was all Cam could say. Marcie lifted one knee over his shoulder, and then the other, and then she was kneeling directly over his face—and he was stunned into silence, gazing up her gorgeous body, her drenched panties less than an inch above his mouth.

The scent of sex was unmistakable, and strong.

She pressed herself down, and he dutifully opened his mouth, letting her grind herself against him, teasing him with the fresh evidence of her latest infidelity. He tasted her through her panties, he breathed in that intoxicating scent. He let her smear her wetness all over his face. She lifted off, briefly, to remove her panties, and then she was freely making use of his willing mouth. Pumping her hips as she rode his face, taking hold of his hands with hers as she used his lips and his tongue to make herself come.

After she came on top of him, she turned around, and fed him some more of her well-used pussy while she took his cock in her hands again, and then in her mouth.

There wasn't a lot of time available in the mornings, before the kids woke up and needed breakfast. But there was time enough for her to make him come, sliding his hardness into her pussy to ride him cowgirl-style, until he was unable to hold back, exploding inside her as he used a pillow to stifle his moans.

There was time enough to take a shower together, too.

A wonderful start to the day.

THE FOLLOWING WEEKEND, they hired a small van and drove it down to London to collect their things from the apartment. Flo was happy to take care of the children in their absence—it was the weekend, so they weren't expected to do any schoolwork.

They were actually in good spirits, bombing down the M40 at just about the speed limit. Marcie might have lost her job, but there would be something else down the line. She might, also, have lost her lover—but there again, they had the distinct feeling that someone else would come along.

Cam liked the idea that his beautiful wife would start dating again, albeit discreetly.

Things were changing. Shaking up the old routines. There was a sense of adventure in the air. And, to top it all, they had a full day and a night without having to worry about taking care of the children—that had a very liberating effect on them both.

That afternoon, they made a start on packing up all their things. Thankfully, there wasn't a huge amount to pack up. The place had been rented as a furnished apartment, so Michael would be able to sleep on a bed during his remaining days in the capital.

In the evening, they had dinner with Michael—a nice, leisurely meal of Chinese food, delivered right to their door.

They watched a movie together, chatting with Michael. Cam would have felt comfortable with the guy having a longer-term relationship with Marcie—he was good friends with her, but it seemed clear to him there was nothing romantic going on. There was a hint of sadness in the air as this chapter of their lives seemed to be concluding—and yet, they were leaving open the possibility of a sequel.

Michael was going to head north, but there would always be an open invitation for Marcie, if ever she was up that way. And similarly, Cam and Marcie made it clear that there was always space available for Michael on their sofa if ever he was in the south-west—and perhaps, if the pandemic ended, and Flo felt comfortable relinquishing the guest bedroom again, there might be a bed for Michael as well. Although, he was also welcome to share their bed any time, just so long as nobody else found out.

A couple of glasses of wine later, it seemed to be one of those magical evenings they would remember for a long, long time.

And then Marcie gave Cam a sharp look, and ushered him out to the bedroom.

'You okay?' he asked her.

'Of course,' she smiled, closing the bedroom door behind her.

'What's going on?'

She stepped toward the en suite bathroom. 'You're going to help me get ready,' she said.

'Get ready?'

'For Michael?'

Cam's eyes widened. Beneath his clothes, his manhood stiffened.

'Come on.' She gave him a little come-hither flick of her head, and he did as she demanded.

When he got to her, she was turning on the shower. She turned to him, and told him to take off her clothes, and then his. As he peeled off her underwear, he couldn't help but notice how stiff her nipples were already, and how wet she was, anticipating a night of sex with two men.

There seemed to be no rush. She stood and let him soap her gorgeous form, massaging her as he coaxed slippery suds over every inch of her body, his fingers gliding over her wonderfully soft, smooth skin, sweeping over her sumptuous curves, around her magnificent breasts, grazing over her erect nipples, brushing over her hairless mound, dipping into her juicy pussy.

Then she helped to wash him, though he didn't receive quite the same laborious soaping, her hands quick and efficient rather than lingering and sensual, except when she indulged in exploring how hard she made his cock.

After they stepped out of the shower, he dried her, and then himself, and she smiled brightly as he told her how beautiful she was, how Michael was going to get so hard when he came up here to see her. She stood in front of the bathroom mirror as he used the hairdryer on her, and gently brushed her long, silky hair until it was a shimmering stream of gold flowing down over her shoulders.

'Will you help me pick out something to wear?' she asked him.

'Of course, sweetheart.'

She stood by the end of the bed while he turned to the chest of drawers, where he found she'd packed everything except a fairly sheer pair of black thong panties, a matching bra, and a pair of black, thigh-high stockings.

'Very nice,' he said.

He helped her step into the panties, and slowly dragged them up her long, shapely legs, slipping them over her hips, her behind, tugging them into place over her mound, noting how very little they really covered—and how easily he could see her sweet pussy through the sheer fabric.

The bra pushed up her breasts a little more, enhancing her cleavage, and then he drew each stocking up her leg, cladding her calves and much of her thighs in soft, black, sheer nylon, the ornate lace tops allowing them to stay up without need for a garter belt.

She pulled a thin, black, sheer top from the almost-empty closet, to go over her shoulders, and then she posed to check herself out in the full-length mirror in the corner of the room.

'You never used to wear such sexy things for me,' Cam said, smiling as he stood behind her to gaze at her exquisite form.

'No,' she admitted. 'I took you too much for granted.'

She turned, and smiled warmly. 'I wore some nice things for you when we were dating,' she said, 'but back then we couldn't afford anything like this.'

'You never wore stockings for me.'

She grinned. 'I always thought my legs were too fat.'

He laughed, 'They *so* weren't. Ever.'

She shrugged, 'I do feel a little more confident these days. You know, since I started going to the gym regularly. Or least, when I did before lockdown.'

'And since then, you've been working out on Michael's cock.'

'I have, haven't I?' she agreed, twirling to check herself out from all angles. 'I do so love getting my exercise on his big, hard equipment…'

She giggled, and fondled her husband's more modest, and yet not inconsequential hardness.

'Are you going to watch him with me tonight?' she asked him, as she sat at her dressing table to apply her makeup. 'Do you want to see me fucking him?'

'If I'm allowed to.'

She smiled. 'I think he'll be okay with it. He's not shy.'

Cam trembled a little to think that he would get to see them, in person, having sex right in front of him. He tried to keep calm as he perched on the end of the bed, watching her apply eyeliner, a touch of mascara, and lipstick, without obscuring her beautiful skin with foundation. Once complete, the makeup seemed to sharpen her pretty face, turning her from a beautiful woman into a beguiling, provocative temptress.

'I think I'm ready,' she said softly, as she checked her hair. 'Can you text Michael, and tell him to come in?'

She passed him her phone, and he obediently tapped out a message before finding Michael's number in her contacts list.

Marcie: You can come in now. All ready xx

He felt a little quiver of electricity surging through his body when he hit the 'send' button. Telling his wife's lover to come and take her.

Then he stood behind Marcie as she gave herself a last

look in the mirror, putting his arms around her before gently kissing her shoulder.

'Are you ready?' she asked him, smiling at him via the mirror.

'Uh-huh,' he said. 'Are you?'

'Oh yes, more than ready.'

She stepped away from him, and walked back over to the chest of drawers, before opening his underwear drawer. She picked something out, and then threw it over to him. A pair of pale, gray, Calvin Klein briefs. He glanced at her, a touch surprised that she'd bought him new underwear.

'You can watch, tonight,' she said. 'But no touching yourself until Michael is finished with me.'

'Okay,' he said, complying with the flick of her eyes to pull on the briefs. He didn't normally wear briefs—hadn't done since he'd been a kid. They seemed ridiculously small, a little on the tight side, but once they were on, he saw that they drew attention to his sizable bulge.

'Very nice,' she said, eyeing him with an approving smile. 'Now, sit,' she added, directing him to the armchair before perching on the corner of the bed, phone in hand.

He sat. He got comfortable. He waited, his heart thumping away inside his chest.

Why was he still so nervous? He'd seen her have sex with him, at least on screen. He'd been physically present a few days ago, although she'd put a blindfold on him to obscure his vision.

Marcie looked up from her phone, asked him, 'Ready?'

He nodded. She pressed the send button on her message summoning her lover.

Cam took a deep breath.

Marcie looked at him, and smiled warmly, seductively. She looked simply delicious. Most men would never under-stand why he would ever want to give up such a goddess to another man. To be honest, a lot of men would never find gratification in their wife's own pleasure.

Cam looked at his wife and saw the nervous anticipation, the quiet excitement in her eyes, and it thrilled him, it stirred his manhood within his tight underwear.

The door opened, and in came Michael.

CHAPTER THIRTY-THREE

'HEY,' Marcie said, smiling.

'Hey,' Michael smiled in return, and then to Cam, before walking over to them.

Marcie gave Cam a little glance that asked him, silently, if he was definitely okay with this. Cam smiled, gave her a little nod.

'You're looking lovely,' Michael told Marcie, as he sat beside her on the end of the bed.

'Thank you.'

Cam could see the bulge in the man's pants as he leaned into Marcie, and he felt pride in his gorgeous wife, and no small amount of wonder that this man was really going to strip off and make love to Marcie, right in front of him. The intensity of the excitement he could see his wife feeling, the raw, animal attraction she felt for this chiseled hunk, was just breathtaking.

Michael kissed her shoulder gently, and then removed her sheer top. A moment later, he was leaning back to find the catch of her bra, and remove that, too. As he did so,

Cam saw Marcie gaze down at his lap, and see the bulge he had noticed a moment or two earlier.

Cam felt a little flicker of excitement at the way his wife laid eyes on the man's package, the way it made her quietly catch her breath, and then turn to look at her husband, a dose of surprise in her eyes.

Well, it was a little strange, to be with Michael in front of her husband. Even after the blindfold incident.

Now, Cam could see everything.

Marcie's bra fell away to expose her magnificent breasts. Then Michael was leaning down to take them in his hands, slipping one of her nipples in his mouth.

Marcie's eyes found those of her husband. Checking him, teasing him, sharing the strangeness of the moment with him. He grinned, and flicked his eyes down, which was enough to point her to the massive erection now ballooning up within his tight briefs. She beamed brightly, ecstatic that she was turning him on, that this thrill ride would make him as hard as it made her wet.

When Michael sat up again, making sure they were both okay with this, Marcie was up, and kneeling on the corner of the bed, kneeling over her lover's lap. She worked at his fly with expert fingers, and then Cam saw the extraordinary sight of another man's hard cock, exposed, right in front of him, his wife's hands wrapping around its base.

Wow.

He'd seen enough pornography in his time, he'd seen other men's equipment before—and large ones, too. But this was real, in person, just a few feet away from him. Just bizarre. And Marcie eyed it hungrily, clutching its shaft tightly, then she gave her husband a sideways glance and licked the colossal erection slowly, from base to tip.

Cam felt a ripple of excitement shiver through his body.

He felt a strange tightness in his chest, a churning of his stomach as though it didn't quite know what to make of this sight before him—horror? Outrage? Red-hot, burning lust? God, he couldn't believe what he was seeing. It was so real, so close. He could smell his wife's sweet perfume—and he could detect Michael's woody cologne.

Marcie held the man's cock in a hand that flashed her wedding ring at her husband, as she ducked down to lick it. She smiled as she flicked her tongue around its tip, monitoring his every response to her depravity.

'Isn't he gorgeous?' she asked her husband.

Cam could only nod. Michael smiled at him, as though they were sharing their mutual amusement at how horny Marcie was right now. It felt oddly reassuring. Friendly. It dispelled any sense that he was a rival, or a threat, and fostered an unexpected feeling of camaraderie.

Marcie gazed down at it, and then leaned in, sank her head down on him, parted her lips and took the first few inches of his manhood in her mouth. It was a stretch, but she seemed delighted by it, lifting up off it again to turn to Cam, smiling, to tell him, 'Honey, I think I might be addicted to *really* big cocks.'

Cam grinned, and briefly glanced at Michael, who was also tickled by her admission.

Then she started bobbing her head on the end of his cock, and Michael's hand was underneath her, clutching one of her breasts, fondling her as she sucked on his hardness. Marcie was moaning, panting a little as she tended to his enormous manhood, but it was the way she kept turning her head to the side, to look at her husband as she sucked on another man, that really got Cam's own manhood throbbing.

It was almost like she was doing it for his benefit, rather than Michael's. Doing it like that, because she knew her husband had a quirky little kink for her promiscuity.

'Oh God…' Michael moaned as she sucked on him.

It was just breath-taking, watching her taking that huge cock in her mouth. It was such a powerful experience, watching it in person, just feet away. The picture quality had been fairly good on his laptop, and via Marcie's security cameras, but this was just incredible. And it wasn't only the sight—it was the wet sounds of her pleasuring him with her mouth, the sweet scents of their fragrances. It was real, and it made it unbelievably difficult not to touch the colossal bulge in his tiny briefs.

'He's so *big*, honey,' she told him, but Cam noticed her eyes were locked on his own bulge.

What seemed to get her going tonight was how this got her husband going.

But Michael wasn't going to last forever, not like that. He wasn't going to last more than a couple of minutes if she kept sucking on him like that. Marcie moved off him, pumping him in her hands a couple of times, but then letting him stand up.

While Michael stood at the foot of the bed and began removing his clothes, Marcie sat back in the middle of the bed, slipping off her panties, which she tossed toward her husband, who caught them, and put them to his face to breathe in the wicked scent of her arousal. Her underwear was already damp. She was ready to take that big cock inside her.

Cam breathed through her underwear as he watched her open her thighs, exposing her bare pussy to them both. Marcie stroked her pussy for a few moments, watching Michael strip off, her gaze taking in the man's buff physique, his rippling muscles. Then she pulled herself to the edge of the bed, offering herself to her lover.

Cam envied her lover in that moment. Her pussy looked so ripe and delicious.

Michael stood there, gazing down at her, that enormous cock just hanging there between his legs, thick and veiny, almost impossibly huge. Witnessing it in person, Cam could hardly believe Marcie could fit it inside her.

Then Michael turned to him, taking him quite by surprise, and said firmly, 'You want to get her ready for me?'

Cam was on his knees in moments. Shuffling to the end of the bed, gazing up at the insanely hot view up Marcie's incredible body from between her legs. She smiled down at him, surprised and delighted that he would use his mouth on her before Michael brought in the cavalry.

As he leaned in, inhaled that powerful, spicy scent of his wife's arousal, and then lightly kissed her just beside her glistening sex, Cam felt a burst of adrenaline shoot through his bloodstream. It wasn't just that he was getting to taste his wife's magnificent sex, worshipping her when she looked so sensational—there was an added buzz because he knew he was preparing her for another man. He was warming her up, getting her juices flowing, paving the way for her lover's enormous manhood to slide inside her adulterous pussy.

Marcie smiled down at him as he kissed his way around her exquisite sex, but then as he planted a kiss on her sensitive pussy lips, then slipped his tongue inside her slippery groove, and drew it slowly up from the bottom to its apex, her eyes closed, her head tilted back, and her mouth opened for a long, low groan.

She tasted delicious.

He loved that, by now, she just opened herself up to

him. There was no insecurity, no concern about whether he might just be doing this because he thought he should, rather than because he wanted to. There were no doubts in her mind that he not only enjoyed feasting on her sex, but downright obsessed about it these days.

He lapped at her tangy juices, and she stroked his hair, appreciating him, loving him, encouraging him.

While he indulged in her beautiful sex, he gazed up her divine body, and saw Michael quietly approach her by the side of the bed, up by her head. Marcie turned, and stopped caressing Cam so that she could take hold of her lover's engorged cock, and bring its tip to her mouth.

He noticed how much wetter she got after Michael slid his manhood into her eager mouth. As she twisted her body so that she could take more of it inside her, so that Michael could stand there and gently fuck her pretty face.

With all that stimulation, with one man's mouth over her pussy while another man's manhood slid in her mouth, Marcie was soon in heaven, moaning quietly only because she didn't want to alert the others in the house to what was going on.

There was no doubt she was fully warmed up.

Cam withdrew, and silently returned to his place on the armchair.

Now, Marcie was soaking wet, her thighs parted wide, ready for her lover to take her. She looked across at her husband as Michael knelt on the end of the bed, lining himself up to take her.

'Take them off,' she breathed, and Cam immediately complied, standing to slip off his briefs, showing her how hard he was to see her with her lover. She smiled brightly, aroused by his own arousal.

It was one of the most difficult things he'd ever under-taken, refraining from touching himself as he watched

Michael touch the length of his mighty cock against his wife's pussy. As the man gently stroked it against her, coating it in her glistening juices. And he couldn't touch himself by stealth, either—as Michael finally nudged the tip of his manhood to her entrance, Marcie was looking straight at her husband.

But while he couldn't pleasure himself as he watched another man enter his wife, he could at least enjoy the look on her face as Michael first slid that colossal thing inside her sensitive pussy. The pure bliss in her expression was just a joy for him, and gave him that glow inside from knowing that while it was another man's cock squeezing inside her, Cam was the husband who had allowed this to happen—so, in a way, Cam was pleasuring her himself.

Once he was inside her, though, her eyes were on Michael.

She gasped at feeling him filling her up so completely.

Cam envied the man his huge penis. And yet, there was something so completely delicious about being a third party in this moment, watching the woman he loved experience the rare treat of a massive cock inside her. The strange, unexpectedly erotic sense that she could have his love, and still enjoy this kind of physical ecstasy from a monumentally large penis.

And it was something of a shock to see it—'in the flesh' was never a more apt phrase.

Although there was no doubt that it turned him on, like nothing he'd ever witnessed before, there was also a clear feeling that he wasn't quite wired to just watch such a thing impassively.

This was the woman he loved. This was the woman who was his whole world, and another man was being about as intimate with her as he could physically be. Part of him was inside her body. His most masculine of parts was inside her body.

Cam watched this other man thrusting that enormous thing into Marcie's tight pussy, and he found it hard to breathe.

A few moments into it, Marcie glanced over to him, to register how he was responding. She must have seen the shock on his face, perhaps saw how conflicted he was in his feelings. He was hard, sure, hard as hell. But it wasn't quite as easy as he'd imagined it would be, taking all this in.

She gestured to him with her eyes, invited him to her.

He hopped up, and stepped to the bed. Veered close to Michael as he approached her, and was nearly over-whelmed by his proximity. It was just so *real*, so visceral. The man's cock sliding inside her again and again, the wet sounds of her copious juices lubricating his penetration. The stifling, earthy smell of their sex, the wetness and the heat of their bodies somehow making the air around the bed humid.

He was so energized, so turned on—and yet his legs felt weak, his muscles trembled, he felt like he could collapse any moment from shock, if he didn't sit down.

He did sit. He parked himself on the edge of the bed, close to where Michael had stood in order to thrust his big cock into her mouth. He sat, and he took Marcie's hand as Michael continued to thrust into her.

Marcie gazed up at him, said, 'You okay, honey?'

He smiled as best he could—he genuinely did not want this to end, no matter how difficult the feelings were to get through.

'He's so big, honey. I can't believe how good he feels inside me.'

The two of them were getting sweaty already, and Marcie was quite flushed.

She reached up, and curled a hand around his head, urging him down to meet her lips. He kissed her, as she wanted, holding her head gently in his hands, feeling the dampness of sweat in her golden hair, tasting the salt of perspiration on her lips—and also, perhaps, something else. Her kiss was sweet, and laced with sweat, but it also drew his attention to the fact that these voluptuous lips of hers had only moments before been wrapped around Michael's tumescent manhood. And when he thought about it, there could be no doubt in Cam's mind that his wife's mouth was seasoned by another man's cock.

It seemed all kinds of wrong.

And yet, at the same time, it was just sex. So Cam happened to be turned on by his wife's dalliance with another man. The proof of that man's contact with her, the evidence of her adultery, merely turned him on further.

Marcie turned onto all fours, and now held Cam's hands as Michael powered into her from behind. It was such a thrill to see her face as this athletic man pounded into her again and again, her entire body shaken with each thrust, her face flushed, her expression almost tortured by the pleasure she was receiving from that huge cock.

Cam was kneeling down on the floor, gazing up at her face as she gripped his hands so tightly—really crushing his fingers—while sustaining a constant barrage of strikes from a really, really huge dick.

She gazed into his eyes with a kind of terror imprinted on her features—it wasn't actually fear, it was just her being totally overwhelmed with sexual energy. As her whining rose in pitch, into more of a hiss than a scream, since she was trying to keep her volume down, Cam tilted up to kiss her adulterous lips, and it seemed to send her over the edge—she was shaking and shivering and jerking, and ultimately collapsing under Michael's weight, as she was totally swamped by her orgasm.

And as she came, Cam looked up to see Michael close his eyes, every muscle in his body tensing up as his own peak arrived. Then he twitched—once, twice, three times, more—and he grunted, and Cam could tell with no doubt whatsoever that this other man was coming, hard, inside his wife.

Marcie opened her eyes and stared straight at her husband as she felt herself filled with her lover's warm come. It was a moment that very nearly sent Cam over the edge.

After that, Michael sat up by the headboard, recovering from his powerful orgasm, and Marcie remained on all fours, turning to take his softening cock in her mouth, to clean him, and perhaps get him ready for another round. Cam wasn't quite sure what to do—he went back to the armchair, supposing that he was supposed to wait and watch, and see if Michael wanted more time with Marcie. At least he got a stunning view, from the armchair. Marcie, from the rear, on all fours, her freshly fucked pussy right there in front of him.

But then Marcie turned and glanced over her shoulder at him, and said, 'Your turn, honey. You can fuck me, now.'

He was surprised at that. He glanced at Michael, and he gave Cam one of those tiny little nods, confirming that it was as she said—his turn.

Cam felt a little self-conscious, worried that his erection would let him down now that there was another man here, while he was supposed to make love to his wife. But he stepped over to the bed again, getting a stupendously close look at his wife's unfaithful pussy, and as he moved in, he spied a little drop of the man's creamy, white come leak out of her sex.

Wow.

It really drove home the point that Marcie had just been fucked by this other man. He had mounted her, he had mated with her, he had potentially fertilized her.

Cam leaned in, and kissed her just beside her pussy, taking a deep breath of that strange, funky smell of sex, sweat, female arousal and a man's fresh come. Wow. It was just shocking. You could not get purer evidence of a gloriously unfaithful wife. Her pussy flushed and rosy red from use, her pussy lips glistening with her juices. A few drops of sticky, white come oozing out of her, put there by her lover only moments before.

Cam felt almost intoxicated by it all.

But there was no danger he was going to lose his erection. He felt like a goddamn seventeen-year-old again, about to enter his first girlfriend. Back then, he'd stay hard even after ten, fifteen pints of beer.

He kissed his wife's pussy, and then pushed up to direct the tip of his flagpole of a cock to her entrance. Then he thrust his hips, and he was inside her, feeling her pussy tight and wet around him—so very wet, in fact, slick from another man's seed.

Marcie glanced round, over her shoulder at him, apparently somewhat surprised at how hard he felt, how big he felt inside her in this moment. She moaned, long and low, and Cam felt like a god, starting to thrust into her in a constant, regular rhythm. She went back to sucking on Michael's cock, seeming to revel in the feeling of two men inside her at the same time, but soon, she had to let it go.

And then Michael was left to sit there and stroke himself while he watched Marcie turn onto her back, to pull Cam onto her so that he could fuck her missionary-style, kissing her unfaithful mouth with passion as he did so, as he made her come as hard as Michael had ever done.

He wasn't as big as Michael, sure. But he was her second cock of the night, and he was a husband who not only tolerated her having other lovers—but actively got off on it. He was a bigger turn-on for Marcie than any huge cock could be on its own.

And when he made her come, the second time, she was left gasping for breath, sweating and flushed to the point where it seemed like fever.

She didn't stop moaning for minutes after Cam had fired his own come deep inside her.

CHAPTER THIRTY-FOUR

HE SLEPT on the couch to let them spend the final night together. It wasn't an entirely selfless decision on his part. He enjoyed lying there with a little peace and quiet, recovering from the high-energy experience of watching, and getting involved with, the coupling of his wife and her lover.

As he lay there, he felt a wonderful underlying tension that made him feel slightly fizzy inside, and even had his tired manhood re-awakening, at least halfway stiff. The tension came from knowing his beloved wife was lying in the arms of another man. That at any moment, the two of them could rouse from their slumber and quietly resume their sexual congress.

He was enjoying one last night of his wife's infidelity before everything would change again.

It took him a while to get any kind of sleep. The city outside the large windows was trying to help him—all was quiet. Unusually so. He hadn't spent a night here, himself, in lockdown. London was strange to be so muted. There wasn't even that low growl of distant traffic to underline everything. But he was too buzzed to fall straight to sleep.

Once, twice, there was the sound of sirens in the distance. He felt bad when he heard those—it reminded him of the very real suffering that came along with this lockdown. The pandemic.

For a while, he went to the windows to stare out at the silent, still street outside. There were no lights on in the buildings across the road. No real signs of life until a lonely fox wandered by, completely unthreatened by anyone.

He paced the living room. He hadn't really spent a lot of time here in this apartment, but there were still memories here. He remembered when they'd first got this place, some years back now, when Marcie's career in London was really exploding.

He remembered their first night here, together. Flo had been on childcare duty that night, too. But she only had to take care of Henry, and he'd been a baby. Had that been the only time they'd had sex in this apartment before the lockdown, and Michael, had come along? After that first night, they were never in this place together. Only ever one or the other.

His strongest memory of this place was walking in here to discover the truth about Marcie and Michael.

It got him fully hard again, thinking about that particular memory. So powerful, the discovery that she'd been cheating. Such a breach of trust. He should have been way more angry about that than he had been. And yet it was such an unbelievably turn-on. His arousal had overwhelmed all other emotions.

It was just sex, wasn't it?

Sure, she hadn't told him that she'd let one of her colleagues move into the apartment after he'd lost his job. But the guy was supposed to sleep on the couch. And then, she was lonely, she wasn't being kept satisfied by her husband. She could have just masturbated, touched herself in the shower. Only there happened to be an attractive man in the next room. Man able to give her a completely different sexual experience than she would ever get from her husband, even if Cam was in the mood.

She could have gone for a run with him. She could have played racketball with him, she could have played tennis with him, she could have gone swimming with him —and there would have been no judgement. She could have gone out dancing with him. No problem. But she had taken a different kind of exercise with him, and society labeled that adultery, and treated it as shameful.

It was only sex.

It was the intimacy that was the issue. She'd taken off her clothes for him. He'd taken off his clothes for her. She had touched him, stroked him, kissed him. She had taken him inside her.

And yet people did that with each other all the time.

Marriage. People got married and promised not to have sex with other people. Well, sure, there was a danger that the woman you committed your life to—the woman you fell in love with—would desert you for another man. That was a danger. But as long as you protected yourself against that possibility, what was so bad about opening up your marriage for sex with others?

Cam lay back down on the couch, and watched Netflix on his phone until he eventually did drift off to sleep.

He didn't sleep through to the morning. His body was too accustomed to waking up erratically through the night because so often one child, or the other, woke up and called out for mom or dad. He woke about 3am, and in the still of the night, he heard a faint giggle from the bedroom. That caught his attention.

He went to the door, but he didn't open it. They would have been fine about him joining them, he was sure. But he wanted to keep out. He just wanted to stay there, listening to the two of them quietly moaning as they were very obviously becoming intimate again. Marcie's gasps as Michael entered her. The steady rise in pitch of her sighs and moans as he drove that huge thing into her again and again, as he pushed her toward orgasm yet again.

Cam listened to them through the door until they came, and fell silent once more. He waited, his heart still thumping, his cock still hard, until he heard one or other of them quietly snoring. They'd fallen straight back to sleep, so easily.

He lay back down on the couch, but didn't touch his stiff manhood anymore. He liked the tension he was feeling. The pressure.

It was easier to drift off to sleep the second time.

The next time he woke, there was a strange warmth emanating from his lap—and a weight pressing down on him from his thighs to his stomach.

Daylight was blasting through the blinds, making Cam wonder how late he'd slept before his attention was rather overwhelmed by the fact that someone was pressing down on his body, and the end of his cock was clamped inside something hot and wet.

Marcie gazed up at him as he rubbed the sleep from his eyes, smiling even though her mouth was full.

'What… hey…' he said, a little out of sorts, but perfectly happy as he realized what was going on.

'Morning,' she said briefly, before sinking back down on his hardness. He brushed her hair out of the way so that he could see her face more easily as she bobbed down on him.

'Wow…' he moaned. 'You're awake already?'

She grinned, and licked his shaft from base to tip. 'I didn't want you to feel left out.'

He laughed. 'Did you get any sleep last night?'

'Not much,' she smirked.

'Where's Michael?'

'Still asleep.'

He watched her sucking on his hardness a while, and it felt wonderful. But it was even better when he thought about the fact that she must have done this with Michael during the night.

'This… is a nice way to wake up,' he said.

She smiled back at him again. 'Michael likes it like this, too,' she said, as though she needed to remind her cuck-olded husband. She nearly made him come, saying that.

She crawled up his body, straddling his waist, pressing her searing sex down against the length of his hard cock, without taking it inside her. It took another glance down between her legs to see that she was wearing panties—a tiny, plum-colored g-string.

'How many times did you guys have sex last night?' he asked her.

She grinned. 'Oh… lots of times.'

He could smell the earthiness of recent sex in the air. He could smell it on her, too, along with the remnants of her perfume. Sweat. Come. Cologne. Perfume. Not strong, yet. The scent of adultery.

'Show me,' he asked her.

She stood, looming over him. She danced for him, slowly, sensually, and slipped her g-string off her hips, allowing it to drop down her thighs, past her knees to the floor, revealing the beautiful v-shape between her legs, her bare mound, her hairless sex. Smiling as she exposed herself for him, loving how she could turn him on, how he adored her.

She stooped to pick up her fallen underwear, and then stood and dropped if on his face.

He chuckled, and held it to his nose, breathing in the strong scent of her adultery.

'More,' he demanded.

She brushed her long, straight, golden hair back over her shoulders and then climbed onto him again, this time straddling his face. Pressing herself down on him, gently brushing her pussy lips over his mouth. She let him lick her, she gave him just enough space to explore her sex, to experience her adultery up close.

Then she pushed back, to take his hard cock within her well-used pussy, and make herself come one more time before they would have to get showered, and dressed, and pack the final few things prior to departure.

She rode him, and he just about held on as she did so, until she was crying out, her body shaking and shuddering over him, and she looked as happy as she had ever been.

CHAPTER THIRTY-FIVE

AND THEN, after a leisurely bite to eat with Michael—the little cafe down the road delivered a full English breakfast right to their door; one of the wonders of the new lockdown economy—they gathered up their last few things, and they were finally out of there.

It felt like the end of an era.

Even lockdown was in the process of being eased, now. People were allowed out in the parks as much as they wanted. Households could visit other households, albeit within a limited 'bubble'—if Cam had wanted to go see his parents in Lincoln, he would have had to argue with his brothers for the privilege of being the one other household to be in his parents' bubble. The government was urging people to go back to the office for work, if they could do so with some kind of social distancing in place.

The numbers of new cases of COVID-19 were dropping in the UK each day, thankfully. Although there were strong feelings that there could be a 'second wave' of the pandemic in the fall.

Cam and Marcie were back in their rented van again,

leaving London for now. Happy to have each other, to have their family. To have this rekindled desire in their marriage. You had to think about the positives when everything around you was so awful.

As they drove, Marcie was flicking through her personal email, and she already had three job offers from companies she'd worked with over the years, suppliers and contractors and clients. People who knew she would be available shortly, since her own company was closing down. She'd be back in a decent role soon enough—they were confident about that.

Then when they turned off the M40 to drive past Oxford, Cam caught a glimpse of what she was looking at on her phone, and asked her what it was. It looked like the photo of a man he didn't know.

'Michael installed it on my phone last night,' she grinned, holding it up so that he could see it more clearly.

Most of the screen was taken up by the picture of a thirty-something man—attractive, dark-haired, with a friendly smile—and underneath it said, 'David, 34'. Beneath that, it read, '5 miles away'. A line of text beneath that read, 'Looking at my phone searching for a reason to stop looking at my phone'. Very zen. There were colored circles at the bottom of the screen, which looked like they could be buttons. An 'X', a star and a heart.

At first, Cam thought it was some kind of employment thing, like LinkedIn or Fish4Jobs.

But then she took back the phone and he saw her swipe to the left, and another image of another man appeared. Dating profiles?

'You have heard of Tinder?' She asked him.

Cam felt his heart singed by an intense heat.

'Uh… yeah, I've *heard* of it.'

She giggled.

'I won't be able to meet anyone else in person, until the lockdown actually ends,' she said, as Cam gazed at his gorgeous wife and his pulse just went haywire. 'But we can have some fun choosing someone, can't we? Maybe connecting with a few guys online…'

Cam felt the familiar tickle between his legs as his manhood started to thicken.

He smiled. When you had a wife open to possibilities, the future seemed bright, and very, very exciting.

AUTHOR'S NOTE

I haven't really felt the need to explain much of the historical context for the events in this novel. The spread of the SARS-CoV-2, the virus behind the coronavirus disease 2019 (COVID-19), from its initial identification in December 2019 into a global pandemic as declared on March 11, 2020, is now well known to everyone. It has affected many millions of people, either directly or indirectly—health wise or economically.

My thoughts, of course, are with those who have suffered the disease, those who have lost loved ones to the pandemic, and those who have lost their livelihoods as a result of the disease—as well as those who have suffered mental health difficulties as a result of the pandemic and its resulting lockdowns, loneliness, anxiety, depression, relationship break-downs, domestic abuse, and the simple loss of a normal life.

In the UK, where I wrote this story, and where this story is set, the government introduced a lockdown to respond to the pandemic on March 23, 2020.

I remember brief conversations early on in the lockdown with other authors in the erotica field as we noticed the first erotic stories going on Amazon flaunting the theme of the lockdown. It was breathtakingly quick that a few other writers had managed to get stories out that made use of the lockdown as a kind of story device. We other authors asked each other whether it was 'too soon', whether there might be a danger that writing a story set in the lockdown could be seen as exploiting the developing crisis for our own gain, even though the situation presented interesting challenges for plotting stories about couples seeking release from overly monogamous arrangements.

At the time, and even now, nobody knew how long the lockdown would last, or how long it would take to tackle the pandemic. It's been an unprecedented crisis in our generation. As I write this in mid-July, there have been 13.5m cases of COVID-19 worldwide, with more than 583,000 fatalities. Governments around the world have imposed lockdowns, and many have eased them as case numbers started to fall again, only to have to re-impose lockdowns as case numbers subsequently rose again.

In the UK, new daily case numbers are thankfully declining just now, but we are still in partial lockdown, with schools closed and social distancing measures firmly in place, albeit without much clarity from officials about how strictly people should be following guidelines—for example, to wear face masks out in public. And like many countries, if not most of the world, we sit on tenterhooks, concerned that there could be a second wave of infections later this year, possibly because lockdowns ease too soon, and people begin to resume travel or social mixing before the virus has fully receded.

I have felt very fortunate to be where I am, riding out this long-term house arrest at my home, with family around me.

But as the lockdown rolled on for weeks and weeks, the pandemic did come to affect me creatively in some unexpected ways.

At first, it was just a case of finding it a little difficult to focus on the usual day job, with so much going on around us. But while we suspected that the lockdown might continue for several weeks, maybe even a month or two, it has now been in place in the UK for 16 weeks. And even though measures were eased very slightly after seven weeks, and a little more after 10 weeks or so, society has fundamentally changed here, as elsewhere.

People don't go out. People don't see their friends. Many people don't even go out to buy essentials, relying on delivery services. Kids are home. Workers are home, if they can do their jobs from home or if they are furloughed. Normal life has gone on pause.

For me, writing stories about couples getting into new and exciting romantic and sexual entanglements, it became increasingly difficult to continue while society was fundamentally altering itself. I was writing about lives that were firmly set in what we had known as 'normal', but society is no longer like that.

As of July 2020, people in the UK are still not allowed to meet new people, those outside their own household or one other household in their 'bubble'. The whole system of people dating has stopped, except for purely online encounters that certainly doesn't extend to actual sex. In fact, the media has pointed out that sex in the UK is currently illegal, unless it is with somebody you live with. Loneliness has been endemic, here, among people who live alone, people who were single with the lockdown began. Some couples who had been dating a matter of mere days when lockdown began had to make rash decisions on whether to move in with their dates just to keep the relationship going physically.

So what was I doing, as an erotica author specializing in couples who find new sexual interest outside of their monogamous relationships?

Was I writing about things as they would become, once lockdown ends and the pandemic is over? But who knows when that will be? And maybe society will *never* entirely return to that kind of normality, now that we have been through this transformative global event. Some medical experts have suggested that this unusual virus may never be entirely conquered. That people might need to wear masks, when they go out in public, for years to come. Maybe even for the rest of our lives.

It started feeling as though I was writing some kind of science fiction — how things might be someday, when life returns to 'normal'.

I mean, I was 30,000 words into a story about a guy who is a driver for the ride share company Uber, who uses his taxi to ferry his wife around to new dates—and in this country, like many others, Uber has effectively ceased to operate aside from a few drivers transporting key workers, or delivering food or parcels.

I stopped writing for a little while, to get my head around all this. Then, after a fair amount of head-scratching, I came to my own, personal solution. Either I would start writing a kind of historical fiction, setting stories in a certain year, or I would write contemporary stories where I acknowledged and accounted for the changes in society going on around us at the time.

And so, I started working on story ideas in which the lockdown is central to the setting. Not avoiding it, not seeking to exploit it as some kind of topical selling point— but just coming up with stories that could, conceivably, happen in the society we find ourselves in today. Among a handful of short story ideas, *A Lockdown Affair* seemed to work, and became much more than a short story—the first draft hit 40,000 words.

After comments from dear friends including my long-time beta reader Anjali, and esteemed fellow author Kenny Wright, the second draft pushed past 80,000 words. Many thanks to them for helping me to get things right. Thanks, also, to the rest of my invaluable beta readers — Dan, Horst, Nick and Robert. The story would not have been nearly as good without their important insights.

So here it is, dear reader, I hope you have enjoyed it. And going forward, I hope that we do get back to a new 'normal' soon, so that people around the world no longer have to deal with the hardships resulting from COVID-19. And in the mean time, I'll aim to keep writing stories that can be enjoyed without completely leaving the realms of believability.

Lastly, if you did enjoy this book (or even if you didn't!) would you please consider writing a review of it on your favorite bookseller's website, so other readers might enjoy it too. Just a sentence or two. That would mean a lot to me.

Thank you!

Max
London, July 17, 2020

ALSO BY MAX SEBASTIAN

OBSESSIVE
Essence of an Affair

From the start of their unusual relationship, Jens Nielsen was always candid about his inability to satisfy a woman in the bedroom. His lovely wife, Effie, was always perfectly understanding, given his condition. Nevertheless he made her an offer that if she was ever tempted by another man, she could have an affair.

Now, for the first time ever, Jens suspects that Effie is taking up his offer—yet the biggest surprise is not that she might actually do it, but that her husband wants to know all about it — and that *knowing* about her affair somehow awakens his desire for his beautiful wife…

Book One in a new trilogy from the author of bestselling hotwife romance *Madeleine Wakes*…

maxsebastian.net/obsessive-essence-of-an-affair

ALSO AVAILABLE

THE MADELEINE TRILOGY
Epic wife-watching romance

His wife flirts with other men. And he likes it.

Hugo and Madeleine Finnell move to New York hoping that a change of scene will help end her depression. With a new job, Madeleine gains confidence and starts drawing the attention of other men — something her therapist encourages.

Hugo watches from the sidelines as others begin flirting with his wife — and his wife flirts back.

Shock, jealousy, and much to his surprise, erotic excitement buffet Hugo as he witnesses this sexy side of Madeleine come alive. Can he stop her as she starts taking things too far? Does he want to?

MaxSebastian.net/the-madeleine-trilogy

Printed in Great Britain
by Amazon